"THEY WENT BY ME LIKE A FLASH.

ORANGE BLOSSOMS

FRESH AND FADED.

BY

T. S. ARTHUR.

"*Take us the foxes, the little foxes, that spoil the vines: for our vines have tender grapes.*"—Solomon's Song.

PHILADELPHIA:
PORTER & COATES.

INTRODUCTION.

AH, if they would never fade—these sweet and fragrant blossoms! If the little foxes would never spoil the vines! They do not always fade, nor are the tender grapes always spoiled. There are many brows on which the orange blossoms are as fresh to-day as when placed there by loving hands in years long past. They will always be fresh and fragrant. Time has no power over them.

But they fade—alas! how quickly!—on so many brows. To keep them fresh—to bring back their sweetness when faded—is the loving mission of our book. It is a book of life-pictures. It takes you into other homes, and makes you familiar with other experiences than your own. It shows you where others have erred, what pain and loss have followed, and how love, self-denial and reason have turned sorrow into joy and threatened disaster into permanent safety.

CONTENTS.

XVIII.

XIX.

XX.

XXI.

XXII.

XXIII.

XXIV.

XXV.

XXVI.

Orange Blossoms.

I.

LITTLE FOXES.

SOBER, half-discontented face at the window—a bright face in the street. The window is thrown open, and a smile goes from the bright face to the sober one, giving it a new and pleasanter aspect. Both faces are young, that at the window, youngest, almost childlike. Yet the window face is the face of a wife, and the street face that of a maiden "fancy free."

"How strangely I was deceived, Bella!" said the lady in the street.

"Deceived! How, Mary? What do you mean? But come in. You're just the one I wish to see."

"I was sure I saw you not ten minutes ago

riding out with Harry," said the young friend as they met and kissed at the door.

"Oh dear, no! I haven't been out riding with Harry for a month."

"Indeed? How's that? I can remember when you rode out together almost every afternoon."

"Yes, but that was before our marriage," replied the young wife in a voice that made her friend look into her face narrowly.

"The husband has less time for recreation than the lover. He must give more thought to business," remarked the friend.

The little wife tossed her head and shrugged her shoulders in a doubtful way, saying, as she did so: "I don't know about the business. But lovers and husbands are different species of the genus Homo. The explanation lies somewhere in this direction, I presume."

"Ah, Bella, Bella! That speech doesn't come with a musical sound from your lips," remarked the friend, smiling yet serious.

"Truth is not always melodious," said Bella.

"How is it as to sweethearts and wives?" asked the friend. "Do they belong to the same class?"

The question appeared to reach the young wife's ears with a suggestive force. Her voice was a little changed as she answered, "I don't know. Perhaps not."

Then, after a moment, she said, "And you thought it was Harry and I that you saw riding out?"

"I was certain of it. But it only shows how one may be mistaken."

The friend had been scanning the young wife for some moments from head to foot in a way that now called out the question, "Do you see anything peculiar about me?"

"Yes," was answered.

"What?"

"A peculiar untidiness that I never observed in the sweetheart."

Bella glanced down at her soiled and ruffled dress.

"My *négligé*," she said, with a little short laugh.

"So I should think. Now, shall I draw your picture?"

"Yes, if you have an artist fancy."

"Here it is: Hair lustreless and untidy; skin dull for want of action and feeling; a wrapper better conditioned for the washing-tub and ironing-table than as a garment for the fair person of a young wife; no collar nor ornament of any kind; and a countenance— Well, I can't give that as I saw it a little while ago at the window, but I'm sure it wasn't the face to charm a lover. Perhaps it might suit a husband, but I have my doubts."

"Why, Mary! You are in a sportive mood."

"No, serious. How do you like the picture? Let me compare it with the original. Fairly reproduced, I believe. I hardly think, though, that you were in this trim when Harry fell in love. But it may be all well enough for a husband. I have no experience in this line, and can't speak by the card."

Bella felt the reproof of her friend, as was evident by the spots that began to burn on her cheeks.

"You wouldn't have me dress in party style every day?" she said.

"Oh no! But I'd have you neat and sweet as a young wife should always be; that is, if she cares for the fond eyes of her husband. I verily believe it was Harry I saw riding out a little while ago!"

Bella threw a quick, startled look upon her friend, who already half regretted her closing sentence.

"Why did you say that? What did you mean?" she asked.

"I only said it to plague you," answered the friend.

"To plague me?" There was an expression in Bella's face that Mary had never seen there before. Her eyes had grown suddenly of a darker shade, and were eager and questioning. Her lips lay closer together; there were lines on her forehead.

"To plague me?" she repeated. "Take care, Mary."

The friend wished now that she had not made that suggestion, and yet, since making it, doubt had reached conviction in her mind. She was sure that she had not been mistaken as to Bella's husband, but who was the lady with whom she had seen him riding out? Bella had said a little while before that her husband had not driven her out for a month, and yet Mary felt certain that she had seen him riding out with a lady at least three or four times during that period. Should she hide the truth, or, trusting to its power for ultimate good, let it appear? There was no time for reflection. She spoke now rather from a desire to help her friend into a better state of perception than from any clear sight in the matter.

"I think," she said, "that, having secured your husband, you have fallen into the error of thinking that personal attractions are not needed to hold him by your side. Now, it is my opinion that, if Harry had found you in your present untidy condition—and you are often in no better plight—in a single instance before marriage, he would have broken off the engagement, and I'm sure that in a suit for breach of promise, if I had been on the jury, a verdict in his favor would have been rendered."

Bella did not smile at this closing sally, but sat looking into her friend's face in a strange, bewildered, troubled way. The intimation that her husband had been seen riding out with a lady, when it fairly reached her thought, gave her a sharp pain. It had never entered her imagination that he could look, with even a passing sense of admiration, into any face but hers—that his heart could turn from her to another for a single instant of time. She had perceived that he was colder, more indifferent, less careful of her pleasures than in the sunny days of their courtship and betrothment, but that he could seek another's society was a thing undreamed of. It was a proverb, this contrast between lovers and husbands, and she had felt that she was proving its truth. That was all. It was an unpleasant truth, and hard to receive, yet she saw no remedy. But now, by a word or two, her friend had startled her into a different view of the case. Was her husband's heart really turning from her? She was frightened at the remote suggestion, for in his love lay all her world.

"You are not really in earnest, Mary, about seeing Harry riding out with a lady this afternoon?" she said in a voice and with a look that revealed fully her state of mind. The color had left her face and her heart shook in her voice.

"I was probably mistaken, Bella," replied the friend, "though I had not doubted of the fact a moment until I saw you at the window a little while ago."

"Did you notice the lady particularly?"

"No; but let the matter pass, dear. No

doubt I was mistaken. It is worrying you more than I could have imagined."

Bella looked at her friend for some moments in a strange way, then giving a low, suppressed, wailing cry, bent forward and laid her face upon her bosom, sobbing and shuddering in such wild turbulence of feeling that her friend became actually alarmed.

"You have frightened me!" said the young wife, lifting her head, at last, as her excitement died away. "Ah, Mary, if I should lose my husband's love it would kill me!"

"Then, Bella," answered her friend, "see to it that you neglect none of the means required for keeping it. If you would continue to be loved, you must not grow unlovely. The charms that won your husband must not be folded up and kept for holiday occasions, and then put on for other eyes than his. You must keep them ever displayed before him—nay, put on new attractions. Is not the husband even dearer than the lover, and his heart better worth the holding? Look back, my dear friend, over the brief moons that have waxed and waned since you were a bride. Put yourself on trial and take impartial testimony. How has it been? Has your temper been as sweet as when you sat leaning together in the summer twilight talking of the love-crowned future? Have you been as studious to please as then, as careful of his feelings, as regardful of his tastes? Do you adorn yourself for his eyes now as when you dressed for his coming then? As a wife are you as lovable as you were when a maiden? Bella, Bella! look to the little foxes that spoil the tender grapes if you would have love's ripened fruitage. Love is not a chameleon, to feed on air and change in every hue of condition. It must have substantial food. Deprive it of this, and it languishes and dies. And now, dear, I have warned you. Meet your husband when he returns home this evening looking as sweetly as when he came to you in your father's house, attracted as the bee is to the flower, and note the manner in which his face will light up. Did he kiss you when he came home yesterday?"

The face of Bella flushed a little.

"Husbands soon lose taste for kissing," she answered.

"If the wife's lips remain as sweet as the maiden's, never!"

"Oh, you don't know anything about it," said Bella. "Wait until you are married."

After the friend said good-afternoon the young wife went to her room and cried for a good quarter of an hour. Then she commenced doing as the friend had suggested. Refreshed by a bath, she attired herself in a spotless white wrapper with a delicate blue belt binding her waist. A small lace collar, scarcely whiter than her pure neck, edged and tied with narrow azure ribbon, was turned away from her swan-like throat, and just below, at the swell of the bosom, was an exquisitely-cut oval pin. Her hair, a rich golden brown, had been made glossy as the wing of a bird, and was folded just enough away from the temples to show their delicate cutting. Two opening rosebuds, red and white, nestled above and in front of one of her pearl-tinted ears. She did look lovely and lovable, as her mirror told her.

Harry was half an hour later than usual in coming home. Bella was sitting in the parlor when he came in, waiting for his return with a new feeling at her heart—a feeling of blending fear and hope; fear lest he was actually becoming estranged from her, and a trembling hope to win him back again. His step was not very light. She noticed that, for her ear had become newly sensitive. He had caught a glimpse of her through the window, and knowing, therefore, that she was in the parlor, came to the door and stood there.

"Bless me!" he exclaimed, after a moment; "how charming you look!"

And he came forward with a pleased smile on his face, and taking her hand, bent down and kissed her.

"Sweet as a rose!" he added, holding her away from him and gazing at her admiringly. How her heart did beat with new delight!

"Dressed for company?"

There was just a little shade of coldness in Harry's voice as he suggested the probable reason for her singularly improved appearance.

"Yes," replied Bella.

"Who?"

"My husband." There was a tender heart-flutter in her voice.

Harry was a little puzzled, but greatly pleased. It was true that he had been riding out that afternoon with a lady, a handsome, attractive woman, who was throwing around his weak, almost boyish, spirit a siren's fascination. She put on every charm in her power to summon, while the foolish wife was hiding hers away, and taking no pains to hold dominion in the heart she had won and was now in danger of losing. Five minutes before, the companion of his ride appeared to his fancy so charming in comparison with his wife that he felt no pleasure at the thought of meeting one who, since their marriage, had seemed to grow every day less and less attractive. But now Bella was his queen of hearts again!

"And you really dressed to receive me, darling?" he said as he kissed her again, and then drew his arm lovingly about her waist.

"Yes, for you. Could a true wife wish to look lovelier to others' eyes than her husband's?"

"I should think not," he answered.

She understood in the words more than he meant to convey.

There was a rose-tint on everything in Bella's home that evening. From the cold, half-indifferent husband, Harry was transformed to the warm, attentive lover. How many times during the pleasant conversation that followed, as she turned her eyes upon him, did she catch a look of tender admiration or loving pride!

"What has made you so charming to-night?" he said as he kissed her for the tenth time. "You look as pure and sweet as a lily."

"Love for my husband," she answered, and then a tear, in which joy's sunlight made a rainbow, stole out from the drooping lashes and lay a crystal drop on her cheek.

She made no confession of her thoughtless neglect of the means by which hearts are held in thrall to love, though her husband half guessed at the fact that something had awakened her to the truth.

On the next afternoon Harry rode out with a lady again, but that lady was his wife. He was never afterward in danger of being won away from faithful love, for Bella grew in his eyes more attractive, more charming, more lovable, every day. And she thus saved him, in his younger and less stable years, from being drawn aside from the right way, and both herself and him from years of wretchedness.

Don't, fair ladies, neglect these personal attractions because you are married. The charms that won are just as potent to retain affection. The beginnings of alienation often lie just here, and many a neglected wife has lost her husband's heart because she ceased to look lovely in his eyes. It isn't in the heart of a man to love a dowdy, careless, fretful, unlovely woman. The husband bargains for something very different from this, and if he finds himself deceived will assuredly repent of his bargain So look to it, young wives, that you lose not, through carelessness or neglect, a single charm.

II.

STRENGTH AND WEAKNESS.

"YOU coward!" ejaculated Mr. Raymond, in a tone of impatience that could not be suppressed, and catching up his fragile little wife, he bore her in his arms out among the breakers, and held her firmly while the foaming surf dashed over them. She was white and shivering when he brought her back to the shore.

"There's no danger. What a coward you are!" said Mr. Raymond, half in anger, as his wife stood with her snowy feet just buried in the edge of a fast receding wave. "Come back into the surf again. See, there are over a hundred ladies in the water now."

But the pale, slender little woman held back, overcome by nervous fears, answering:

"No, Henry, I do not care to go in again; I'm

all in a tremor; the water is too cold for me." Her teeth chattered as she spoke.

"Cold! Pshaw! the water is warm as milk. You're afraid; that's the trouble. I wouldn't be such a coward for a kingdom. Come along! Another dash among the waves will tone up your nerves and put courage into your heart."

And saying this, Mr. Raymond, a strong, stout, warm-blooded man, with animal courage enough to face almost any danger, partly dragged and partly bore his weak and frightened wife back again among the seething waters, where in his thoughtless cruelty he permitted a wave to break entirely over her. She did not expect, and so was not prepared for, this. The briny fluid entered her mouth and nostrils, strangling and terrifying her to such a degree that when her husband carried her to the shore she was unable from nervous exhaustion to stand.

Weak brandy and water, and half an hour in bed, restored Mrs. Raymond's nervous system to its normal condition, but no persuasion could induce her to bathe again. Mr. Raymond scolded, taunted and ridiculed her for this cowardice, but all efforts to overcome her timidity were in vain. Had he permitted her to make her way gradually into the surf, to try for a little while the smooth water inside of the breakers, she might have gained courage, and at last found herself unterrified among the rushing and foaming waves. But he was too impatient a man for this.

From the seashore Mr. Raymond took his wife to Niagara, where he lost patience with her again. He wanted her to pass with him under the great sheet of water, but the bare idea made her shiver.

"There's no more danger for you than for me," urged her husband. "Ladies go under the Falls every day. Come, now, be a brave little woman. It will be something to talk about."

"No inducement would tempt me, Henry," answered Mrs. Raymond.

"Well, I always did hate a coward!" broke from the lips of Mr. Raymond as he turned in brief anger from his wife and strode the room with the sweep and strength of a vigorous animal. Without a thought for the fears of his wife, he did not see the sudden going out of light from her countenance, nor the pain and fear that swept over it.

Always did hate a coward! And had he not over and over again called her a coward? These were the hardest words that ever came from her impulsive husband's lips, and the hurt went very deep.

"And so you will not go under the Falls with me?" he said, in a cold, half-offended way, turning from a window where he had stationed himself after his flurry about the room.

"Yes, I will go." Mrs. Raymond did not smile, nor speak cheerfully, nor even look into her husband's face. But her tones were firm. She spoke in earnest.

"You will?" Mr. Raymond's voice leaped with a sudden surprise, in which pleasure was mingled.

"Yes." Ah, if he could have looked past her sober face and seen the struggling fears in her heart—fear of mortal danger contending with fear of losing her husband's love!

"I always did hate a coward!" Already had passed from his thoughts the memory of these unguarded words. But could she forget?

Never! "If he hates a coward, I must exhibit no more fears." Not in any utterance of words was this resolve taken. But still it was the fixed law of her life for all the time to come. What were bodily harms, or death, even, to loss of her husband's love? Nothing—nothing. But had she banished fear from her heart? Had her sensitive organization, in which fear of external danger was almost an idiosyncrasy, changed in a moment? Oh no! She was the same as to this, but a stronger fear held weaker fears in subjection.

And so in an hour from that time Mrs. Raymond passed under the avalanche of water that came thundering down into the abyss below. Scarcely with a higher courage or a more shrinking consciousness of life peril did martyr of old advance to the stake or scaffold. Pale lips, and colorless face, and trembling hands, that grasped the stout arm of her husband, were all in evidence of what she suffered, but these were scarcely noted by Mr. Raymond, who felt exhilarated by the scene, and exultant at having overcome the vain terrors of his nervous wife.

"You see there is no danger," he said, lifting

his hand to the great moving wall of waters that shut them from the world. But his voice was drowned in the cataract's thunder. Soon she began to draw upon his arm. Her terror did not lessen by familiarity; she was panting to return. But Mr. Raymond, with something of the feeling that men have who force a timid horse to the very side of a locomotive and hold him there to cure him of fear, kept his wife under the fall until she came near fainting. How near, he never knew. Mr. Raymond praised and complimented her for her bravery without having the most distant perception of what she had endured. His praise was grateful, and she was glad that she had gone with him, though whenever thought went realizingly to the scene under that terrible sheet of down-rushing water which shook the earth in its fall, a shudder crept through her heart.

Next, Mr. Raymond proposed a trip in the "Maid of the Mist." Twice since their visit to the Falls had Mrs. Raymond watched this fragile little steamer as she went bravely—recklessly, it seemed to her—almost to the edge of the leaping torrent, which seemed to grasp after the tiny vessel, eager for its destruction. No money would have tempted her, no power forced her, into that peril. But now, trying to shut her eyes to danger, she said "Yes," and prepared to go. But to remove all perception of danger was simply impossible. Firmly grasping her husband's arm, and without a word expressing her terror, Mrs. Raymond stood, with pale, closed lips and eyes wildly dilated, as the boat steamed up into the very spray of the Falls. His was the enjoyment, hers the suffering. Death might come to her in almost any of his usual forms, and she might be aware of his approach, yet remain peaceful in soul compared with the agitations that rent her on this occasion.

"What a brave little woman you have become!" said the pleased husband as the boat headed round and left the point of danger. The praise was grateful, but no adequate compensation for the pain he had forced her to endure.

"And now for Montreal and the Rapids!"

"I would prefer going back and spending a week at Saratoga," answered the wife, her heart shrinking at thought of going through the Rapids of the St. Lawrence, the perils of which were greatly exaggerated in her imagination. She had read of them and heard of them from summer tourists, and the dangers of the passage were vivid impressions on her mind.

Mr. Raymond understood his wife in this objection as well as she understood herself, but that only made him the more fixed in his purpose to go down among the Rapids. He must cure her of this foolish weakness which was interfering so much with his comfort and her enjoyment. And so the shrinking, fearful, reluctant little woman was forced to encounter new alarms and to suffer in a degree that it was impossible for her husband to comprehend. Thence he would proceed to the White Mountains; and though he knew his wife's fear of a horse, he coolly planned an ascent in which she must make one of the party. But excessive nervous excitement, continued through so long a period, wrought its legitimate effects upon her delicate organization. On the morning selected for the ascent Mrs. Raymond was too ill to leave her bed. At first her impatient husband accused her of pretence, but he was quickly disabused of that error, for, hurt by the allegation, she made an effort to get up and dress herself, but fainted and fell upon the floor.

It was nearly a week before Mrs. Raymond could be removed. Then, by short journeys, her husband bore her back to New York, their place of residence, with a feeling of discouragement in his heart. Weakness, timidity, nervous fears—these were so far outside of his organization that he could neither sympathize with nor tolerate them. He admired boldness, freedom, strength, courage, but, with the instinct of a nature such as his, despised their opposites. Not being a man of much self-denial, or very considerate of others, Mr. Raymond made little effort to conceal from his wife what he really felt and thought, but always treated her weakness as something blameworthy. It took months for her to recover fully from the effects of this summer tour. But for the feeble babe that lay in her arms when the next season came round she would have been forced through the same ordeal. That gave the stay-at-home argument its full value, and she did not leave the city, except for a couple of weeks' residence at the house of a friend on the Hudson. It was a pleasant summer to her compared with the pre vious one, but Mr. Raymond fretted over it as dull and stupid. He wanted the exhilarant ocean, the bold cataract, the lofty mountain and the fleet courser. There was joy to a temperament like his even in the face of danger.

A few years went on, and the tremulous nerves of Mrs. Raymond did not grow any firmer in the face of bodily peril. She was a weak, timid, shrinking woman still, only more successful in hiding her fears from the intelligent eyes of her ruddy, robust, iron-nerved husband, who, to use his own boastful words, did not know the quality of fear.

But there is more than one kind of strength and courage. That which Mr. Raymond possessed is shared with the lion and the bear: it was animal courage and strength. The courage to look disaster in the face, to stand up bravely in the front of adverse opinions, to walk steadily onward in the path of duty though men sneer and blame, to be true to honor and virtue amid the sorest temptations, to do right even though friends and fortune are lost,—this is the higher form of courage, this is to have real strength. And the day was at hand in which

Mr. Raymond was to be tried by the truer standard.

Mrs. Raymond had noticed, with concern, a growing abstraction on the part of her husband. His wonted cheerfulness was gone, and gradually lines of care and trouble began to show themselves on his face. He went out alone in the evening more frequently than before, and to her questions answered that he had business engagements. Then he had calls from men not known to Mrs. Raymond, who would sit late in his private room, and sometimes their voices, in loud and earnest talk, would startle her with vague anxieties. That something was going wrong she felt sure, but had not the remotest intimation of its nature, though she had time and again endeavored to win the confidence of her husband.

The truth was, commercial ruin impended, and Mr. Raymond was beating about with more of blind desperation than calm judgment in search of the way to extricate himself. To take this weak, fearful, timid little wife into his counsels was never thought of for a moment. He must save her from shock and harm if possible The storm that was lowering in his sky must not strike upon her, for at the first touch of its chill winds leaf would wither and blossom fall. Now he felt for her a deeper and more pervading tenderness. The threatened danger he could fully comprehend, and if the evil lowering in the sky was so fearful to him, would she not die in terror at its first frown? Carefully he sought to guard her, and jealously he concealed all intimations of peril. But she was not deceived. Great peril she knew to be at hand, though in ignorance of its nature.

One evening two men were alone with her husband. She had noticed, on their being announced by the servant, an expression on his face that startled her by its strangeness. He had risen up quickly, and, as it seemed to her, in a slightly agitated manner. Half an hour subsequently, as Mrs. Raymond passed the door of her husband's office, or private room, whither he had taken his two visitors, she was startled by hearing one of the men say in an urgent voice:

"It's your only chance, Mr. Raymond."

There was dead silence for a few moments. Mrs. Raymond held her breath, listening for the answer.

"It takes a brave man to look ruin in the face." Was that her husband's voice? How full of bitterness! How depressed! How shorn of its confidence!

"A braver man than I," was responded. "But why talk of ruin, with the means of safety within your grasp, Mr. Raymond?"

"I do not like the means."

"Does a drowning man hesitate when the means of escape are offered?"

There came no reply to this question.

"Think of all the terrible consequences that must follow, Mr. Raymond. It will kill your wife!"

The groan that parted the lips of Mr. Raymond was audible to the startled listener's ears.

"Mercantile dishonor, ruined fortunes, a tainted name, even—for against every unfortunate man there are some to whisper of fraud and wrong: think of these things, Mr. Raymond"—thus urged the tempter—"and then decide the question. Get beyond this extremity, and all will be well. No wrong is intended, and none need ensue. This money pressure is but temporary. Keep your credit unsullied, and when this sudden storm is over you will find yourself on smooth water with a sunny sky above. Everything depends on your keeping afloat now. If you go under, all is lost now and for ever. Desperate diseases require desperate remedies."

"If I stood alone," said Mr. Raymond, in a tone so full of trouble that it brought tears to the eyes of his listening wife, "I would not hesitate. The remedy you propose is worse than the disease, and I would die rather than take it. But other lives hang on mine. Ruin will not pause when I go down, but trample ruthlessly on other hearts."

The door of the room swung firmly open, and the apparition of a woman startled the inmates.

"You do not stand alone!" said a brave voice, and Mrs. Raymond moved to the side of her husband. Her step was strong, her form lifted to its full height, her cheeks flushed with quickly-moving blood, her mouth calm and resolute, her eyes full of strength and courage. "And therefore the stronger reason why you should hesitate. Take no further counsel of these men," she added, her tones growing almost severe; "the little I have heard them say tells me that they are not safe advisers. If the ruin they predict is to fall, let it fall, but keep your honor unsullied. I am brave enough to stand by your side in any trouble that God in his wisdom may send, but not brave enough to meet the consequences that will surely follow if you go forward in the way that is now proposed."

Mr. Raymond turned and looked into the face and upon the form of his wife with an expression of surprise, doubt and astonishment

"Are you brave enough," he asked, "to meet wide-sweeping ruin? to give up this luxurious home? to go down into poverty and neglect?"

"If my husband comes out of the fiery trial as gold from the crucible—yes," was calmly answered.

"My good name will suffer."

"Through false assertion!" Mrs. Raymond spoke quickly.

"Yes, for I have not purposely wronged any man."

"The good heart will be my tower of

strength," she said, a bright smile touching her lips.

"You are answered." Mr. Raymond looked from his wife to the men who a little while before had nearly drawn him away from the path of honor and safety. His countenance grew almost stern. "Let the worst come. My feet have touched the solid rock, and shall rest thereon, immovable."

And silently the baffled tempters withdrew. Not to advise Raymond for his own safety had they come, but to secure an advantage for themselves by means that would have wronged others and surely disgraced the unhappy, bewildered and almost desperate man they were dragging to the brink of a precipice.

"Tell me all, dear husband—all, all! I am strong enough to bear the worst, and brave enough to stand by your side facing the whole world. Misfortune comes not alone to us. It falls upon thousands and tens of thousands, and shall we not bear it patiently? Not from without is real happiness, but from within. Reverses and changes cannot rob us of love, peace and the blessing that God sends always to the pure of heart."

Mr. Raymond told her all, and she listened to the statements which left no shadow of hope without blanching cheek or quivering lip. The timid, feeble little woman, who shuddered in sight of the cataract and grew pale and faint as the surf swept toward her fragile form, stood up without a shrinking nerve as the tempest of misfortune grew black overhead. Brave, hopeful words came from her lips, and strength from her strong heart passed to the fainting and fearful heart of her husband, who, but for her courageous bearing, would have stumbled in the path of duty, and sullied through the weakness of terror a good name which he still bears proudly before all men.

III.

LOVE NOT CONSTRAINED.

MRS. EARLY had been fretted at the breakfast-table. The butter-knife not being in its place beside the butter-plate had given occasion for a sharp reprimand.

"Don't let me have to speak of that again," said Mrs. Early to the servant in a tone of voice that made her husband's flesh creep, as we say.

Mr. Early glanced into her face, but its expression was so disagreeable to him that he turned his eyes away. At the same time there came into his thoughts these lines of Shakespeare's:

> "A woman moved is like a fountain troubled,
> Muddy, ill-seeming, thick, bereft of beauty,
> And while it is so, none so dry or thirsty
> Will deign to sip or touch one drop of it."

When it is known that Mr. and Mrs. Early had been man and wife for only about six months, it will be admitted that something was going wrong. The young husband had plucked his rose, the sweetest to him that the garden bore, but somehow it was losing beauty and fragrance.

The morning meal passed almost in silence. Mr. Early kept his eyes for most of the time on his cup and plate. It was never pleasant to look at his wife when she was out of humor. The expression of her face hurt him. Why was she out of humor? You know the cause. A careless or hurried servant had forgotten the butter-knife in setting the table—that was all.

Mr. Early only took one cup of coffee on that morning. He usually drank two. Finishing the meal before his wife was done, he pushed back his chair, and rising, said, "I'm in a hurry this morning."

He did not come round the table to kiss his wife—a little ceremonial which she had so perseveringly required at every daily parting that her matter-of-fact husband began to rebel at the constrained salutes—but turned off abruptly and went into the hall to get his hat. Particularly was the kissing humor absent on this morning. Kissing was with him a sign of love, and he saw no image of love in the troubled fountain of his young wife's spirit.

"Why, Frank!" cried Mrs. Early in surprise, and with reproof in her tone. He understood what she meant, but it was always a hard thing for him to act against his feelings. Just then his wife was unlovely in his eyes, and he didn't want to kiss her.

"Good-morning! I'm in a hurry," and he started for the street door.

Mrs. Early waited until he was near the end of the hall, and then, springing up from the table, ran after him. He heard her coming, but did not pause. Opening the door, he passed out and shut it behind him. He felt that there was something hard, almost cruel, in this, but the fountain, in his eyes, was "muddy," and he had no desire to "sip" or touch one drop of it.

Mrs. Early stood in surprise and disappointment for some moments, and then going into the little parlor, sat down and cried. Unfortunately, she did not clearly understand the case —did not see how, if there was defect of love on her husband's part, it was because she had made herself less lovely in his eyes.

When Mr. Early returned at dinner-time he was in a repentant mood, and wished to atone by words and acts of tenderness for his neglect of the morning. But his wife gravely declined the proffered kiss, and looked at him with sober, accusing eyes.

"Oh, just as you please!" was the slightly-offended remark of Mr. Early, and taking up a book, he sat down and read until the bell announced dinner.

The meat was overdone, and Mrs. Early scolded about it sharply.

"A poor sauce for a bad dinner!" So Mr. Early thought, but of course kept his thoughts to himself.

Trifling omissions in setting the table, which a quiet word aside to the servant would have instantly supplied, were made the occasion of sharp reprimands that were especially disagreeable to Mr. Early. He ate in silence and with contracted brows. Strangely oblivious to the real effect upon her husband of her table-lecturings and complainings, Mrs. Early kept up her fault-finding almost to the end of the meal. She was in an unhappy humor, and gave voice to it, as a kind of relief, without reflection. If she could have known just what was passing in her husband's mind, her lips would have been closed in sudden silence. You may think it strange that her perception was at fault. Her husband thought it strange. Indeed, he felt that she must have known how unpleasantly her conduct was affecting him, and this gave him less patience. It seemed to him that she was giving annoyance willfully.

Mr. Early left the dinner-table, as he had left the breakfast-table, abruptly, and went away to his business. The parting kiss, as in the morning, was omitted. This time the young wife did not ask for it. There was considerable crying through the afternoon, and some thinking. After the crying came the thinking. There was a calmer state, but perception was at fault in the main. Pride came in to dim the clearness of her mental vision.

"I'll not beg for love!" she said to herself. "If he has no kisses to give, I will not gain them through solicitation."

So, when her husband came back at day's decline, she met him with a composed manner, slightly reserved, and without an intimation that she desired or expected the kiss he had prepared himself to give. We say, prepared himself to give, not from love, but from constraint. The kiss was not offered. There was a manner about the young wife that caused him to withhold it—a manner not usual, and not quite understood.

During tea-time no jar occurred. If everything was not just to Mrs. Early's mind, she repressed complaint. Once or twice her husband saw a cloud forming and began to brace himself for a storm, but there fell no rain, flashed no lightning. A few quiet sentences passed during the meal. They felt better on rising than when they sat down. Early looked into his wife's face, soberer than usual, yet veiled with a kind of tender depression that touched his feelings. "Have I been unkind?" he said to himself. The very question softened him. His wife came round the table and stood by his side. They walked from the room together into the lower hall and up the stairs. On the way he drew his arm about her waist, then bent down and kissed her lips—not with constraint, nor with a careless dash, but with a soft, lingering pressure born of a loving impulse. The low, sweet thrill that ran through the heart of Mrs. Early was almost new to her.

"What does it mean?" she asked herself, in a kind of surprise, as she leaned toward her husband, yielding to the closer pressure of his arm. On reaching their sitting-room, Mr. Early withdrew his arm gently, and taking up a book sat down to read. Neither was yet entirely at ease. Something unpleasant had arisen between them, and it was not yet wholly removed.

Mrs. Early's thoughts were still more than usually active. Seeing that her husband was getting absorbed in his volume, she took a late magazine and tried to find interest in its pages. She had not read far before a passage arrested her attention that made her heart beat quicker. She read it again, and then began pondering its meaning. We give the passage:

"Love is not constrained, but spontaneous. It is dimmed by solicitation, it is hurt by chidings. If you would be loved, you must pût on the graces of loveliness. Thousands of young wives have poured out unavailing tears for the love they might have kept by sweet deportment.

They fret over things disagreeable in their households, they scold their servants at meal-times, they veil their countenances with peevishness, dissatisfaction or anger, and then demand kisses and signs of love! But love is repelled, not won. From all this comes estrangement, not conjunction."

Almost stealthily, after reading the passage twice, did Mrs. Early glance across to her husband. His face was in repose; his lips wore a pleasant expression; his book was interesting him. Rising, she quietly left the room. Sitting down in another apartment alone, she began reviewing her conduct in the light of this new revelation, and saw it as she had never seen it before. Her cheeks burned as she remembered how rarely a meal had passed of late without its quietness being marred by reprimands addressed to the cook or waiter. She was almost always fretted at the table because of some neglect or deficiency which a little forethought on her part might have remedied, and so very few meals were really enjoyed by either herself or husband.

"I will reform all this!" said Mrs. Early when the whole case stood out clearly before her.

"I don't wonder now at the variable temper of my husband, hitherto a mystery—at the fact that clouds have fallen so often and so suddenly over the sunshine of his face. The fault was my own. As for kisses, I will win, not demand them, in the future. If they are withheld, I will look for the cause in myself, and not in my husband."

On the next morning, a little before the breakfast-hour, Mrs. Early went down to the dining-room and kitchen to see if things were being done in right order. Two or three serious omissions met her eyes. She repressed her quickly-rising anger, and instead of scolding until her blood was heated, calmly but seriously pointed out the neglect, for which there came an instant acknowledgment and a promise not to be careless again.

Still, even with this care and forethought, all defects were not foreseen and mended. On taking the cover from the sugar-bowl on sitting down to the table, the vessel was found empty. This was a thing of frequent occurrence, and was usually accompanied by a sharp reproof, given volubly and with angry, flashing eyes.

A slight premonitory shiver ran along the

nerves of Mr. Early. There had been an enjoyable calm and pleasant sunshine, but here came the cloud again, suddenly darkening the summer sky. He paused for the storm to break.

But there was no storm. There was scarcely a dimming of the light in his wife's face. She lifted the empty bowl in a quiet way and handed it to the servant, speaking to her aside and in an undertone. The servant said, "Oh, how could I have forgotten?" with sincere regret in her voice, and quickly supplied the omission.

When Mrs. Early looked across the table and saw the expression of her husband's eyes, which were fixed upon her, she had her reward. Admiration was slightly veiled by wonder.

How very small this incident! What a trifle it seems! But little things are pivots on which the motion of greater things depends. They are the keys by which we often unlock treasure-houses of happiness or misery.

When Mr. Early arose from the breakfast-table his wife did not spring up as usual to demand her parting kiss, but sat with a gentle, subdued aspect, looking at her husband with love-lighted eyes. He came round the table, and, stooping, touched her lips in a pressure worth more than all the kisses she had extorted from him in a month—worth more, as her full heart acknowledged to itself that instant.

There was no impediment, no constraint in love after that. It came full and free, drawn toward its object by the magnetic force of loveliness.

IV.

GROWING COLD

HERE was an ardor about the young lover that showed how deeply his heart was interested, and his betrothed might almost be said to live only in his presence. He flew to her side like steel to the magnet when evening set him free from business; and she awaited his certain coming with a trembling joy that pervaded her whole being. The days were long that kept them apart, but lightning-footed the hours of evening. How eagerly they looked forward to that blessed time when they would hear the words spoken that were to make them one! And the time came at last, though with slow-pacing steps. Hand in hand and heart beating to heart, they entered a new path of life, carpeted with flowers, and moved onward with springing feet that took their measure to Love's delicious music.

Swiftly passed the first seasons of their new existence. It was the warm, fragrant, blossoming spring-time, and the sunshine filled the air with vernal warmth.

"Shall we ever grow cold to each other?" said the young husband, leaning toward his bride and speaking in a tone of peculiar tenderness.

This was occasioned by the presence, in a small company, of a married couple, not two years wedded, who were known to have lost much of young love's ardor. Their indifference was so apparent as to have become a subject of remark with their friends and acquaintances.

"Never, Leonard, never!" was almost tremulously whispered back. "That is impossible! Those who truly love, love on for ever."

"And with us it is true," said the husband—"true, warm, eternal love!"

And each believed that it was so. Let us follow them a little way on their life-journey.

Leonard Williams was a young, ambitious merchant, who was trying, unwisely, to do a large business on a small capital, and Leonard Williams and his wife were a young couple who thought rather more of making an appearance in the social world than was consistent with their means and prospects. He had too large a store, and too many goods in it, and they lived in too large a house, with too much furniture in it.

A tranquil spirit is not possible under such circumstances. Overwearying mental labor and absorbing care must attend them. It has ever been so—it was so with Leonard Williams. Even before the waning of the first year his fine brow began to wear a shadow and his eyes to have an absent expression. There was a failing warmth in his manner toward his bride that chilled her heart, at times, as if cold airs had blown upon it suddenly. She was too young, too inexperienced and too ignorant of the world to comprehend the causes that were at work undermining daily the foundations of their happiness. She only felt that her husband was changing, that warmth was diminishing and the cloud and the shadow coming in the place of sunshine.

Daily and weekly and monthly the change went on, he getting more and more absorbed in business, and she finding a certain poor compensation for heart-weariness in dress, gay company, pleasure and fashionable dissipation. The coldness of feeling, as well as of exterior, was mutual. A few years longer, and all the little tender courtesies that marked their intercourse when alone failed utterly. Williams would meet his wife on his daily return from business without a changing countenance or tender word, and she met him at evening and parted with him on each succeeding morning with an air of indifference that iced over the surface of his feelings.

And so the years went on, he struggling and striving with the world in the arena of business, and she trying to find in the unsubstantial, gilded exterior of things that pleasure she failed to extract from the real.

How like mould on a rich garment, or rust upon burnished steel, did indifference creep over the pleasant surface of their lives, dimming the mutual attraction! Williams had energy of character and a mind that found new strength in difficulty. A man of feebler intellect, less hope and less suggestion, starting wrong, as he did, would have been driven to the wall in a few years. But Williams discovered his error in time to prepare himself for the impending consequences. At the close of five years from the day of his marriage he resolutely looked his affairs in the face, and saw that, instead of being worth many thousands of dollars, he was just upon the verge of bankruptcy. It took him two years to get safely past the dangers that beset his way. One cause of his trouble lay in the extravagance of his style of living. It rather startled him to find, on examining his private account, that twenty thousand dollars had been drawn for personal expenses. One-half of that sum, added to his capital, would have made all safe.

"This will never do!" he said to himself. "We are living too extravagantly. There must be a change."

But what would his fashionable wife say to this? Would she be willing to give up her elegant home and retire from her gay position? A feeling of discouragement came over him as these questions arose in his mind.

"She must give it up, she must retire!" he said to himself, with some warmth. But he did not wish to make known the fact of his deep embarrassment, for he had no confidence in her power to endure reverses. If she sunk down in weak distress, the burdens he had to bear would be so much heavier, and they were quite heavy enough already. After viewing the matter on all sides and pondering it deeply, Williams came to the conclusion that the only economical change likely to meet his wife's approval was a change from their own home to a fashionable boarding-house. A close calculation satisfied him that to do so would lessen their annual expenses about one thousand dollars.

"Anna," he said to her, one evening, breaking through his cold, abstracted silence, "we are living at too costly a rate."

Mrs. Williams turned her eyes upon his face with the manner of one who had heard unpleasant words, but did not fully comprehend their meaning.

"It would cost us less to board, and you would be freed from household cares," he added.

"Don't think of it, Leonard!" was her prompt reply, spoken in very decided tones. "I cannot be induced to give up my elegant home. As to household cares, I am not troubled by them."

"It is a question of economy," said Williams

"If that is all, the question may as well sleep," replied his wife, almost indifferently "for it costs quite as much to live in a first-class hotel or boarding-house as in your own home."

Williams had no more to say. A deep sigh fluttered on his lips; his gaze withdrew itself from the countenance of his wife and fell to the floor; his head sank low upon his bosom, and thought went from his home to wander amid the seething reefs toward which his vessel was driving, hoping to find some narrow passage through which he might steer in safety to a smooth haven. He felt cooler toward his wife after that, and she was conscious of the coldness without imagining the cause.

No change in the style or cost of living took place. That heavy burden he had to carry in addition to his other heavy burdens, and it required all of his strength.

During the two years that elapsed before his feet were on firm ground again he appeared to have lost all interest in his home, his wife or his children. Mrs. Williams frequently said, lightly, speaking to friends or acquaintances, that she had no husband now, Mr. Williams having united himself to business in a second marriage. If she spoke thus in his presence, he would part his lips in a forced smile, or perhaps say jocosely that she had better have him before the courts for bigamy.

Fashion, show, pleasure, filled up all the time of Mrs. Williams which was not devoted to maternal duties and household cares, and business was the Moloch at which Mr. Williams sacrificed all social and home affections.

At forty, with a family of interesting children springing up around them, they were but coldly tolerant of each other. Never having seen, from the beginning of her married life, any good reason for economy or self-denial, Mrs. Williams had failed to practice these virtues, but had suffered the opposite vices of extravagance and vain self-indulgence to grow rankly as offensive weeds. Her demands upon her husband's purse had, therefore, always been large, and they steadily increased, until he was learning to hold the strings more tightly, and to question and object whenever she made what he thought large requisitions. Thus alienations were constantly engendered, and, at times, there was strife between them. Roughness on his part and petulance on hers often came in to help the work of estrangement.

Twenty years of a false life, twenty years in

which two married partners, warm and loving at the first, went on steadily growing cold toward each other through the interposition of sordid and worldly things, twenty years of a home intercourse but rarely brightened by love's warm sunshine breaking through the leaden clouds of care or folly,—what a sad heart-history is here! And is it not the history of thousands of over-earnest business-men and their thoughtless, unsympathizing, fashionable wives, who seek outside of hearts and homes what they can never find—that tranquillity of soul after which all aspire, but to which so few attain? Alas that it is so!

Ah that we could write from henceforth a better record of Leonard Williams and his wife, that we could tell you how, growing at last weary of their vain existence, they turned back, athirst for the pure waters whose sweetness had once refreshed them, finding again the fountain of eternal youth! But it was not so. Habits of thought and feeling were hardened into that second nature which is rarely broken up. If, occasionally, the restless heart returned along its life-journey, seeking for some of the lost flowers and vanished fragrance, their sweetness was perceived only as the dim delight of a dream, not real enough to inspire an effort to seek their restoration. And so they moved on in the coldness of twilight. Age found him a sordid, irritable, unhappy man, and her a nervous, restless, vain, disappointed woman.

There are such, reader, all around you. But keep your heart warm. Do not suffer it to grow cold toward your wife or husband. Shut out the vain things of the world. The home-loves are warmest, the home-lights brightest, and they will grow warmer and brighter with years if you feed them with the pure oil of unselfish affection.

V.

LITTLE THINGS.

KATY CLEVELAND has been married only a single month. What ails the sweet young bride? Her eyes look as if she has been weeping. That curve upon her lips is not the arching beauty of a smile. Has Edward spoken unkindly, or refused some darling request? Has he left her to be gone a week, or failed to return at the appointed time after a few days' absence? No, none of these. Then why has grief visited her gentle bosom?—for grieving she is as she sits there by the window still as an effigy.

Do not smile at the answer we give you: Edward has only forgotten the expected kiss at parting, and gone forth to his daily business, leaving a shadow upon the spirit of his young wife.

You smile in the face of our caution! It is such a little thing! And you say, If Katy Cleveland is going to make a bracket to hang troubles upon out of every trifle like this, she will soon have her whole house tapestried with gloom.

But it was no trifle to Katy. The young husband's kiss may be nothing to you—not even held to the value of a pepper-corn—but it was of priceless value to the bride. She had even come to look forward to the daily partings and meetings with a pleasant anticipation of the unfailing kiss, that sweet token of love.

But the token had been withheld at last, and on the closing day of their "honeymoon." How ominous! Was the husband's shadow already thrown across the threshold of their home?

Acts we all instinctively regard as the representatives of thoughts or feelings. The kiss, with Katy, was an expression of love, its denial an evidence of failing warmth on the part of her idolized young husband. She had no other interpretation. No wonder, therefore, that tears dimmed her eyes; no wonder that a veil was on her countenance. It was the bride's first sorrow.

Away to his store Edward Cleveland had gone, wholly unconscious of the shadow he had left behind him. He did not even remember that in parting he had withheld the usual kiss. Thoughts of business had intruded themselves even into his home, and claimed to share the hours sacred to domestic tranquillity. The merchant had risen for the time superior to the husband.

When Edward met his wife at the falling of twilight it was with a lover's ardor. Not only one kiss was bestowed, but many. In the warm sunshine of his presence the clouds which had veiled her spirit for hours were scattered into nothingness.

And yet the memory of that forgotten kiss remained as an unwelcome guest. On the next day; and the next, and every day for a week, the expected kiss was given, yet ever and ever, in her hours of loneliness, would thought go wandering back to the hour when her husband left her without this token of his love and trouble the crystal waters of her soul.

At the end of a week the kiss was forgotten

again. Nor was this all: Edward had shown on one occasion a spirit of impatience and spoken words that smote upon her feelings with a sharp pain. He had not meant to speak unkindly, had not even felt so, but Katy had seemed unusually obtuse in some matters about which Edward sought to interest her, and her dullness provoked him.

"You are a little simpleton!" He spoke half in sport, half in earnest, his brows slightly contracting. "Why, a girl fourteen years of age could see through it all!"

He observed that the color on her cheeks deepened, that the expression of her eyes changed and that she turned her face partly away from him, but he never imagined the degree of pain his lightly-spoken censure had occasioned. It never entered into his heart to conceive of the darkness of the veil which suddenly came between her spirit and the sunlight.

And so Edward felt a degree of contempt for the quality of her understanding. "A little simpleton!" Ah! if the words were half-playfully spoken, they had a meaning. He would not have said them if he had not discovered a feebleness of comprehension below what he had believed to exist. Could the young wife's thoughts reach to any other conclusion? No!

These were little things, trifles, compared with the great troubles of life that come to all, and that were in store for Katy Cleveland as surely as for the rest. But they need not have been, and would not have been if Edward had thought as much out of himself and had felt toward Katy as tenderly as in the beginning. How very guarded was the lover in all his words and actions! He never forgot the parting kiss, never was betrayed into a lightly-spoken word that carried with it a sting for the heart of his betrothed. Oh no! Had he deceived Katy as to his real character and feelings? We cannot give a freely-spoken yea or nay to this. He had not meant to deceive her. And yet certain semblances were put on, and the lover appeared to have more perfections than really existed in the man.

"Ah, well, is not this ever so?" Perhaps it is. With certain qualifications to the sentiment, the lover is always a dissembler. If not, when he assumes the husband he thinks it no longer needful to give voice to the tender sentiments that pervade his bosom. It is enough for his wife to know that he loves her. But she looks for signs and tokens as of old, and these failing, she sits often athirst by the dried-up fountains from which once gushed out refreshing waters.

Almost timidly did Katy look into her husband's face when he returned home. Every hour during his absence, and almost every minute of every hour, had she thought of his depreciating words, and she felt that he too must be thinking of them all the time, and with something of disappointment, if not alienation. But she was in error here. Edward had forgotten them almost as soon as uttered, and nothing would have surprised him more than the fact that Katy was grieving over them. He met her with the most ardent of kisses, the sweetest of smiles and the tenderest of words, and she was happy again.

But the evening did not pass wholly free from shadows. Edward was showing more and more of the true external of his character, which had many aspects not yet seen by his wife. He had selfish qualities, as all men have, and peculiarities that to some would show themselves as offences. One fault was impatience. This he had repressed, though often under strong temptation to let his feelings leap into unseemly words. He was, moreover, a man disposed to musing in silence. His business fully occupied his thoughts during business-hours, and intruded itself even into the times and seasons that should have been sacred to domestic peace. A thorough mercantile education had given him habits of order and punctuality. He was one of your minute men, orderly, punctual, a little sarcastic and impatient. Ah, Katy Cleveland! you have a trial before you with this husband of yours, who is far from being the perfect man your girlish imagination pictured. And yet he loves you as the apple of his eye, and would on no account give you pain.

"There it is again!" Edward had gone to the bookcase which stood in their sitting-room to get a volume. Vexation was apparent in his tones.

"What's the matter?" inquired Katy, whose heart began to beat quicker.

"Who is it that disarranges these books so shockingly?"

"No one, dear. Nobody touches them but myself," replied Katy.

"Then it is time you had learned a little order. Just look here! Do you see this volume of Byron upside down, and out of its place in the series? And here are two books laid on the tops of others, instead of being set in upon the shelf, and here is another with the front instead of the back turned outward. Such disorder annoys me terribly! Of all things, I like to see order, and most of all in a woman. I hardly expected to find it so seriously lacking in my wife!"

Edward was annoyed, and did not very carefully modulate his tones. They struck very harshly and with an angry intonation upon the ears of Katy, whose heart was too full to permit her to make answer.

"The fact is," continued Edward, "I am a little disappointed in you."

Ah! This was too bad! The blow given, with not a thought of its force, reached instantly the fountain of tears, and they gushed in a flood over the cheeks of Katy.

Now, what had Edward said to occasion such a burst of grief? He was not conscious of cruel words. Only lightly had he laid his hand upon her—lightly, if not lovingly—and this was the effect! Must he never speak out when he saw affairs go wrong? Must he let all things fall into disorder, and yet hold his peace? This was asking too much. It was unreasonable.

"Katy"—he spoke rather sternly—"I thought you a reasonable woman, but all this is very unreasonable!"

Now, Katy, for all her sensitiveness, had some spirit, and there was sufficient pride in her heart to cause it, even in pain, to lift itself indignantly against the one who thrust at her too sharply, even if that one were her husband. Her tears ceased to flow, and she made answer:

"And I thought you a kind and reasonable man!"

People who utter harsh words usually evince surprise, often indignation, when coin of like quality is returned to them in exchange. Edward Cleveland was for a moment or two half confounded at this unlooked-for response. He had in as mild a way as possible (?) pointed out a disorderly habit that was exceedingly annoying, and, lo! his wife assumed an air of injured innocence.

"And pray, madam, in what respect have I shown myself lacking in kindness and reason?"

Edward turned full upon his wife as he made this interrogation and looked with knit brows into her face.

"In making the position of two or three books on a library shelf of more importance than a kind and gentle demeanor toward your wife, who has no thought or wish but to please you."

Well and timely spoken, Katy Cleveland! There are always two sides to every question, two aspects in which to view all misunderstandings between individuals, husband and wife not excepted. Far better it was to give Edward this revelation of your thoughts than to hide them away from his perceptions and leave him under the wayward influence of his own partial views. It was a statement of the case altogether unexpected, yet so forcibly put that the young husband found himself shamed by an irresistible conviction of wrong.

"Right, Katy dear!"

It took a few moments for common sense

and kind feelings to overcome the young man's pride. But the closing sentence of his wife had dispelled his trifling anger and left but small resistance. He spoke cheerfully, even tenderly, shutting the bookcase door at the same moment, and drawing an arm around her waist, pressed her closely to his side.

"Yes, you are right, darling!" he said. "The position of a book is a small matter compared to words and tones that make the heart bound with pleasure or flutter in pain. These little things annoy me sometimes. It is a weakness. But I will overcome it and never speak to you in unkindness again, though every book in the house be scattered on the floors."

Katy smiled lovingly into his face through eyes that swam in tears.

"I did not dream that such things annoyed you, Edward," she made answer. "Father never seemed to notice them, though mother has scolded a great deal about my want of order."

"Men are different in this respect. Anything in disorder is sure to disturb me. I have many times wished it were otherwise. But habits are strong."

"Bear with me a little while," Katy made answer, "and I will endeavor to reform my bad habits. Want of order is, I believe, one of my most serious failings, but it shall not stand between me and my good husband as an originator of strife. Only, Edward—"

The young wife paused. A slight unsteadiness of voice betrayed itself on the last word.

"Say on, love. Only what?"

"Have patience with me. New lessons are not learned in a day. I shall often forget—often act but imperfectly."

"And will you have patience with me also, Katy?"

"With you! In what?"

"Patience with my impatience. One of my besetting sins lies here. I feel quickly and speak quickly. When things are not just to my mind anger stirs in my heart."

"It will be very hard for me to bear with your displeasure," said Katy, growing more serious. "If you speak to me harshly or unkindly, I shall not be able to keep back the tears. Will you have patience with them, dear?"

"Yes, yes, and kiss them away or smile them

into rainbows," replied the husband with lover-like ardor.

Here was a good beginning. Katy's reaction upon Edward—a reaction that surprised herself almost as much as it surprised him—had brought him back to reason. She had held up a mirror before his eyes and rather startled him with his own distorted image.

But the world was not made in a day, as the old adage has it, and habits of mind are too real things to be overcome and set aside on the first earnest effort. Katy's want of order and punctuality and Edward's impatience came into rather strong conflict ere a week had passed, and there were frowns and anger on one side and tears upon the other. After a brief estrangement, good sense and right feeling brought back the discordant strings of their life into harmony again.

One of the little things that annoyed Edward Cleveland was his wife's habit of lingering in conversation with friends when she knew that he was waiting for her. As for instance: They were at a social party, and the hour for returning home had come. They left the parlors together, he going to the gentlemen's dressing-room for his hat and overcoat, and she to one of the chambers for her bonnet and furs. Of course he was ready first. It did not take him two minutes to draw on his coat and take up his hat. At the end of the fourth minute he began to think it time for Katy to make her appearance. But Katy and an old friend were in earnest conversation about some matter in which both had an interest, and she had not at the end of five minutes even taken her bonnet from the bed. At the end of ten minutes she said: "I must be going. Edward is waiting for me."

And she drew on her bonnet and tied the strings.

"How becoming!" said the friend, referring to the bonnet. "I never saw you look so well in anything."

This turned their talk into a new channel, and five minutes more were consumed, at the end of which period Katy said, as she hastily took up her furs:

"I'm forgetting myself! Edward is waiting."

But the friend started a new subject, and five minutes more were consumed. When Katy came at last, with slow steps, talking still to her friend, and her husband met her on the stairs, she saw that his face was clouded. To him the time he had been walking impatiently the dressing-room floor seemed full an hour; to her the time she had been chatting with a friend not over five minutes.

Edward was able to keep back from his tongue an indignant rebuke only long enough to get fairly out of the house. Then he said:

"Katy, this is insufferable! And if you treat me so again, I'll leave you to get home as best you can."

Upon the pleasant state of feeling left by the evening's social recreations what a chilling pall was this to fling! Katy had drawn her hand within his arm, and was leaning toward him, but the pressure of her hand relaxed instantly.

"More than half an hour have you kept me waiting with my heavy coat on, momently expecting you to appear."

"No, Edward, it was not ten minutes," replied Katy, in a husky voice.

"Beg your pardon! It was three times ten minutes! But one ten would have been more than twice too long. I never saw such a thoughtless creature!"

Katy had done wrong, and she saw it, but not to an extent that warranted such an angry state of feeling in her husband. The time she had talked with her friend passed so quickly that she could not believe more than ten minutes had flown away, but even to keep her husband waiting, under the circumstances, for ten minutes, she felt to be wrong, and had he not spoken so angrily, she would have acknowledged her error and promised never again to offend in a similar way. As it was, she simply remained silent, while he, in the excitement of his unhappy state, added other words of rebuke no more carefully chosen.

It was very, very hard, under the circum stances, for Katy, suffering as she was from the indignant rebuke of her husband, to think clearly and feel rightly. The punishment was, in her view, altogether beyond the offence. He talked on, but she remained silent.

At last he began to feel that he was saying too much. Katy had not meant to offend him. Hers was only a thoughtless act, which his impatience had magnified into a crime, and which he had punished as if it had been a crime. Had his young wife given way to her feelings, she would have wept herself to sleep that night, refusing to be comforted. But there was common sense, right feeling and a great deal of true perception in that thoughtless little brain of hers. She knew that her husband loved her, and she knew that she had done wrong in trespassing on his naturally impatient disposition So, as soon as they were home, and she could say what was in her mind in a manner to give it the right effect, she spoke to him these words in a low voice that slightly trembled:

"Edward, forgive my thoughtlessness. I will try and not offend you again in this particular. And forgive, also, the frankness that accuses you of a far greater wrong than mine. I do not remember anything in the marriage contract to which we both assented that gave either of us the right to be angry with or to speak harshly to the other. We pledged mutual love, forbearance and kind offices, and little things, no matter how annoying, should not make us forgetful of our pledges. I was wrong, very wrong, but wrong from thoughtlessness. Oh, Edward, if you had only spoken of it in kind remonstrance, I would have seen my error quite as clearly and resolved to do better quite as earnestly, and loving instead of painful emotions would have trembled in my heart. It is not good for us to be angry with one another. The trite old precept of bear and forbear must never be forgotten if we would be happy together. I am not perfect, and cannot attain perfection in a day. Bear, then, with my infirmities for the sake of the love in my heart—a love that to save you, dear husband, would smile even in the face of death! Such love should cover a multitude of small offences."

Edward Cleveland caught his young wife to his heart, and while he held her there tightly covered her lips with kisses.

"Oh, these little things, these little things!" he said. "How like foxes do they spoil our tender grapes! But, dear Katy, it must no longer be. Do not try my faulty patience overmuch, and I will hold my hand hard against the weaknesses of character which have already troubled our peace."

"Speak freely and frankly, Edward," was the reply, "only speak kindly. I will never of set purpose give pain or annoyance. The dearest wish of my heart is to make you happy; the light of my life is in your loving smiles."

It was far better thus to understand each other. A world of unhappiness in the future Katy saved herself and husband. A true word firmly spoken will bring a man to reason quicker than a gallon of tears. Calm, firm remonstrance is always better in a wife than weeping or moody silence. The first a husband can understand; to the latter he has no key of interpretation.

From that time Katy was more considerate and forgiving of her impatient husband; she knew his heart to be full of love for her, and the little things that some wives would have magnified into barriers of separation she swept aside with a gentle hand, and set herself to the work of preventing their future interposition. She had her reward.

VI.

IN DANGER.

"HANNA," said Mr. Lea to his wife on meeting her at tea one evening, "I find that a previously made engagement will prevent my going to the opera to-morrow night."

The countenance of Mrs. Lea fell. Evidently her disappointment was great.

"I'm sorry, dear, but it can't be helped. You are to go, however. I've taken care to provide a substitute, and one altogether suitable, I hope. Lewis Steele will be your escort."

Mrs. Lea did not evince pleasure at this communication, but the look of disappointment gradually went out of her face.

"He'll be around to take a cup of tea with us," added the husband.

"Will he?" There was a covert interest in her voice not perceived by Mr. Lea.

"Yes. I invited him."

"I'm sorry," remarked Mrs. Lea after a brief silence. "I would rather bear the disappointment than go to the opera in company with any one except my husband."

"But Lewis, you know, is such an intimate friend."

"Yes, I know," she answered, in a quiet, absent manner.

Mr. Lea did not press the subject. He saw that his wife would accept the escort he had engaged, and with grace enough to put him at his ease.

Next evening came, and Mr. Steele called as per engagement. Mrs. Lea, in her opera cloak and tasteful head-dress, looked charming, and there were few handsomer or more attractive men than her companion for the night. In the eyes of her husband Mrs. Lea had never looked more beautiful than on this occasion, and he half regretted the proud satisfaction he would have known in sitting beside her in the public gaze, amid the fashion and beauty of the town. But he had other and more congenial pleasures on hand.

Mrs. Lea was in danger. Not that she was a

vain, weak or unprincipled woman. Not that she was cold toward her husband. Her danger lay in his indifference to the wants of her nature, in his selfish neglect, in his inadequate appreciation of her character.

Being an intimate friend of Mr. Lea's—his groomsman, in fact, at the wedding—Steele had always been a guest, without formality, admitted and confided in as if he were a brother. There was, as time proved, a closer assimilation of tastes between him and Mrs. Lea than between her and her husband. Steele was fond of music and art, and so was Mrs. Lea, and many evenings they spent together singing and playing while Mr. Lea, on some excuse, absented himself, and passed the hours in more congenial companionship.

Yes, Mrs. Lea was in danger, and not only in danger, but gradually awaking to the painful consciousness of the fact, and yet more painful consciousness of a spell-like thraldom which she had not strength to break. And Lewis Steele, her friend and her husband's friend, was in danger also. Yet into neither mind had the tempter cast a thought of evil. The hour had not come for that.

Something occurred to separate the friends with whom Lea passed the evening at an earlier hour than had been anticipated, and at ten o'clock he found himself on the street, alone, and in the neighborhood of the Academy of Music.

Instead of going home to await his wife's return, Mr. Lea acted from the moment's impulse, and buying a ticket, went in to see and hear the concluding part of the opera. His first thought on entering was to search for his wife, and if a vacant seat was near, to join her and her companion. The parquette circle was crowded. For a little while he stood at one of the doors, looking in upon the gay assemblage; then he ascended to the balcony, where he found a single vacant place. Accepting this, he turned his eyes to that portion of the house in which he had selected seats, and soon saw his wife and Mr. Steele. They were in earnest conversation, and apparently indifferent to the music or action of the opera.

"She's a splendid woman; there's no mistake about that." It was the remark of a person just behind him.

"Did you say her name was Lea?" So

queried the individual to whom this remark was made.

"Yes. Her husband is a lawyer, I am told."

"Who is that with her?"

"A former lover, it is said."

"Ah!"

"A handsome fellow, isn't he?"

"Yes, and if as unprincipled as handsome—"

Colson came forward upon the stage at this moment, and the sentence was not completed. Lea neither saw nor heard her, though she sang one of her most effective parts. His eyes were on his wife and her companion, who, intermitting their pleasant talk, turned their attention to the prima donna, yet every now and then exchanging words and glances.

"Where is her husband?" The conversation began again.

"Mrs. Lea's husband?"

"Yes."

"Heaven knows! Asleep somewhere—besotted, or blind. If he had half an eye, he would see what is becoming patent to all. Now look at them! Doesn't that speak for itself? See how lovingly they lean toward each other, and how she hangs upon his sentences. A hundred eyes are on them, and yet they are unconscious of the notice their demeanor toward each other is attracting. There is only one saving clause."

"What?"

"The young man is spoken of as the soul of honor."

"What is his name?"

"Steele."

"I never heard of him. But soul of honor or soul of dishonor, he is not in his right place to-night. In fact, the flaunting of such an intimacy with a married woman in the face of a public assemblage is dishonorable, and the man who so little regards the decencies of common life will not hesitate at anything beyond."

"If he had a true respect for her," remarked the other, "he would so conduct himself as not to give cause for a breath of detraction. A handsome married woman cannot often appear in public places unaccompanied by her husband without eliciting observation and remark. There must be no lover-like unconsciousness of outward things in her and her male attendant such as we see in the case before us. This cannot possibly exist without tainting the good name."

8

A brief silence followed. Mr. Lea's heart was leaping in strong throbs. He was startled, amazed, bewildered, frightened, in face of a new and unsuspected danger. Had he been really blind that he now saw such a gulf at his feet? Had the earth just yawned, or had the chasm been there all the while and his unconscious feet upon the brink?

"Her face is pure as well as beautiful." The conversation went on again.

"Yes. I have always admired it for that very purity. I believe her to be innocent now. But even innocence should be guarded. No heart is free from guile. The best may be tempted. And of all dangers, I think that most perilous in which a loving, sympathetic woman, neglected by a cold, indifferent husband, is thrown into intimate companionship with an agreeable man who fully appreciates her and responds to her feelings and sentiments. If he stand in the relation of a former lover, so much the worse."

"And that, as I understand it, is the relation held to Mrs. Lea by the gentleman now in her company?'

"So people say."

"Are they much talked about?"

"Yes. I've heard this intimacy referred to of late several times."

A grand chorus filled the house with its multitudinous harmonies, silencing all conversation and attracting every ear. As it died away the curtain fell. One act more, and the performance would be over. In the interval a free and easy movement prevailed through the house. Some stood up and many passed to the lobbies, among whom were the two men whose conversation had so startled Mr. Lea. He remained, with scarcely a movement of the body, his eyes riveted upon his wife and her companion, who were so interested in each other as to be almost oblivious of things around them. Presently they arose and went out into the lobby. For a moment or two there was a debate in Lea's mind. Then he got up and went into the lobby also. It was filled with ladies and gentlemen, some promenading and some passing to the stairways. Among these he moved, searching for his wife, but after sweeping around through the whole area he failed to meet her. Thence he passed to the foyer, which was more crowded than the lobby. Entering at the north door, he moved toward the south, fronting a large mirror in which the forms and faces of all advancing in that direction were reflected. He had walked for half the distance of this splendid room, when, for a single instant, he caught the image of his wife's face in the mirror. It was partly turned from her companion, who was leaning toward her, evidently in the pause of some utterance, and awaiting a reply. He saw both their faces at the same moment, and was strongly impressed by each expression. There was something evil and alluring in the face of his friend—a look wholly new to that open, frank, honorable countenance. In the face of his wife he read surprise, repulsion and pain. All this, as we have said, was the revelation of a moment. A group of promenaders came between, and hid their reflection in the mirror.

Pressing forward to catch another view, Mr. Lea was almost upon them before their forms were again visible. His wife had withdrawn her hand from her companion's arm, on whose face he saw blank regret. The rich color, which had increased so highly the beauty of her countenance, had faded out, a strange pallor succeeding. Her eyes were cast down, but lifting them, she met the gaze of her husband reflected from the glass almost directly in front of which she was now standing. Lea saw a flashing change in her face as their eyes met It was not a guilty change, but full of a glad surprise. Turning instantly, she caught his arm with a clinging grasp—he felt her hand thrill to his heart—and said:

"Oh, Henry! I'm so glad to see you here."

Mr. Steele turned more slowly, schooling himself by a hasty discipline in the brief lapse of time which would intervene ere he looked into the eyes of the friend against whom, in a moment of passion and weakness, he had meditated the deepest of all wrongs. Both men saw, in that interval, the duty of concealment, and both exercised a rigid self-control. There was polite recognition, an easy reciprocation of commonplaces, such as pass between friends on meeting, and then a formal transfer of the lady to her husband in courteous phrases.

"Will you see the last act?" inquired Mrs. Lea as the orchestra began to play.

"As you like," was answered.

"Just as you like, Henry. I am ready to go or stay."

"We will remain," said Mr. Lea. And they passed from the foyer into the balcony, and took the seats vacated by Mrs. Lea and Mr. Steele ten minutes before. The last-named individual had signified his intention of retiring from the house. Ere the curtain arose, Mr. Lea had determined the exact place in which he sat a short time before, and marked the two gentlemen sitting directly behind. He was sure of their identity by the fact that one had an opera glass pointed toward them, and that they were evidently surprised at something and curiously interrogating each other. The simple work which Mr. Lea had taken in hand for the concluding half hour of the performance was to present himself and his wife to the eyes of all who had misjudged her during the first part of the evening, and to let it appear that she was gratified with her change of companionship, and that between her and her husband there existed a mutual confidence and affection. He talked with her of the acting and the music, admiring fine passages and entering into the spirit of the performance, through her appreciation, in a higher degree than he had ever entered before. So skillfully did he conceal from his wife all signs of what he had seen and heard in the balcony and foyer that she felt an assurance that he was wholly ignorant in regard to any danger having been in her way. But he understood very well why she held so clingingly to his arm as they walked homeward that night, and why she responded with such a penetrating tenderness in her voice.

Mrs. Lea was never again in danger. From that period of awakening her husband grew more and more into a just appreciation of her character and its needs, of her purity, taste, intelligence and high womanly qualities, and of his duties as her husband. In public places he was always her attendant, thus protecting her good name and elevating her in the eyes of all.

Alas! how many, standing just on the verge of danger, as Mrs. Lea stood—pressed to the verge by a husband's blind indifference—have suffered their feet to pass over! For the sake of those who are on the right side, yet walking in doubtful ways and amid allurements, we strike a note of warning, and so strike it that the indifferent, unsympathizing husband as well as the unguarded wife may hear.

VII.

TEN YEARS AFTER MARRIAGE.

TEN years since the wedding-day. Mrs. Howland was alone. She had left her husband in the little room where they usually sat together through the evenings while she put the children to bed.

Mrs. Howland did not feel inclined to return to the family sitting-room, where she had left her husband, but remained in the chamber with her sleeping little ones in a musing, brooding, unhappy state of mind. Something of coldness and alienation had been growing up between her and her husband for a long time past. The old tenderness of manner which had been so sweet was all gone. He was kind, thoughtful in regard to her comfort, honorable and true but getting more formal and less affectionate in manner every day. His wife, who had loved him very tenderly and still loved him, had failed to give in her life the adequate response to his—had, in the fret and fever of a disciplinary existence, suffered herself to walk amid disturbing and discordant elements instead of taking her place serenely by his side. And so inharmonious things had been permitted to jar where all might have been peace.

It was pressing upon the mind of Mrs. Howland that her husband had ceased to love her, and this conviction was taking all the sweetness from her life. It did not once occur to her that she was herself growing unlovely, that she had laid aside nearly all the external things by which, when a maiden, she had sought to win him — the sunny countenance, the alluring voice and manner, the scrupulous attire, the deference to his tastes and opinions, the guard upon her temper, the womanly elevation of character that made her seem as one who ruled in the kingdom of her own soul. This was the being he had loved, this the woman he had taken to walk with him through life. Alas for the fading ideal! He had found, instead, one who made scarcely an effort at self-government, whose feelings and impulses were her springs of action. Deeply, passionately, she loved him, but only a wise, self-abnegating love blesses both itself and the object of its devotion. Without some change on the part of Mrs. Howland it was impossible for them to grow together as one.

For nearly half an hour after her children were asleep the mother sat in her wretched mood, apart from her husband and feeling no inclination to join him. "All love has died," she said. "I am nothing now." And as she said this her heart shivered with an instinctive realization of what her words involved. Then fear for the loss of a thing so precious as a husband's love seized upon her soul and inspired a new purpose. A love worth winning was surely worth an effort to retain. And was not the way to win the way to keep? A new light broke into Mrs. Howland's mind. She began to see things in herself that were very far from being in harmony with her life when a maiden—things that would certainly have repelled a lover, and were they bonds for a husband?

These thoughts startled the awakening wife. Then old memories were revived, bringing back old states. Pictures warm with the hues of love came out of the dim past.

"Is the cup broken and the wine spilled?"

she asked of herself. "God forbid!" came from her lips in audible utterance. Then she left the chamber where her children slept, and with silent feet went slowly toward the apartment in which she had left her husband alone. On the way she paused, stood still for a moment, then returned. The gas was burning low. She threw up the light and caught a reflection of herself in a toilette glass. One glance sufficed. That was not the style in which she had appeared before her lover. Taking down her hair, she applied comb and brush rapidly for some minutes, and then arranged the glossy masses with taste and skill. Next the soiled and tumbled wrapper was removed and her person attired in a neatly-fitting dress, around the neck of which was laid a snowy linen collar fastened by a small coral pin, her husband's gift of other days. Already her cheeks were in a glow and her eyes filled with light. One long glance at herself in the mirror revealed a wonderful transformation. How the old memories were crowding in upon her! How soft her heart was growing! How full of tenderness was every thought of her husband! Her lips were athirst for kisses!

And now Mrs. Howland left her chamber again. Her slippered feet gave no sound as they moved over the carpet, and she came to the open door of the sitting-room without betraying a sign of her approach. There she stood still. Mr. Howland was not at the table reading, as she had left him, but at his secretary, which was open. He was reclining his head on one hand and gazing down upon something held in the other, and seemed wholly absorbed. For more than a minute he remained in this fixed attitude, his wife as still as himself. Then a long sigh trembled on the air, and then lifting the object on which his gaze was directed, Mr. Howland pressed it to his lips, kissing it almost passionately three or four times. A wild throb leaped along Mrs. Howland's veins. Then her heart grew still as in the presence of some unknown but stupendous evil. Something impelled her to spring forward and read this mystery, and something as strongly held her back. As she stood, pale now and in a tremor, the object was kissed again, and then returned to a drawer in the secretary from which it had been taken. In this act for an instant the miniature of a lady met the gaze of Mrs. How land! Locking the drawer, her husband placed the key in his pocket, and then resting both arms on the writing leaf of the secretary, buried his face in them and sat motionless.

Turning away as noiselessly as she had approached, Mrs. Howland fled back to her chamber in wild affright, and sat down panting and in bewilderment. As soon as thought began to move in a determinate way, the first result was a flood of indignation, a burning sense of wrong, and it was only by an effort that the outraged wife could hold herself back from confronting her husband and demanding to see the miniature. A calmer but not less painful state succeeded, in which conscience whispered of indifference and neglect. Had she turned, habitually, her most attractive or her least attractive side to her husband? Had she kept herself lovely in his eyes—lovely in temper and lovely in person? Her heart sunk; it grew darker and darker around her; life seemed crushing out.

"Who is it?" This question marked a change in the current of Mrs. Howland's thoughts. Rapidly she passed in review one lady friend after another, but without an incident to fix suspicion. Then times and seasons in which her husband was absent from home were dwelt upon. Once a week regularly he went out in the evening, occasionally twice. The regular absence was for the purpose of attending a literary society—at least so he had informed his wife. Now, for the first time, doubt of his truth crept in, and this doubt was as the sweeping away of all the sure foundations on which her soul had rested.

For a long time Mr. Howland remained sitting at his secretary with his face buried in his arms. At length, rising with a slow, weary motion, as of one exhausted by bodily or mental exertion, he drew out his watch.

"Half-past nine!" was ejaculated in surprise. And then he looked through the door over toward the chamber whither his wife had gone with the children, and stood listening for some sound. All was silent. For a short time he moved in an uneasy, irresolute way about the room, and sitting down, tried to find interest in the pages of a book. But in a little while the volume closed in his hands. Thought was too busy in another direction to dwell even with a favorite author.

"Ten o'clock!" The bell was ringing its clear notes from a neighboring steeple. Mr. Howland started up, and turning out the light, went over to the sleeping-room. His wife was in bed. He spoke to her, but she did not answer.

"Are you asleep?" No motion nor response of any kind. She lay with her face nearly hidden under the bedclothes. He looked at her in a strange, earnest manner for some moments, and then, moving about noiselessly, prepared for rest. The day had been one of much activity, and Mr. Howland was weary enough for sleep. Soon after his head touched the pillow he was in the land of dreams. His deep breathing had scarcely given evidence of the fact ere a light movement on the part of Mrs. Howland showed her to be awake. Presently she drew the clothes from her face and raised herself cautiously. The heavy breathing of her husband was not interrupted. She sat up in bed: he still slept on; she glided from beneath the covering, and groping in the darkness, found her husband's vest, from which she took a key.

"Mother!" The slight noise made in opening the chamber door had disturbed one of the children. Mrs. Howland stood still, holding her breath. The call was not repeated, and she went out, groping her way along the passage with a hand on the wall. Entering the room she sought, she closed the door behind her and drew the bolt, fastening herself in. Now all her motions became hurried and nervous. After lighting the gas she went to her husband's secretary, and with the key in her possession unlocked one of the private drawers. Her hand shook so that the key rattled on the scutcheon before a way was found into the wards. The first object that met her view as the drawer came open was a morocco miniature case, which she seized upon with a clutch as eager as that of a bird of prey, and bearing it to the gaslight, unloosed the clasp and exposed the face of her rival.

It was a young and lovely face, and the eyes looked up into hers with a tender and sweet expression. Away from the pure forehead the hair of golden auburn fell smoothly back, and lay in curls upon her neck, that was whiter and purer than alabaster. The lips were full, soft, and arching as if for a flight of arrows,

Love's witchery was in the pictured countenance.

Still, very still, did the wife sit and gaze down upon her rival's face—that face on which scarcely an hour before she had seen her husband's kisses laid. Still, very still, she sat, the tears creeping out of her eyes, falling slowly over her cheeks and dropping upon the miniature. Was she jealous of that rival? No! Her heart was too glad for jealousy, too full of joy, too wild with a new-born happiness. The bride of ten years ago was the rival of to-day, and the heart of her husband was true to his marriage vows! It was no fault of his that he could not love what had become unlovely. Not unlovely in the poorer signification of that word, as indicating changes wrought by the wearing hand of time, but unlovely through indulgence in impatience and fretfulness, and in the neglect of self-discipline—unlovely also from carelessness of attire and personal neatness.

With the image of herself as she was ten years before, and with the image of her husband fondly, passionately kissing that image, dwelling in her imagination, Mrs. Howland went back to her bed. She had suddenly awakened as from a dream, a long, weary, troubled, exhausting dream, and the language of her heart was, "Thank God that I am awake!"

As they sat at breakfast on the next morning, Mrs. Howland noticed a change in the expression of her husband's face as he looked at her across the table, letting his eyes dwell upon her with unusual interest. It was a pleased, almost admiring expression. She was in no doubt as to the cause, for she had attired herself with scrupulous care in a clean, bright morning-wrapper, and wore a cap fastened at one side with a ruby hairpin and ornamented with two or three small pink bows and a sprig of flowers. A plain linen collar pinned with a cameo was around her neck. And, better than all, she had banished every sign of discontent and fretfulness from her face.

"How sweet mother looks this morning!" said Mr. Howland, glancing at one of the children who sat near her and smiling one of his old, bright smiles.

"Don't she!" answered the little one, lifting her rosy mouth to mamma for a kiss.

"Me kiss too, mamma so beautiful!" and little Allie scrambled down from her chair in new-born admiration of her mother, and put up her mouth also.

"And me too," exclaimed Mr. Howland, passing around the table and laying his lips softly and lingeringly upon the lips of his wife. He saw, as he looked across the table on resuming his seat, that her eyes were dim with tears. He knew they were tears of pleasure, but did not imagine how deeply her heart was stirred nor how full of precious memories and golden hopes the moment was crowded.

Ten years after marriage. Love's lamp was burning low, the oil nearly exhausted, the wife grown so unattractive that the husband's heart was turning back in worship of the bride. But the lamp has blazed up again: there is a supply of oil. A beauty beyond any bridal beauty invests the wife, and it shall grow more womanly, more luxuriant, more enchanting, as the days succeed each other and years progress, until the soul puts on her garments of eternal youth.

VIII.

A HINT TO HUSBANDS.

"WHY didn't you make them all crust—solid to the centre?" said Mr. Rodney, in a fault-finding tone, as he let the biscuit he had taken drop heavily on his plate. "You might shoot a man with a thing like that!"

Mrs. Rodney's face colored. She was hurt at her husband's tone and manner.

"I meant to have had them right, James," she answered, with just a sign of choking in her voice. "But—"

Not permitting his wife to finish the sentence, Mr. Rodney broke in upon her captiously: "Oh yes, of course *but* did all the harm. No one except *but* is responsible for anything that goes wrong in this house. I wish you'd turn him out: I'm tired of his presence. *But* spoils the coffee and burns the steak, dries the biscuits into canister shot, and lets the milk sour. *But* hinders and mars everything. He's a bad fellow, and I wish, my dear, that you'd get rid of him."

Mr. Rodney thought himself quite clever in this speech, and the satisfaction thence derived almost put him in a good humor.

Two children sat at the table, one of them a boy nine years old, the other a girl in her eleventh year. The boy, imitating his father, took one of the hard biscuits, and bouncing it in his plate, called it a canister shot, but the girl, sympathizing with her mother, broke her biscuit in two, saying:

"See! mine is soft and nice inside, and I like crust." She buttered it, and began eating with the true relish of hunger. The boy followed her example, and Mr. Rodney, feeling, it may be, a slight rebuke in his daughter's treatment of the case, broke, with an affected display of strength, his biscuit also, and found in its delicate flavor a sweeter morsel than he had anticipated. But his wife ate nothing. His ungracious spirit had destroyed her appetite.

It happened that on the next evening Mr. and Mrs. Rodney, with their two children, were to take tea and spend the evening at a neighbor's.

"I must apologize for my biscuits," said the lady hostess as the meal began. "Unfortunately, they are baked too much. In spite of all we can do, cooks will sometimes spoil everything."

The apology, ill-timed as such excuses often are, was needed in this case. The biscuits were scarcely presentable. But Mr. Rodney, away from home, was the model of good breeding, and with the blandest of smiles, as he pressed open the tenacious mass of hard-baked dough with his fingers, at cost, apparently, of no effort, made answer:

"They are very good, ma'am—very good. I like well-baked bread, and these are just the thing. Overdone is not half so bad as underdone. The dryer the baking, the quicker of digestion."

"I only wish my husband were as easily satisfied," returned the lady, pleased with the tact and politeness of her guest.

"A very fine cup of coffee," said Mr. Rodney, looking in smiling approval across the table. "I don't know when I have tasted better."

Five mornings in the week he tasted better, but never said a word in its praise. If, on the sixth or seventh morning, the standard went down to that of which he was now drinking, Mrs. Rodney received unpleasant intimation of the fact.

Was he really deceived? In the pleasant social sphere that pervaded the company, did taste find a new sense, and extract from common things a more exquisite flavor? It may have been so in a degree. But the true explanation is found in a courteous desire on the part of Mr. Rodney to please and to appear well.

"Did you make this salad?"

Mrs. Rodney had just taken a mouthful of the chicken salad as her husband asked the question, and was tasting the rancid oil.

"Yes, I made it." Pleasure and approval had been perceived in Mr. Rodney's tones, and satisfaction mingled with pleasure in the lady's voice as she thus replied.

"It is charming. I must get you to teach my wife your secret. She makes a fine salad, I will admit, but not equal to this."

Mrs. Rodney swallowed with an effort the mouthful of salad she had taken. It came near choking her, and she did not try another.

With some curiosity and some surprise she watched the apparent enjoyment with which her husband ate the offensive mess, even accepting a second supply. She did not feel at all complimented by his reference to her skill in salad-making. That was "the unkindest cut of all." It was not possible for her to help contrasting this excess of approval in her husband with his excess of condemnation the evening before—this uncalled-for praise of a friend's housekeeping with his uncalled-for condemnation of his wife's. As all women do, she laid these things up in her heart and pondered them.

During the whole evening Mr. Rodney was in admirable spirits, the very embodiment of cheerful good humor. Mrs. Rodney was a little more quiet than usual, sometimes dull and absent-minded. The fact was, she could not forget the difference between her husband at home and her husband abroad—his treatment of those who were nothing to him and his treatment of his wife, who should have been all to him.

As the children were along, Mr. and Mrs. Rodney went home at an early hour. On the way back Mr. Rodney was talkative, and had many pleasant things to say of the friends with whom they had spent the evening, but Mrs. Rodney was irresponsive and almost silent. She could not forget.

"Don't you feel well?" asked Mr. Rodney, at last becoming aware that his wife was far from being in like fine spirits with himself. They were at their own door.

"My head aches a little." It was true, but her heart ached more. Something whispered into the dull ears of Mr. Rodney a remote suggestion of what the truth might be, and then followed certain remembrances that set him to thinking in a new direction. It was his turn to become silent: speech died on his lips as he passed his own threshold. A certain heaviness of atmosphere weighed on his bosom like a nightmare. What could it mean? Self-love was not ready to take the blame, and went searching about for the offending agent.

"If *she* were more cheerful and even tempered." Who was *she?* His wife, of course.

Mr. Rodney sat down to read, and Mrs. Rodney went over to their sleeping-rooms with the children, who were soon in bed.

But the evening's excitement kept them awake.

"What are they talking about?" said Mr Rodney, looking up from his book. His wife had joined him.

Mrs. Rodney did not answer.

"Just listen to their tongues!" and the father arose, adding, in a pleased, interested voice, "I must enjoy it with them," and stepped lightly from the room. As he reached the door opening into the chamber where the children lay, and stood just on the outside, he heard this remark from the little girl:

"They weren't half as good as those we had last night, and father praised them and said he liked hard biscuits. I wonder what mother thought? I guess she remembered what he said about her biscuits, that were twice as good."

"If father chooses to praise anybody's things, hasn't he got a right to do it?" demanded the brother, in a hectoring kind of way.

"I s'pose he's got the right," was answered, "but that isn't the thing. 'Twasn't kind to talk to mother in the way he did, and then praise another woman before her face for doing ten times as bad. That's what I look at."

"Oh pshaw! You don't know. Hasn't father got a right to speak when he pleases?" said the embryo tyrant.

"I'll tell you what I do know." The child's voice rose to a clearer tone.

"What do you know?"

"That mother's coffee is twice as good as Mrs. Glenn's, and yet father never praises it. But if it happens to get wrong once in a while, don't mother hear something! I guess she does! Did you taste that chicken salad?"

"Yes." The boy's tone was not quite so arrogant.

"Could you eat it?"

"No."

"And father said it was charming, and that he must get Mrs. Glenn to teach mother how to make chicken salad! It was a shame! And mother sitting right there! I couldn't help looking at her, and I krow she felt bad. He's always finding fault with what she does, and I wish he wouldn't do it. It wasn't true, neither."

It's an old saying that listeners never hear

any good of themselves: Mr. Rodney proved the truth of the adage on this occasion. He did not linger to enjoy more, but silently retired, something wiser than when he left the family sitting-room. Mrs. Rodney did not ask him about the children's talk, and he was not inclined to be communicative on that subject.

Next morning Mr. Rodney surprised his wife, and the children also, by saying, after tasting his coffee,

"This is delicious!"

Was it earnest or irony? Mrs. Rodney's color heightened. She looked doubtingly at her husband.

"As good as Mrs. Glenn's?" asked his daughter, glancing at her father with an arch expression.

"Yes, you saucy little rogue! and a great deal better. Mrs. Glenn cannot begin to make coffee like this."

"But she can beat mother at chicken salad. Mother's oil has no taste to it."

"Annie! Annie!" Mrs. Rodney spoke to the child in a reproving voice.

"Fairly hit!" said Mr. Rodney in good

humor. "But you know, dear," he added, trying to put himself right with the child, "that we must seem pleased with the entertainment others provide for us. It would have been very impolite in me to have shown that I tasted the rancid oil."

"You needn't have said anything about it," frankly answered the artless child.

"I guess you're about right, dear," said Mr. Rodney. "I overacted my part, but I won't do so again. This steak is very tender." Mr. Rodney looked from his daughter to his wife, thus changing the subject.

"I'm glad you like it." There was a pleased manner about Mrs. Rodney that her husband did not fail to observe. She felt better all day for the few words of approval which had escaped her husband's lips. At dinner-time no fault was found with anything—a rare occurrence; rarer still, he expressed satisfaction with a dish provided with the design of giving him pleasure. The biscuits at tea-time were a failure again, the careless cook having spoiled them by overbaking. Mr. Rodney, not appearing to notice their hardness, said:

"You have the art of giving a peculiar sweetness to everything you make. These are very toothsome."

It cost little or no effort to say these few words, yet were they far sweeter to the ears of his wife than was the food to his taste. What a new sphere of pleasantness and tranquillity pervaded, during the evening that followed, the home of Mr. Rodney! It was as though husband and wife had passed from dull, shaded rooms into wide apartments down into which, through crystal ceilings, the light of heaven was falling. The old charm came back into Mrs. Rodney's face, softening yet elevating its beauty, and her voice stirred memories and feelings in the breast of her husband which, long sleeping, had seemed dead.

"I have been blind, but now I see." Thus spoke Mr. Rodney with himself as he lay musing on his bed that night. "These common things of our daily lives are as husks that contain sweet kernels if we will but rend them to extract what nestles within. If we chew the husks alone, we shall find dryness and bitterness. I have tasted both husk and kernel, and know where sweetness and nutrition lie."

After that, Mr. Rodney was charier of complaint and more lavish of approval. The new life which pervaded his household was so sunny and cheerful that, no matter how rough the world went with him on the outside, his soul became peaceful within its walls. He had, in being kind and just, taken thorns from a pillow whereon, until now, he had failed to secure tranquil repose.

IX.

A YOUNG WIFE'S SORROW.

DON'T just like the tone of Martha's letters," said Mrs. Barton to her husband one day. Martha was a daughter who had been married for three or four months, and was then living several hundred miles away from the town in which her parents resided.

"Nor do I," was the answer. "If Edward is in anything unkind to her, I have been greatly deceived in him."

"There are peculiarities of character and temperament in every one that only a close intimacy can make apparent. And Martha has these as well as Edward. It is not improbable that something unseen before has revealed itself since marriage, and stands as a source of irritation between them."

Mr. Barton sighed. He was very fond of

Martha. She had been a pet with him since childhood, and this separation, in consequence of her marriage, was a great trial. The thought of her being unhappy pained him.

"Suppose," he said, "we send for her to come home and make us a visit. It is nearly four months since she went away."

"I was going to suggest something different."

"What?"

"A visit to Martha."

"That will be out of the question, at least for me," said Mr. Barton.

"I did not mean," replied Mrs. Barton, smiling, "to include you in the visit."

"Oh, then you propose to take all the pleasure to yourself? Now, it strikes me as a better arrangement to have Martha pay us a visit. It will do her a great deal more good than merely to receive a visit from you. She will get back for a little while into her old home, and see father and mother both. And then I will come in for a portion of the enjoyment, which is to be considered."

"I've thought of all that," replied Mrs. Barton, "and yet favor the visit to Martha. The reason is this: If I go there, and stay a week or two,

I will have an opportunity to see how she and Edward are getting along together. We must live with people, you know, to find out all about them. There may be some little impediments to happiness lying right in their path which I may help them to pick up and cast aside—some little want of adaptation in the machinery of their lives which prevents a movement in harmony that I may show them how to adjust."

"I guess you are right, taking that view of the case," said Mr. Barton.

The visit of Mrs. Barton was made accordingly. After the first brief season of gladness that followed the meeting with her mother had passed, Martha's countenance showed some lines not written there by sweet content. The mother asked no questions, however, in the beginning, calculated to draw Martha out. She wanted a little time for observation. The young husband was bright, cheerful, attentive and fond, as he had appeared to her before the wedding day. But on the second morning after her arrival she noticed that he did not talk quite so freely as usual at the breakfast-table, and had something very much like a cloud over the sunshine of his countenance. Martha's manner was a little constrained also, and her face a little sober. Once or twice during the meal Edward exhibited a feeling of annoyance at things not rightly ordered.

Mrs. Barton was already beginning to see the little impediments and obstructions to which she had referred in talking with her husband. But she did not encourage Martha to speak on the subject. She wanted to see more and understand the case better. On the third day the cause of trouble between Edward and Martha—for a discordant string was really jarring in the harmony of their lives—became more clearly apparent to the mother. The little external restraint which had been assumed at the beginning of her visit by both of the young people was gradually laid aside, and she saw them in the real life they were living.

The basis of the difficulty lay in the total unfitness of Martha for the position she had assumed—that of housekeeper, we mean—and, in consequence, her young husband, in whose ideal of home perfect order had been included, found everything so different from his anticipations that a graceful acquiescence was impossible.

"I don't know what has come over Edward," said Martha to her mother on the morning of the fourth day, after her husband had left for his place of business. Her eyes were swimming in tears, for Edward had spoken hastily and with ill nature at the breakfast-table. "He used to be so kind, so gentle, so considerate of my comfort and feelings, but he seems to be growing more impatient and harsh in his manner every day."

"Has the reason of this never occurred to you?" Mrs. Barton's manner was grave.

"I can imagine no reason for the change," replied Martha.

"He is disappointed in something, evidently. He does not find in you all he had expected."

"Mother!" The young wife had a startled look.

"It must be so, Martha, else why should he be different from what he was? He has had an ideal of a wife, and you have failed to reach this ideal."

The face of Martha, which had flushed, became almost pale.

"And I am free to own," continued the mother, "that you fall considerably below my ideal. I do not wonder at Edward's disappointment."

Tears began to fall over the young wife's cheeks.

"I'm sure," she said, sobbing, "that I have been to him all that I know how to be. If love would draw upon me favors and kindness, he would never look at me, as he does sometimes, with cold eyes and a clouded face, nor speak in angry impatience, words that hurt me worse than blows."

"But you have not done for him all that you know how to do," said Mrs. Barton.

"I fail to comprehend you, mother," was replied to this.

"You do not make his home as pleasant as it should be. There seems to be no anticipation of his wants, and no provision against discomfort. Everything is left to your two servants, who do pretty much as they please."

"Why, mother!"

"It is true, my daughter. I have looked on with closely observant eyes since I have been here, and must say that I am disappointed in you. In every case that Edward has shown impatience in my presence, the source of annoyance lay in your neglect of a plain household duty. It was so this morning and so yesterday."

"He was annoyed at the burnt steak this morning," said Martha, in answer. "That wasn't my fault, I am sure. I'm not the cook."

"It is your place to have a competent cook," said Mrs. Barton.

"If I can find one, mother."

"The one you have now is not to be trusted to prepare a meal."

"I know that, but how can I help myself?"

"And knowing that, you never went near the kitchen to see that she did not spoil the steak intended for your husband's breakfast. It might have taken you ten or fifteen minutes to superintend personally the preparation of this morning's meal, and so made it worthy of being set before your husband, but instead of this you sat reading or talking from the time you were dressed until the bell rang. When we went down there was no butter on the table, no knife and fork to the dish of meat, no salt, nor any napkin at your husband's plate. The tablecloth was soiled, and you scolded the waiter for not putting on a clean one. The meal opened in disorder, which you might have prevented by a little forethought, and progressed and ended in annoyance and bad feeling. Now, who was to blame for all this?"

"But, mother, you don't expect me to go into the kitchen and cook?" said Martha.

"The captain who undertakes to sail a ship must know all about navigation. Is it more unreasonable to expect that a woman who takes upon herself the obligations of a wife should know how to conduct a household? Is a woman less responsible in her position than a man? If so, what moral laws give the distinction? I have not seen them. The captain does not trust the ship wholly to the man at the helm. He takes observations, examines charts and sees and knows for himself that everything is done at the right time and in the right place. His thought and his will are active and predominant in every part of the ship, for on him rests all the responsibility. And it is so everywhere in man's work. You ask if I expect you to go into the kitchen and cook. I answer, Yes, in case there is no one else to prepare your husband's food. If you have an incompetent cook, or one not to be trusted, then it is your duty to make up her deficiencies by a personal attendance in the kitchen just as often and just as long as the case may require. You contracted to do this when you became a wife."

"I don't remember that the subject was even referred to," said Martha, who did not yet see clearly, and who felt that her mother's view of the case actually degraded the wife into a household drudge.

"Was it stipulated," answered Mrs. Barton, "that Edward should engage in business, giving himself up to daily care and work in order to secure for his wife the comforts of a home? I don't remember that the subject was even referred to. And yet it was as much implied in the act of taking a wife as the other was implied in the act of assuming the relation that you now hold. Do you suppose for a moment that he isn't active in every part of his business?—that he trusts an incompetent clerk as you trust an incompetent cook? Thought, purpose, hands, are all busy in his work, and busy throughout every day—busy for you as well as for himself. He can't find time for reading during four or five hours of every day, nor time for calls on pleasant friends; no, no. His work would suffer, losses might follow and comfort and luxury fail for the wife he toils for. But this wife is too indolent or too proud to go down into her kitchen and see that his food is made palatable and healthy, to be present in all parts of his household with taste, order, neatness, economy and cleanliness. I don't wonder that he is disappointed and dissatisfied."

Martha's perceptions were beginning to be a little enlightened. She did not make any reply.

"Let me tell you how I have found it in your badly-managed household," resumed the mother. "Perhaps seeing through my eyes may help you to a better appreciation of things as they actually are. Twice since I have been here there has been no water in my room, and I have had to come down in the morning and get it for myself."

"Oh, mother! That is too bad! To think that Margaret should have been so careless!" The daughter's face crimsoned.

"Now, if you had been a careful housekeeper, or a thoughtful one, you would have visited my chamber to see that all was right there. You would never have left your mother's comfort dependent on the uncertain administration of a servant. Next, the room hasn't been dusted twice since I have been here. My fingers are soiled with everything I touch, and I am sure it hasn't been swept under the bed or bureau for a month. But this only affects your guests—is only so much taken from their comfort. Let us look at some things that involve the comfort of your husband, for these are of highest consideration. You asked him yesterday morning to get you some pink-lined envelopes. He brought them at dinner-time. He asked you to darn a rent in a black alpaca coat, so that he could wear it. Did you do as he requested? No; you read and toyed with fine needlework all the morning, but never touched the coat, and when he asked for it what reply did you make? Oh, you hated darning above all things, and told him he'd better direct his tailor to send for it. The day had become unusually warm, and he had to go out after dinner wearing a thick cloth coat, just because you had almost willfully neglected to perform so slight a service for your husband. Do you imagine that he never thought of your failure to do for him what he had asked?—that he didn't feel your indifference to his comfort? Your kiss, de pend upon it, Martha, touched his lips coldly, and your loving words, if any were spoken, were as sounding brass and tinkling cymbal in his ears. He looked past all lip affirmations and saw the failure in deed.

"And failure in deed seems to be the rule under your administration of his household instead of the exception. Most especially is this the case in what appertains to the dining-room and kitchen. The meals are always badly cooked and badly served. The slovenliness with which Margaret sets the table is a disgrace to herself and a standing rebuke to her mistress. I haven't seen a really clean dish—as I regard cleanliness—since I have been here, nor a clean knife or fork. Your cruet-stand is offensive to the eye. There is a smeared mustard bottle with a smeared spoon, a ketchup-bottle with half an inch of tomato ketchup at the bottom, and an oil bottle empty. Pepper and vinegar bottles I will not describe. The cruet-stand itself is as dark as lead, and the napkin-rings and spoons not much better."

"Pray stop, mother!" said Martha, interposing, with a face rather nearer to scarlet than white.

"No; I must say a word or two farther. Can such things be, and escape your husband's observation? Can such things be, and not prove a daily offence and annoyance to him? Can such things be, and not irritate him, at times, into unkindness? He would be more than mortal, my child, were he temper-proof against assaults upon good-nature like these."

Martha was not a fool, though there are too many in her position, we are sorry to say, to whom the word most significantly applies. She saw through her mother's clearer vision the blindness in which she had been and the folly of her defective household administration; saw that in holding herself above domestic duties and manipulations she was governed more by pride and indolence than a just regard for wifely or womanly dignity; saw that to hold fast her husband's love she must do something more for him than offer loving words; for life, being real and earnest, demanded earnest work from all—from the delicate wife as well as from the more enduring husband.

On the next morning, as Edward lifted his cup to his lips, he said, with a smile of pleasure:

"What fine coffee, Martha! I don't know

when I have tasted anything so delicious. Your handiwork, I infer?"

And Edward looked from his wife to her mother.

"No," replied Mrs. Barton; "it is none of my handiwork."

"But it's mine," said the young wife, who could not keep back the acknowledgment, her pleasure in seeing her husband's pleasure was so great.

"Yours?" Edward set down his cup and looked across the table in real surprise.

"Yes, mine. I made the coffee this morning."

"You did? Well, as I said, it is delicious! I wouldn't give this cup of coffee for all the stuff that has been made in the house since we entered it."

The steak was praised next.

"Did you cook this also?" asked the husband.

"I superintended the work," was answered.

"It is only necessary for some people to look at things and they will come all right," said Edward, "and I shouldn't wonder, Martha, if you belonged to the number."

There was a compliment and a reproof in the sentence, and both were felt.

"Do I need to say another word, my daughter?" said Mrs. Barton when she was alone with Martha again.

"I think not, mother," was answered. "Since our talk yesterday I have been looking at my place as a young wife from a new stand-point, and I find that I have not understood my duties. But they are very plain now, and I shall not need another reminder. Young girls fall into some strange notions about a wife's condition. They think of it as something more ornamental than useful—as invested with more queenly dignity than a homely administration of service in the household. She is to be loved and petted and cared for with untiring devotion and tenderness, but caring for her husband in the unattractive uses of a family in the kitchen, if need be, does not enter some imaginations as a thing at all included in the relation of husband and wife."

"And coldness, irritation, ill-nature, and too often alienations, are the consequences," said Mrs. Barton. "You felt a change in your husband. Did not the cause present itself?"

"Not until you pointed it out to me."

"Can it be possible that you were so blind, my daughter?"

"I was just so blind, mother!"

"Do you wonder that Edward was annoyed at times?"

"I wonder that he had so much forbearance," was the reply. "I wonder that he did not speak out plainly and tell me my duty."

"You might not have understood him," said Mrs. Barton. "He could not have said all that I have said. There would have been the appearance of a selfish regard for his own comfort. Young wives do not always understand a husband's reproving words, which are more apt to blind than to enlighten, for they are usually spoken under the impulses of chafed feelings. It is better, therefore, that I should have helped you to see clearly in a matter involving so many consequences."

X.

LOOKING FOR WRINKLES.

THERE had been a domestic storm in the household of Mr. Nicholson, and such storms, we regret to say, had become rather frequent in that household. Mr. Nicholson was a man of amiable temper and kind feelings, but with defects of character that were often particularly annoying to his wife, a quick tempered woman, who, when once fairly aroused, made everything stand around her, as the saying is. Mr. Nicholson was apt to forget and neglect—two faults with which Mrs. Nicholson had no patience, especially when this forgetting and neglecting interfered with matters bearing a relation to her daily round of duties.

A thorough business-training, from youth up to manhood, and consequent habits of order, with a methodical routine of doing things, en sured to Mr. Nicholson success as a merchant.

Without these important adjuncts to business his naturally easy and amiable qualities would have sadly interfered with his material interests. But neglect and forgetfulness were out of the question where order and routine were strictly observed. It was out of his business where Mr. Nicholson's peculiar weaknesses were seen. He was one of the class of men who keep their wives waiting, and who deserve the scolding they not unfrequently receive—who forget to execute the little household commissions entrusted to them, and neglect from day to day and from week to week the doing of things absolutely necessary to be done in order to secure comfort at home.

"Edward," Mrs. Nicholson might say as her husband is leaving for his place of business in the morning, "won't you stop at the store as you go down and tell Mr. Perkins to send up a bag of salt and a gallon of vinegar?"

"Certainly," Mr. Nicholson answers, and in a way so cheerfully acquiescent that his wife feels pleasure in his manifest willingness to oblige. But scarcely is Mr. Nicholson ten paces from his own door ere some matter of business intrudes itself, and so fully occupies his thoughts that he passes the store of Mr. Perkins, and even nods to Mr. Perkins himself, without once thinking of the salt and vinegar. Nor until salt and vinegar are thrown upon him from the face and lips of his aggravated wife at dinner-time is he again consciously aware that such articles exist.

"It is too bad, I declare!" he may answer; or, "What a terrible memory I have!" or, "I deserve a good scolding!" But Mr. Nicholson never resents his wife's use of salt and vinegar in such cases. Her anger is but a passing storm, and he knows that the sky will soon be clear again. Still, these outbreaks are by no means agreeable, and it is one of his chief regrets that Mrs. Nicholson's handsome face is so often marred by unbecoming passion. He tries to be more thoughtful in regard to her wishes, but habit is strong, and he goes on offending.

There had been, as we have intimated, one of these too often recurring storms in the household of Mr. Nicholson. His wife had said to him one morning—it is a little remarkable, knowing his particular infirmity, that she so steadily persisted in burdening him with commissions, not the half of which were ever attended to—

"Edward, won't you stop at Mr. Blackwell's as you go along and ask Mrs. Blackwell to send me up that pattern of a basque I lent her? Margaret is coming this morning to make one for me. She can only give me a part of to-day. Now, don't forget it, please."

"A basque pattern did you say?" Mr. Nicholson was always ready to oblige his wife.

"Yes. Mrs. Blackwell will know the pattern I mean. Tell her I would have sent for it, but that I have only one girl this week, and she is so cross that it is almost as much as my life is worth to ask her to do anything out of the kitchen."

"Hadn't you better send a note?" suggested Mr. Nicholson.

"It is not worth while. Mrs. Blackwell will know what I mean. It is a pattern I lent her a few days ago. Now, don't forget, Edward. Remember that Margaret will be here this morning, and she can't do anything until she gets the pattern."

"I'll attend to it," said the husband as he parted from his wife. But he didn't attend to it, and it was a foolish thing in Mrs. Nicholson, knowing his infirmity, to entrust him with any commission of importance. Almost past the door of Mrs. Blackwell he went without a thought of the basque coming into his mind, and he kept on to his store, remaining altogether oblivious to the subject.

In due time Margaret arrived as per engagement. Everything was ready for her except the basque pattern, and that was still to be received from Mrs. Blackwell. Mrs. Nicholson was considerably annoyed by this delay, and talked out her feelings to Margaret pretty freely, as women of her peculiar temperament are wont to do on such occasions. She had two or three theories touching the matter. Now she was certain her husband had forgotten to call at Mrs. Blackwell's, and now she was quite as sure that he had called, and that Mrs. Blackwell did not see fit to put herself to any special trouble in sending the pattern home.

"Let me go for it," said Margaret. But Mrs. Nicholson answered:

"No. I'm certain Mr. Nicholson called, and in that case I wish her to send it home. She ought to have done it, anyhow, before this."

Hour after hour passed, but no pattern came. Beyond measure was Mrs. Nicholson annoyed, and had she not cause for annoyance? No lady-reader will gainsay this for an instant. It was a trying case. Two or three times Margaret renewed her request to be permitted to go after the pattern, but the more the subject was pondered by Mrs. Nicholson, the stronger became her conviction that the neglect was all on the part of Mrs. Blackwell.

Finally, after waiting two or three hours, until it was too late to finish the basque on that day, even if the pattern were at hand, Margaret went away, leaving the disappointed Mrs. Nicholson in the worst possible humor with herself and with every one else.

The day was just burying itself in shadows when Mr. Nicholson, weary in mind from business cares and pleased to get home, stepped across the threshold. His little pet, May, had been watching at the parlor window during the space of half an hour, and at the first glimpse of his form had sprung away from her position and was at the door, ready to be caught up into her father's arms almost as soon as he had swung it open. And she was so caught up by her loving father, and almost smothered with kisses.

"Is that you, Edward?"

It was the voice of Mrs. Nicholson calling from one of the upper rooms.

The response of her husband brought Mrs. Nicholson down with quickly-moving feet. She found him just inside of the parlor door, with the happy little May in his arms, looking very cheerful and utterly unconscious of any approaching storm.

"Just to think of it!" said Mrs. Nicholson, going off at once in an excited tone of voice; "Mrs. Blackwell never sent that basque pattern, and Margaret, after waiting here for several hours, went away without touching the garment she came expressly to make."

"I declare!" exclaimed Mr. Nicholson. "Now, isn't that too bad!"

"Isn't what too bad? You don't mean to say that you didn't call at Mrs. Blackwell's?"

There was an outflashing of indignation from the eyes of Mrs. Nicholson at the very thought.

"I do mean to say that very thing!" replied

Mr. Nicholson, with some penitence of manner. "It is all my fault. What could I have been thinking about? I'm very sorry indeed!"

"Sorry don't mend the matter!" retorted Mrs. Nicholson. "It's a shame for you to do so! Here I've had Margaret waiting nearly all day without being able to take a single stitch in my basque, which I expected to wear to-morrow, and all because you did not choose to take the trouble to stop at Mrs. Blackwell's and ask her to send home the pattern I lent her."

"Don't say 'didn't choose,' my dear." Mr. Nicholson's countenance changed.

"It is just what I do say, and what I mean," answered Mrs. Nicholson with blinding indignation. "If you had cared a particle about my comfort or convenience, or had possessed the smallest inclination to obey me, you never would have neglected that small request. I have cause to be angry!"

"I'm very sorry," said Mr. Nicholson.

"Oh, don't say sorry again!" Mrs. Nicholson interrupted. "I hate the word, and have no faith in it. Sorry!"

Little May, with a half-frightened look, drew

her arms tightly around her father's neck, and laid her head down upon his bosom.

For some moments longer the indignant woman stormed, and then, as there was no re-action from her husband to keep alive the tur-bulent spirit that possessed her, anger wasted its strength down to feebleness and silence.

The hush of sadness followed, as in all such cases, and tears succeeded to passion. Mrs. Nicholson, after having poured out her vials of wrath, felt more unhappy than while bottling up her indignation. Not a word of angry retort had passed her husband's lips; she would have felt better if he had betrayed some darker shades of feeling, and thus brought himself down nearer to the level upon which she had descended. But he only remained passive, with his loving little May clinging to his neck.

At tea-time but few words were exchanged by husband and wife. The cloud on May's spirits had nearly passed over, and she chatted away, and asked her usual score of childish questions.

After tea the gas was lighted above the cen-tre-table in the sitting-room, and Mrs. Nicholson sat down with her work-basket.

Little May had a box of painted paper toys, and amused herself with these, talking to her father about them, and enjoying the interest he seemed to take in the curious figures they exhibited.

Very few words had been addressed by Mrs. Nicholson to her husband since they left the tea-table. What she said was of but small moment, but the tones of her voice were subdued and timid, showing repentance for the harsh words she had used and a changed state of feeling.

"What a funny-looking old woman!" said little May to her father, laughing suddenly, in a merry voice, as she held out for his examination one of the pictures. Then, as if a new thought had crossed her mind, she left her chair, and climbing into her mother's lap, commenced a close examination of her face. With eyes and fingers she searched it all over in so curious a way that both father and mother were amused as well as interested.

"What are you looking for, pet?" inquired the latter.

The question seemed a little to confuse the child, and she left the mother's lap and resumed her place at the table with a perceptibly heightened color.

"Say, darling, what were you looking for in my face?"

"For a wrinkle," answered little innocence, smiling, yet flushing to a deeper crimson.

"A wrinkle!" The hand of Mrs. Nicholson passed with an involuntary movement over her face.

"A wrinkle!" Mr. Nicholson laughed out aloud. "What does little puss mean?"

Little puss, as her father often called her, now threw an arch look upon the mother, and said:

"Don't you know what Aunt Mary read in the paper yesterday?"

"No, dear; what was it?"

"Why, that a wife gets a new wrinkle in her face every time she scolds her husband. And I wanted to see—"

The child's voice was lost in the merry laugh that rang from her father's lips as he caught her in his arms and bore her with a triumphant air around the room.

"Well, pet," he said as his merriment subsided, "did you find a new wrinkle?"

For a moment or two Mrs. Nicholson was

fluttered, and her face became all aglow from a quicker heart-beat. But her perception of the ludicrous was strong, and her good sense a balancing quality, and she quickly joined in the merry laugh that was all at her expense.

"No, there isn't a single wrinkle in her face," answered May, positively.

"Nor shall one be seen there for twenty years to come," said Mrs. Nicholson, throwing a tender look upon her husband, "if no other cause should produce them."

May's bedtime had come, and the child was borne away by her mother, who gave her many loving kisses ere she left her alone with the angels who watch over sleeping children.

She said nothing about the wrinkles as she rejoined her husband, but there were merry twinkles in both their eyes and right feelings in both their hearts.

Mrs. Nicholson, who is a handsome woman and just a little vain of her beauty, has quite reformed her ways in the matter of scolding her husband. There are dangers attending that peculiar domestic recreation that she is unwilling to encounter.

XI.

A NERVOUS WIFE.

MY friend Wilkins married a sweet young girl of a quiet, amiable disposition, but in no way skilled in those domestic arts without a knowledge of which the wife's duties are always felt to be hard in the beginning. He was the envy of more than one who had aspired to the possession of her hand. I knew him to be industrious, intelligent and kind-hearted, and I felt sure that he had taken a life-companion who would be faithful and loving. The promise was bright enough to warrant a prophecy of more than ordinary happiness.

They removed to another city. Ten years afterward, in passing through that city, I called upon Wilkins, who met me with the old, frank cordiality. Eyes and face were in a glow of pleasure when, still grasping his hand, I inquired after his wife. His countenance changed instantly.

"Poor Mary!" he said in a sad, discouraged way. "She has no health."

"I'm sorry," was my natural response.

"Sickness and the loss of two of our children have so worn down body and mind that she is now but a shadow of her former self. Worst of all, her nerves are completely shattered. But you must see her. To meet an old friend will do her good. You will take tea with us and spend the evening?"

I assented, and then made farther inquiries about his family and worldly condition. His story was not a very bright one. The birth of their first child was followed by a prostrating sickness which brought the young mother to the utmost verge of life.

"She has never had good health since," said Wilkins in a depressed voice. "My income was small, and we could not afford the amount of household assistance in the beginning that she really required, and so everything was against her restoration to sound health. Children came rapidly, bringing with them more exhausting cares. And the death of two of our little ones to which I have referred seemed to complete the work of ruin. She is now a hopeless invalid, a poor, weak, nervous, unhappy creature, a mere wreck of what you saw ten years ago, moving like a tearful ghost through her daily round of duties, and only kept alive by the constant and careful attention of a physician. I don't think the doctor has been out of my house for two weeks at a time for six years, and I'm sure has received more than fifteen hundred dollars of my money in that time. The fact is, what with doctor's bills, nurses, medicines and the hundred nameless expenses a sick and nervous wife entails upon a man, my fortunes have been marred. They keep me poor."

Wilkins spoke in a fretful voice. It was plain that he had grown impatient under the trials to which the bad health of his wife had exposed him.

I called at his store again toward evening, and went home with him. Had I met Mrs. Wilkins in the street, I would not have recognized in her the happy bride who, ten years before, blushing in beauty, I had seen giving her hand in a life-partnership, with such loving confidence in the future, to the husband of her choice. Her countenance was wan and wasted, all the beautifully rounded outlines gone; her eyes, deeply sunken, were languid almost to indifference; her hair, once richly luxuriant, had fallen off, until scarce half of it remained, and that looked dry and crisp, with here and there a premature line of gray. She stooped slightly and her motions were lifeless.

A faint smile parted her lips as I grasped her hand with all the warmth of a genuine friendly interest. But it faded almost as soon as it was born. I tried to talk with her in a cheerful strain, and did succeed in awakening a brief interest in the olden time. But the present was too painfully real a thing: it would not let her thoughts indulge in pleasant fancies. I could not help asking about herself and her children, and this turned the current of her feelings into its wonted channel, and I listened to her sad heart-stories and painful experiences in sickness until my own feelings were deeply shadowed. I pitied her. What a sombre, suffering life had been hers! Into what a world of misery instead of happiness had marriage translated her!

As she talked I observed her husband carefully. It was plain that he had but little sympathy with his wife's state of feeling. He was a sufferer with her, though in a lighter degree, and as his sufferings originated in her, there was plainly a lack of kindly patience toward his companion. Several times he interrupted her, trying to draw the conversation into another channel, and once or twice he threw in depreciating sentences, as if she were exaggerating the unhappy story of her life.

I learned that Mrs. Wilkins rarely, if ever, went out of her own house. Her duties were very arduous, and her ability, from ill health, small. Every day she worked to bodily exhaustion, and usually in pain. There was no recreation of any kind, bodily or mental. It was a living death. No wonder she was a drooping, wretched, nervous woman.

On the next day, having thought the matter over, I called to see my friend at his store, my mind made up to have a plain talk with him. I referred to his wife, expressing in regard to her my earnest sympathy.

"Poor Mary!" he replied; "her case is hopeless, and mine too, I fear."

"While there's life there's hope," said I, using the physician's half-despairing axiom.

He regarded me a little curiously.

"How often do you take her out riding?" I inquired.

He shook his head. "Can't afford carriage-hire; much as I can do to pay the doctor. No, no, neither of us has time or money to spend for riding out."

"Change and fresh air you will find better and cheaper medicine than doctor's stuff. Do you take her to the seashore once a year, or to the springs, or the mountains?"

"You are jesting," he replied, with the air of one who felt that an undue liberty had been taken.

"Far from it, my friend," I answered, seriously. "I feel too warm an interest in you to jest on a subject like this."

"The seashore, the springs, the mountains, are summer luxuries beyond the reach of our ability." He spoke sadly.

"Do not name them as luxuries in your case. If the enervated votary of pleasure and fashion needs them for recreation and to impart a new zest to the year's succeeding round of gay existence, how much more essential are they for the sick, the nervous, the exhausted toiler in l.fe's field of earnest labor! I fear, my friend, that you have not thought wisely of your wife's true position—that in some sense you are to blame for her present ill health and state of mental depression."

"How?" Wilkins looked surprised.

"The human soul," I answered, "is not a piece of senseless machinery, not made up of a series of iron wheels that can do their work as well in the dark underground chamber as in the broad daylight. Even the flower must have change—air, sunlight, morning, evening and the advancing seasons—for its healthy growth and maturity. But the human soul is of higher organization, and of multitudinous wants compared with the flower. Shut up the flower from the warm sun and the refreshing air, and will it not grow sickly—nay, will it not fade, wither and die? You are treating your wife with less consideration than you would treat a house-plant. No wonder that she is dying daily."

Wilkins really looked amazed, and I was for a little while in doubt whether he were offended at my freedom or astounded at his own blind ness touching the nature and wants of the human soul he had adjoined in a life-companionship with his own.

"Nature's two best physicians," I went on, "are pure air and exercise. And what is better, they charge nothing for attendance."

"To a large part of mankind," answered Wilkins, "time is money. It is so in our case."

"Don't make that too positive a conclusion. Increase the strength and you diminish the hours of labor—nay, more, you remove from them the cause of extreme exhaustion. My word for it, if you had spent a hundred dollars a year in giving your wife change of scene, sea-bathing and mental as well as bodily recreation, your doctor's bill would have been reduced by more than that amount. How often do you take her to concerts or other places of public amusement?"

"We haven't been to a concert for five years," said he

"And yet I remember that she was passionately fond of music."

"We can't afford it," remarked Wilkins, gloomily.

"Better go without a dinner occasionally.

Health of the soul is quite as essential as health of the body. If you starve the former, what is there in mere eating and drinking worth living for?"

"Mary wouldn't go if I were to purchase tickets. She has housed herself so long that she has no desire to step across the threshold of her prison-house."

"For which, speaking frankly, and to an old friend, you are, in a great measure, to blame. And unless you at once and with a purpose not to be set aside by first difficulties open wide the doors of this prison-house, and actually compel the drooping prisoner to go forth, a few years will close up the history of a wretched life."

"Ah!" said he, "I can feel the force of what you say! But how and where to begin? That is the question."

"I notice," was my reply, "that Herz, the celebrated composer and pianist, is in your city, and will give, this evening, one of his concerts. Take her to hear him."

The eyes of Wilkins dropped to the floor. I saw what was in his mind. The tickets were one dollar each, and the expense, therefore, larger than he felt that he had a right to incur for a simple amusement. He had too many lemands for dollars in other and more important directions.

"I am going to invite her," said I, "and I don't believe she will refuse me."

"I'm sure she will not go." Wilkins was quite positive.

"We'll see. You will take a note of invitation from me at dinner-time. I will enclose tickets for you both, and say that I will call at tea-time and make one of the company at the concert."

Wilkins was incredulous, and half opposed me, but my interest in his unhappy wife was too strong, and I resolved to have my own way. The tickets and invitation were accordingly sent.

I called at my friend's store, late in the afternoon, to go home with him.

"Well," said I, cheerfully, "what word from your good wife? Will she be ready for the concert?"

"I'm afraid not." Wilkins shook his head and looked gloomy.

"What did she say?"

"That it was impossible for her to go out; that she couldn't leave the children; and, finally, after I had met every objection with a reason that could not be gainsaid, she declared that she didn't feel like going and couldn't think of it."

"The ice is very solid and hard to break through." I smiled as I spoke. "It is that want of inclination which must be overcome. She'll go if we insist upon it."

But Wilkins was of a different opinion. "I know her a great deal better than you do," was his answer.

At tea-time I went home with him. There was a change in Mrs. Wilkins: a glance revealed this. The languor and exhaustion so painfully apparent on the previous evening were scarcely visible. Her eyes were brighter, her countenance more elevated, her lips had a firmer outline. I saw that some attention had been given to her dress, and, though not in concert trim, it was plain enough that it would not take her a very great while to be in presentable condition.

Wilkins was in error. His wife did go to the concert, and surprised both him and herself by the amount of pleasure she received from the exquisite performance of Herz. Indeed, she expressed her satisfaction in lively terms and with a glowing face in the intervals of many of the pieces.

"How is Mrs. Wilkins?" I asked of my friend as I entered his place of business on the next day.

"Better than for many months, I am pleased to say," was his answer. "She seemed, this morning, almost another woman. That music was like an elixir to her soul."

"I had faith in it," said I. "Depend upon it, Wilkins, you have been consenting to your wife's death by murder and suicide—murder on your part and suicide on hers. My next recommendation is Cape May. Give up your business for a week, and borrow the money to pay expenses if you haven't the ready cash on hand, but take your wife to Cape May immediately. It will not cost half as much as her funeral. Sea air, sea bathing and a sight of old Ocean will put new life into her veins."

"She can't possibly leave home. We have too many young children."

"She'll have to leave home, and her young children too, for ever, if you don't do something to save her." I spoke with some feeling, for I was a little provoked at my friend's inclination to throw difficulties in the way. "Just make up your mind that the thing has to be done, and I'll answer for your wife. The fact is, it's my opinion that she'll say 'Yes' on the first proposition."

And so she did. A little management was practiced. I accepted another invitation to tea, and during the evening gave as graphic a description as was in my power of the novelty, excitement and wonderfully beneficial effects of a week at the seashore. My own experience was quite to the point, having regained strength almost by magic after a long period of extreme nervous exhaustion.

"You must take your wife to the seashore. It is just what she wants," said I, after the way had been fully prepared.

Wilkins followed up with such a hearty acquiescence that the point was carried under scarcely an appearance of objection. Difficulties were, of course, suggested, but these were pronounced of such slender importance that they were waived almost as soon as presented. Two days afterward I had the satisfaction of seeing them off in the steamboat. As I shook hands with them at parting, I could see in the countenance of Mrs. Wilkins some reviving traces of her old girlish beauty and the rekindling in her eyes of the light of other days.

A year afterward, in passing through the city, I made it my business to visit my old acquaintance. He received me with a warmth of manner and cheerfulness of spirit which satisfied me that his state of mind had considerably improved.

"How is Mrs. Wilkins?" I made almost immediate inquiry.

A broad smile went over his face as he re plied: "A thousand per cent. better than when you saw her a year ago."

"I am delighted to hear you say so. How did the Cape May prescription answer?"

"Admirably. It worked like a charm. Mary came back another woman. It was to her almost like discovering the fountain of eternal youth. I never saw such a change in any one."

"Didn't she fall back into old habits of mind and body after her return to the city?"

"No."

"How did you prevent this?" I inquired.

"By acting on the hint you gave. I hired a wagon for an afternoon once a week while the pleasant weather lasted, and showed her all the fine scenery within ten miles of the city. It cost me two dollars each time, but it was cheaper than paying the doctor, and the medicine cured more radically. You can't imagine what a change in her feelings took place. Nothing outside of the narrow circle of home interested her before: thought seemed asleep or palsied; but now she takes an interest in everything. Her soul has awakened from its dead torpor."

"Was it not starved into more than infantile weakness?" I remarked.

"Perhaps so," he said, thoughtfully. "The mind must have its appropriate food as well as the body."

"Nothing is truer than that," I replied. "And like the body, it must have the alternations of shade and sunshine, fresh air and exercise. It must have change and recreation as well as seasons of labor. Without these, mental health is impossible, and without mental health there can be no true bodily health."

Husbands, I fear, are not thoughtful enough

about their wives in this particular. I am very certain if every toiling housekeeper and worn-down, nervous, exhausted mother whose pale face is hardly ever seen beyond the portals of her own door were forced abroad occasionally into the social world—if she would not go willingly—and taken yearly to the springs, the seashore or the mountains for a few weeks, that hundreds and thousands of wives and mothers who are now sickly, nervous and unhappy would be in the enjoyment of good health and cheerful spirits, giving light to their homes and happiness to the hearts of their husbands.

Try the prescription, ye men with sickly, toiling, exhausted wives whose pale faces haunt your homes like ghosts of former blessings. Pity them wisely and hold them back while you may from the low resting-places under the green turf toward which they are descending with rapid feet.

XII.

ONLY A HUSBAND.

"THANK you!" What a musical ring was in the voice of Mrs. Archer! what a pleasant light shone in her eyes! She had dropped a glove, which a gentleman had lifted from the floor and placed in her hand.

Mr. Archer, the lady's husband, saw the little act of courtesy and noticed its reward. He would have given almost anything for just such a musical "Thank you!" for as bright a glance as she had thrown upon a stranger. Once, tones and glances like these had been his reward for any little attentions he might happen to offer; now, all the small courtesies of life were withdrawn, and no matter what the act or its quality, his wife received it with a cold indifference singularly in contrast with her manner toward other men.

Was it a defect of love? Did Mrs. Archer really think more highly of other men who showed her polite attentions than she did of her husband? Sometimes a chafed feeling of impatience, sometimes of jealousy, and sometimes of mournful regret for sunnier days in the far-away past, would trouble the husband sorely. But these were pushed aside or suffered to die for lack of aliment, and the dull, cold routine of every-day life permitted to have its usual course.

On the occasion referred to above, Mr. Archer and his wife were spending an evening at the house of a friend where company had been invited. For days previously the countenance of Mrs. Archer had worn its usual dead calm, its accustomed placidity, its matter-of-course aspect. She had talked with her husband, in a kind of dead-level tone and manner, on all subjects that happened to come up, whether of first or third importance. Or if interest happened to rise into anything approaching enthusiasm, it was accompanied by something of sharpness that left on the mind of Mr. Archer an uncomfortable feeling as if he were blamed for something. And this had been the wife's aspect even after she had donned her company attire, and up to the moment when she made her appearance among the guests of the friend to whose house she brought, tied up, as it were, in a closely-compacted bundle, her smiles and courtesies for public dispensation.

As he had noticed on many previous occasions, so did Mr. Archer notice on this, the remarkable difference between his wife's home and company manners—between her treatment of her husband and her treatment of other gentlemen who happened to enter into conversation with her or offer any polite attention. The answer to their words always went forth from lips wreathed with smiles and eyes sparkling with pleasure; to his words from a cold, placid mouth, and with half-indifferent or averted glances. And yet Mrs. Archer was a faithful wife in all her dutiful relations, and in her heart a loving wife to her husband. If smiles did not play in sunny circles over her countenance as in former times, she made the household smile with order and comfort arranged and secured by her ever-busy hands. Her thoughts were no wandering truants to other and forbidden fields, but home-guests, nor were they busy for herself, but for the husband and children in whom her own life was bound up. It was not that love for her husband had grown dull—answering not as mirror answereth to face—that her countenance did not light up at his coming, that she did not meet his words and attentions with smiling glances. Had she not given him her heart when she gave him her hand?—had she not promised to be a faithful wife? Was she not true in all of her relations? What more was required of her? It never entered into her thoughts that her husband was weak enough to desire a daily repetition of the love-glances with which, in the season of young love's ardor, her eyes were ever beaming when they turned upon his face.

And yet it was even so. It was because he hoped to live all his after-life in the warmth of those glances that he had wooed and won her in the bright days of her young womanhood. And when he saw the light growing daily dimmer and dimmer, and felt its genial warmth diminishing, a shadow fell upon his spirit. Very kind, very attentive, the husband remained, but his wife became aware of a certain coldness toward herself that was far from being as pleasant as the lover-like manner with which he had formerly treated her, and many times she sighed for the tones and glances she saw him give to other ladies, as he sighed for like tokens of interest from herself. Both were in error, and both in a certain sense to blame.

On the evening referred to, the contrast between the manner of his wife to himself and to other men who showed her little attentions was felt with more than usual distinctness by Mr. Archer. He was not jealous, for he knew the truth of her character, nor offended, but hurt. Almost any price would he have paid for the bright return another received for a simple act, the double of which on his part would scarcely receive a passing notice.

Not long after this Mr. Archer saw his wife drop her handkerchief. Stepping forward from where he stood talking with a lady, he lifted it from the floor and placed it in her hand. His eyes were fixed upon her countenance, but she did not so much as return his look nor make the slightest acknowledgment, merely receiving the handkerchief with a quiet indifference in striking contrast with the way in which she had taken the glove from another's hand. Mr. Archer was disappointed. The drooping flowers in his heart were pining for sunbeams, and he had hoped for a few bright rays. But they were not given.

A lady to whom Mrs. Archer had been introduced that evening, and who was a stranger to both herself and husband, sat by her side They had been conversing with some animation, and were interested in each other. This lady was struck by the marked difference with which Mrs. Archer received these two slight attentions from different gentlemen. She had observed the polite response made when the glove was handed to its owner, and was pleased with the graceful manner of her new acquaintance. The cold, almost repulsive, way in which she accepted the handkerchief was therefore noticed the more distinctly. She saw that the individual who presented it was disappointed, if not hurt. Her inference was natural.

"That gentleman is no favorite of yours," she remarked.

"What gentleman?" Mrs. Archer looked curious.

"He who lifted your handkerchief just now."

"Why do you think so?" There was a slightly amused expression in the corners of Mrs. Archer's mouth.

"You treated him very coldly, almost rudely, I thought—pardon me for saying so: quite differently from the way in which you treated the gentleman who picked up your glove a few minutes ago."

A smile spread over the countenance of Mrs. Archer.

"Oh, he's only my husband!" she made answer.

"The one who lifted the glove?"

"No, the one who gave me my handkerchief."

"Only your husband!"

The lady spoke in a tone that Mrs. Archer could not help feeling as a rebuke.

"He's my husband," she said, "and doesn't expect me to be particularly ceremonious. He picked up my handkerchief as a thing of course. The other was a mere acquaintance—half a stranger, in fact—and a more formal acknowledgment of his polite attention could not have been omitted without rudeness or a want of regard for etiquette."

"I am afraid," remarked the lady, guardedly, so as not to give offence, "that some of us are scarcely just to our husbands in this matter of exterior courtesy. I know that I have not been, and a lesson I once received will never be forgotten."

The eyes of Mrs. Archer turned by a kind of instinct toward her husband. He was standing near a brilliant gas-lamp, the light of which was falling clearly on his face. His glance was upon the floor. There was a shadow on his countenance which the strong light, instead of obliterating, made more distinctly visible—a look of disappointment that was almost sad.

A new thought flashed into the mind of Mrs. Archer and touched her with a feeling of tender self-upbraiding. Was it possible that her husband had felt her manner as cold or indifferent? Was it possible that he had noticed the blandness of her manner toward one who was but little less than a stranger, and contrasted it, as the lady had done, with her seeming indifference to himself? Her eyes were still on his face when he lifted his own from the floor and turned them full upon her. They were dull and spiritless. A little while they lingered upon her, and then moved slowly away, as if seeking some object pleasanter to look upon. For some time Mrs. Archer continued gazing at her husband, but he did not look toward her again. She sighed, and letting her eyes fall, remained lost in thought for some moments. Then turning to the lady who sat by her side, and who was observing her closely, she said, with a smile half forced:

"You have set me to thinking."

"And in the right direction, I hope," was frankly responded.

"I think so."

Watching for a good opportunity, when she knew her husband was near her and could not help noticing the fact, she purposely disarranged a light scarf that was laid over her shoulders. Instantly he stepped forward and drew it into place.

"Thank you, dear," she said, quickly, a smile on her lip and a pleasant light in her eye. They were not counterfeit, but real, for Mrs. Archer truly loved her husband, and was pleased with any little attention at home or abroad. But he being "only her husband," she had, like far too many others, omitted the form of acknowledgment because he must know that the feeling was in her heart.

What a change came instantly into her husband's face! What a look of pleased surprise, almost grateful in its expression! Verily, she had her reward! How tenderly he leaned toward her! and what a new meaning was in his tones as he remarked on some topic of the hour! And did not her heart leap up at these signs of the affection that was in his heart, still warm and lover-like, still pleased with tokens of kindness and ready to reward them twenty fold? Away back, through many years, her thoughts went to the May-time of their young love, when they lived in the light of each other's eyes and thought no music as sweet as the melody of each other's voices.

The time seemed long to Mrs. Archer that they were required by etiquette to remain, for she desired to be alone with her husband. Not much was said by either as they walked homeward that night, but the hand of Mrs. Archer clung with a closer pressure than usual to the arm of her husband, and the arm held the hand, with a returning pressure, firmly against a heart that beat with quicker pulsations.

Both time and place were soon propitious. They stood in their own chamber looking with a new expression in their eyes into each other's face.

"Dear husband! I love you, and I am proud of you. You are not like other men!" Mrs. Archer drew an arm around his neck and laid her lips upon his lips.

"God bless you for the words!" he answered, with a joyful thrill in his voice.

"You did not doubt my love?" she said, in half surprise.

"No, no! But words and tokens of love are always grateful. You are dear to me as my life. Let us keep the golden links that bind our hearts together bright as in the beginning, burnishing them daily with small, sweet courtesies. Forgive me if in aught I have shown coldness or indifference: there has been neither in my heart."

Ever after the golden links were kept bright, burnished daily by the small, sweet courtesies of which the husband had spoken.

XIII.

THE FIRST SHADOW.

IDA was a bride. Onward through a year of patient waiting had she moved toward this blessed estate, all her thoughts golden ones, all her fancies radiant with love and beauty. And now she was a bride, a happy bride. He who had won her was worthy to wear her as a crown. Kind, honorable and gifted, his praise was on the lips of all men.

Yes, Ida was a happy bride. It was the blooming, fragrant spring-time of her life. Singing-birds were in all the trees, musical waters gliding through the peaceful landscape, and a cloudless sky was bending over all. The blessedness of this new life was greater than she had even imagined in all the warmth of her maiden fancies.

A moon had waxed and waned since the lover

became the husband—a moon dropping the sweets of Mount Hybla. It was evening, and Ida stood by the window looking out through the dusky air, waiting and wishing for the return of her husband, who was later than usual from his home. At last her glad eyes caught a glimpse of his well-known form, and starting back from the window, she went with springing steps to meet him at the door, opening it ere his hand could ring the bell.

"Dear Edward!" What a gushing love was in her voice! She raised her lips for a kiss, and a kiss was given. But somehow its warmth did not go down to her heart.

"Are you not well, dear?" she asked, tenderly, as they entered their pleasant little parlor, and she looked into his face and tried to read its expression, but the twilight was too deep.

"Quite as well as usual, love." The voice of her husband was low and gentle, but it had a new and changed sound for the young wife's ears—a sound that made her heart tremble. And yet his arm was around her, and he held one of her hands tightly, compressing it within his own.

It grew dark in the room before the gas was

lighted. When the strong rays fell suddenly upon the face of her husband, Ida saw a change there also. It was clouded. Not heavily clouded, but still in shadow. Steadily and earnestly she looked at him, until he turned his face partly away to escape the searching scrutiny.

"You are not well, Edward." Ida looked serious, almost concerned.

"Don't trouble yourself. I'm very well."

He smiled and patted her cheek playfully, or rather with an attempt at playfulness. Ida was not deceived. A change had passed over her husband. Something was wrong. He was not what he had been.

In due time tea was announced, and the little family of two gathered around the table in the neat breakfast-room.

"Burnt toast and dish-water tea, as usual!" These were the first words spoken by the young husband after sitting down to the table, and the manner in which they were uttered left Ida in no doubt as to the state of his feelings. How suddenly was the fine gold dimmed!

A few hours earlier the young husband had called in to see his mother, an orderly, industrious woman and a notable housekeeper. As usual, he was full of the praise of his beautiful young wife, in whom he had yet seen nothing to blame, nothing below perfection. But his mother had looked at her with different eyes. Living in the world was, with her, no holiday affair, and marriage no mere honeymoon. She was too serious in all her views and feelings to have much patience with what she esteemed a mere play-day life. A little jealous of her son's affection she was withal, and its going forth to another with an ardor so different from what it had ever gone forth to herself made her feel cold toward the dear little wife of Edward, who was its favorite object.

"It is time," she said, with a distance of manner that surprised her son, "for you and Ida to be a little serious. The honeymoon is over, and the quicker you come down to sober realities, the better. There is one thing about Ida that rather disappoints me."

Edward was too much surprised at this unexpected announcement to speak. His mother went on:

"She's no housekeeper—"

"She's young, mother. She'll learn," he said, interrupting her.

"She had no right to marry until she knew how to make a cup of tea!" The old lady spoke with considerable asperity.

"Mother!"

"I say just what I mean. Not a single cup of tea have I tasted in your house that was fit to drink. I don't know how you can put up with such stuff. You wouldn't have done it at my table, I'm very sure."

"Please, mother, don't talk so any more about Ida! I can't bear to hear it."

"You can bear to hear the truth, Edward. I speak for Ida's good, and your own too. She is a wife now, not a mere sweetheart. And she is your housekeeper besides, with something more to do and care for than dress, music, party-going and enjoyment. I must say, as I said a little while ago, that I am disappointed in her. What are girls thinking about now-a-days when they get married? Surely, not of their husbands' home-comforts."

"If you please, mother, we will change the subject," said the young man, who was exceedingly pained by the strong language he had heard. He spoke so firmly that the matter was dropped, and not again alluded to at that time.

We have now an explanation of the change in the young husband's state of mind. There were some truths in what his mother had said, and this made it so much the harder to bear. The first shadow had fallen, and it dimmed the brightness of this new and happy life.

Still the defects of Ida—very small to his eyes, even after they were pointed out by his mother—were things of no moment. He had not intended her for a household drudge. Was she not loving-hearted, accomplished and beautiful? True, he had intended her for the presiding genius of his home, and there were sober, matter-of-fact things to be done in all homes. But her devotion to these would come in good time.

How Edward came to speak as he did about the tea and toast was, almost on the instant he had given utterance to his words, a mystery to himself. He regretted the start he gave to his young wife, and trembled for the effects of his unkindly uttered words. He would have given much could he have recalled them. But they were said beyond the power of unsaying.

The reference of his mother to the indifferent tea with which she had been served at his table had not only mortified him, but made things distinct in his memory which before were only seen dimly and as matters of indifference. Where all was so bright, why should he turn his eyes upon a few fragments of clouds skirting the far horizon? He would not have done so if left to himself. The clouds might have spread until very much larger than a man's hand before their murky aspect would have drawn his happy vision from the all-pervading brightness.

Ida's hand, which was raising a cup to her lips, fell almost as suddenly as if palsied; paleness overspread her countenance; her lips had a motion between a quiver and a spasm. From her eyes, which seemed bound as by a spell to her husband's face, tears rolled out and fell in large drops over her cheeks.

Never before since Edward had looked upon that dear young face had he seen its brightness so veiled. Never before had a word of his been answered by anything but smiles and love responses.

"I'm sorry, Edward." How the sad, tremulous voice of Ida rebuked the young husband's unkindness! "It shall not be so again."

And she kept her word. Suddenly he had

awakened her from a bright, dreamy illusion. She had been in a kind of fairy-land. By an unlooked-for shifting of scenery, the hard everyday working world, with its common working-day wants, had struck with an unlovely aspect upon her startled vision, the jagged edges of the real wounding painfully her soft ideal. But once awakened she never slept again. It was the first shadow that fell dimly and coldly upon her married heart—the first, and to the life-experienced we need not say the last.

Very, very tenderly spoken were all the words of Edward to his young wife during the shadowed evening that followed this first dimming of their home-light. And Ida, who felt the kindness of his heart, tried to smile and seem as of old. But somehow she could not force into existence the smiles she wished to send out as tokens of forgiveness. Thoughts of the bad tea and burnt toast, the "usual"—ah! there lay the smart!—evening entertainment she had provided, or rather suffered to be provided by unskillful hands—were her own any more skillful?—for her returning husband, haunted her all the while.

"It shall not be so again!" Not idly uttered

were these words. All the evening she kept repeating them to herself with a steadily-increasing purpose and a clearer vision. "Edward shall never have another occasion for rebuke."

Several times during the evening the young husband was tempted to refer to the conversation held with his mother in explanation of his conduct, but he wisely kept his own counsel. Of all things, he dreaded an estrangement between his wife and mother.

On the next morning Edward noticed that his young wife left their chamber earlier than usual and went down stairs. Not, however, to fill their home with music, as she had often done. Her matinée was the singing tea-kettle, not the stringed piano. She had a heightened color when she took her place at the breakfast-table and poured for her husband the fragrant coffee which she had made with her own hands after discovering that her cook was ignorant of the art. But how did she know the art? That was almost accidental; the recollection of some good housewife's talk had served her in the right time. The warm praise bestowed by Edward on the coffee was ample reward.

Ida bought a cook-book during the day—

that sounds unromantic, but it was even so—and she studied it for hours. During the afternoon her mother-in-law came in, and Ida urged her to stay to tea. The old lady accepted the invitation—not, we are sorry to say, in the very best spirit. She had opened the war on Edward's "butterfly" young wife, and she meant to follow it up. When Edward came home and found that his mother was there, his spirits fell. He saw by the corners of her mouth that she had not forgotten their interview of the preceding day, and that her state of mind was not a whit more charitable. Ida's face was a little shadowed, but she was cheerful and very attentive to his mother, and, happily, ignorant of her true feelings. She passed often between the breakfast-room and the parlor, evidently with household cares upon her mind.

Tea was at length announced. Edward's heart trembled. His mother arose, and with rather a cold air accompanied her children to the room where the evening meal awaited them. The table had an attractive look, new to the eyes of both Edward and his mother. It was plain that another hand besides the servant's had been there. Ida poured the tea, and Edward served the hot biscuit and cream toast. The eyes of the latter were on his mother as she lifted, with an air which he understood tc say, "Poor stuff!" the cup of tea to her lips. She tasted the fragrant beverage, set the cup down, lifted and tasted again. The infusion was faultless! Yes, even to her critical taste. Next the biscuit was tried, and next the toast. Mrs. Goodfellow herself could not have surpassed them.

"Have you changed your cook?" The old lady looked across the table curiously at Ida.

"No, mother," answered the young wife, smiling. "Only the cook has found a mistress."

"Is this all your work, Ida?" The old lady spoke in a half-incredulous tone.

"Yes, it is all my work. Don't you think, if I try hard, I'll make a housekeeper in time?"

This was so unexpected that the husband's mother was delighted. Ida had gone right home to her matter-of-fact, every-day heart.

"Why, yes, you precious little darling!" she answered, with an enthusiasm almost foreign to her character. "I couldn't have done better myself."

The shadow passed from the heart of Ida as

her eyes rested on the pleased countenance of her husband. This was the first shadow that had fallen since their happy wedding day, and it moved on quickly, but its memory was left behind. It was like the drawing of a veil which partly conceals yet beautifies the countenance.

Ida's husband was a man like the rest, with man's common wants and weaknesses, and her married world was one in which hands must take hold of common duties. But she soon learned that in the real world were real delights, substantial and abiding.

Bravely did she walk in the new path that lay at her feet. She had her reward. Tea and toast but expressed her household duties, none of which were rightly performed during the delicious honeymoon. But she failed in nothing afterward, and soon learned that the ground in which true happiness takes deepest roct, and from which it springs up with strongest branches, is the ground of common, homely, every-day duties.

XIV.

NOT APPRECIATED.

HE last sad rites were over. She had fallen by the way ere life's meridian was reached, and left husband and children to a sorrow that mocks for a time at consolation. Seven years she had been a wife, six years a mother, and now a lonely-hearted man and three little motherless ones were left in the dwelling where the sunshine of her loving presence would never again appear.

Mr. Newcomb was a sadder man now than when he followed the palled coffin to its final resting-place. And there were reasons why his heart should feel a deeper depression. A few friends and neighbors had returned with him from the place of graves, and they had lingered for a short time in the desolate rooms, speaking together in muffled tones of the departed, and of those she had left behind her.

Two women talked in this wise, and it so happened that Mr. Newcomb heard every word. They thought him in one of the upper chambers, but he was sitting in an adjoining room, and their voices came in through an open window and smote his ears with intolerable pain.

"Poor Alice!" said one. "It is a blessed relief for her."

"But a dreadful loss to her children," was answered. "Dear little babies! My heart aches for them. And I pity Mr. Newcomb, also. It is a great loss, though he never did rightly appreciate her, poor thing!"

"I can't get up much sympathy for him," said the other, "and it isn't any use to try. His wife was not appreciated, as you say. He did not understand her disposition, nor give her credit for the virtues she possessed. She was faithful and loving, but sensitive—so sensitive that the lightest word of unkindness was felt as a painful stroke."

"And that reminds me," said the neighbor, "of one of the bad habits he indulged in—of bantering her in company and showing off her little faults or peculiarities. I have been so provoked with him that I could with difficulty keep my tongue from reproach."

"She was plain, and I think that annoyed him sometimes."

"Plain! The beauty of her pure spirit was ever shining through her face, and if his eyes were not clear enough to see it, he was unworthy of her."

"She was not as bright as some other women, and it always struck me that he indulged in depreciating contrasts."

"She was good, true, faithful, loving," was answered, "and these are better qualities in a wife than mere brilliancy. Do you remember that evening at Mrs. Bolton's about a year ago?"

"Very well."

"She was there, you know."

"Yes. I recollect."

"He flirted with pretty Miss Gardner, who has only her face to recommend her."

"I remember. It lowered him in my opinion I don't like to see married men too particular in their attentions to showy young girls."

"Nor I. Well, I happened to catch the expression of Mrs. Newcomb's face when her husband was standing at the piano turning the music while Miss Gardner sung. She was looking at him. Oh, it was inexpressibly sad! A little while afterward I turned again to the place where she had been sitting all alone, but she was not there. 'What ails Mrs. Newcomb?' I heard a lady ask some minutes later. 'Dear knows!' was the almost pettish reply. 'She's gone off up stairs to have a cry all to herself. Something's gone wrong, I suppose. She's a hard body to get on with. I pity her husband.' I pitied *her*, poor child! for I could understand her heart."

"He went a great deal into company without his wife."

"Yes, and if you asked for her, there was always an air, or tone, or expression in his face that made you feel as if he did not regard her as of much consequence. 'Where is Mrs. Newcomb?' you would inquire. 'She doesn't go out,' or, 'She's a queer little home body,' or, 'The baby's sick,' or, 'She doesn't enjoy company.' These were the reasons he would give. It has been on my lip a dozen times to answer, 'Why don't you stay at home and keep her company?' And I wish now that I had. It might have quickened in him a perception of duty, and caused a few more rays of light to fall on her not always sunny pathway."

Mr. Newcomb heard no more. But wasn't that enough to give him the heartache for years? No, he had not appreciated his wife, now lost to him for ever. She was neither a brilliant nor a handsome woman, but true as steel to duty. Love for her husband was a passion that involved all the elements of her life. But the delicacy of her perceptions too soon revealed the sad truth that for some cause she had failed to win from her husband a love in any degree answering to her own. This so shadowed her feelings that she often appeared unamiable in his eyes, when she was only in strife with hidden anguish. Gradually he grew indifferent, and simply because he did not understand her. He imagined her incapable of deep affection, when every chord in her soul was thrilling in too painful sensibility.

And so the darkening years went on, and the fevered pulses began to take a slower beat. Mr. Newcomb grew more and more indifferent to his nervous and at times fretful but daily fading wife. Others saw that her days were numbered, but he did not take the alarm "Mrs. Newcomb looks very thin and feeble," remarked a friend. "She isn't quite so strong as she was, but she's tough," replied the husband. Tough! At the very moment her overstretched heartstrings were beginning to yield! And he was in robust health—ruddy-faced, clear-eyed, round-limbed and with every muscle in full vigor. He could not sympathize with the feeble woman moving about his house like a shadow, nor comprehend how he was daily extinguishing a life that looked vainly to him for the food upon which it alone could exist.

"Tough!" If she did linger on for a time, it was pitying love for her babes that kept her alive, gave strength to her feeble limbs and endurance to her sinking heart. And as she became weaker, he seemed rather to recede than draw near—to grow cold toward her instead of tender and compassionate. And so her day went down in clouds and rain.

No, she had not been appreciated. Mr. Newcomb was a good sort of a man, taking the general acceptation of the words—a pleasant neighbor, an agreeable friend, an honest citizen—but he had not proved a good husband to the woman he had taken to be his wife, simply because he had not rightly comprehended her quality nor reached her consciousness. She was of finer spiritual texture than he had imagined, and died because she could not live in the earth-laden atmosphere he compelled her to breathe.

"Not appreciated." There are Mrs. Newcombs all around us. Their pale faces haunt us at every turn; their mournful funerals shadow our streets; their orphaned babes sit weeping for love in many a lonely dwelling. And the ruddy-faced Mr. Newcombs—smiling, affable, "such good company," favorites at every feast—are around us also. We send a word of truth to their hearts; may its passage be sure and quick, like the passage of an arrow!

XV.

SMILES FOR HOME.

AKE that home with you, dear," said Mrs. Lewis, her manner half smiling, half serious.

"Take what home, Caddy?" and Mr. Lewis turned toward his wife curiously.

Now, Mrs. Lewis had spoken from the moment's impulse, and already partly regretted her remark.

"Take what home?" repeated her husband. "I don't understand you."

"That smiling face you turned upon Mr. Edwards when you answered his question just now."

Mr. Lewis slightly averted his head and walked on in silence. They had called in at the store of Mr. Edwards to purchase a few articles, and were now on their way home. There was no smile on the face of Mr. Lewis now, but a very grave expression instead—grave almost to sternness. The words of his wife had taken him altogether by surprise, and, though spoken lightly, had jarred upon his ears.

The truth was, Mr. Lewis, like a great many other men who have their own business cares and troubles, was in the habit of bringing home a sober and too often a clouded face. It was in vain that his wife and children looked into that face for sunshine or listened to his words for tones of cheerfulness.

"Take that home with you, dear." Mrs. Lewis was already repenting this suggestion, made on the moment's impulse. Her husband was sensitive to a fault. He could not bear even an implied censure from his wife. And so she had learned to be very guarded in this particular.

"Take that home with you, dear! Ah, me! I wish the words had not been said. There will be darker clouds now, and Gracious knows they were dark enough before! Why can't Mr. Lewis leave his cares and business behind him, and let us see the old, pleasant, smiling face again? I thought this morning that he had forgotten how to smile, but I see that he can smile if he tries. Ah! why don't he try at home?"

So Mrs. Lewis talked to herself as she moved along by the side of her husband, who had not spoken a word since her reply to his query, "Take what home?" Block after block was passed, and street after street crossed, and still there was silence between them.

"Of course," said Mrs. Lewis, speaking in her own thoughts—"of course he is offended. He won't bear a word from me. I might have known beforehand that talking out in this way would only make things worse. Oh dear! I'm getting out of all heart!"

"What then, Caddy?"

Mrs. Lewis almost started at the sound of her husband's voice breaking unexpectedly upon her ear in a softened tone.

"What then?" he repeated, turning toward her and looking down into her shyly upturned face.

"It would send warmth and radiance through the whole house," said Mrs. Lewis, her tones all a-tremble with feeling, and scarcely able to give utterance to her words.

"You think so?"

"I know so! Only try it, dear, for this one evening."

"It isn't so easy a thing to put on a smiling face, Caddy, when thought is oppressed with care."

"It didn't seem to require much effort just now," said Mrs. Lewis, glancing up at her husband with something of archness in her look.

Again a shadow dropped down upon the face of Mr. Lewis, which was partly turned away from his wife, and as before they walked on in silence.

"He is so sensitive!" Mrs. Lewis said to herself, the shadow on her husband's face darkening over her own. "I have to be as careful of my words as if talking to a spoiled child."

No, it did not require much effort on the part of Mr. Lewis to smile as he passed a few words lightly with Mr. Edwards. The remark of his wife had not really displeased him; it had only set him to thinking. After remaining gravely silent, because he was undergoing a brief self-examination, Mr. Lewis said:

"You thought the smile given to Mr. Edwards came easily enough?"

"It did not seem to require an effort," replied Mrs. Lewis.

"No, not much effort was required," said Mr. Lewis. His tones were slightly depressed. "But this must be taken into the account: my mind was in a certain state of excitement, or activity, that repressed sober feelings and made smiling an easy thing. So we smile and are gay in company at cost of little effort, because all are smiling and gay and we feel the common effect of excitement. How different it often is when we are alone, I need not say. You, Caddy, are guilty of the sober face at home as well as your husband." Mr. Lewis spoke with a tender reproof in his voice.

"But the sober face is caught from yours oftener than you imagine, my husband," replied Mrs. Lewis.

"Are you certain of that, Caddy?"

"Very certain. You make the sunlight and the shadow of your home. Smile upon us, give us cheerful words, enter into our feelings and interests, and there will be no brighter home in all the land. A shadow on your countenance is a veil for my heart, and the same is true as respects our children. Our pulses beat too nearly in unison not to be disturbed when yours is irregular."

Again Mr. Lewis walked on in silence, his face partly averted, and again his wife began to fear that she had spoken too freely. But he soon dispelled this impression, for he said:

"I am glad, Caddy, that you have spoken thus plainly. I only wish you had done so before. I see how it is. My smiles have been for the outside world—the world that neither loved nor regarded me—and my clouded brow for the dear ones at home, for whom thought and care are ever-living activities."

Mr. and Mrs. Lewis were now at their own door, where they paused a moment, and then went in. Instantly on passing his threshold Mr. Lewis felt the pressure upon him of his usual state. The hue of his feelings began to change. The cheerful, interested exterior put on for those he met in business intercourse began rapidly to change and a sober hue to succeed. Like most business-men, his desire for profitable results was ever far in advance of the slow evolutions of trade, and his daily history was a history of disappointments in some measure dependent upon his restless anticipations. He was not as willing to work and to wait as he should be, and, like many of his class, neglected the pearls that lay here and there along his life-path because they were inferior in value to those he hoped to find just a little way in advance. The consequence was, that when the day's business excitement was over his mind fell into a brooding state, and lingered over its disappointments or looked forward with failing hope in the future, for hope, in many things, had been long deferred. And so he rarely had smiles for his home.

"Take that home with you, dear," whispered Mrs. Lewis as they moved along the passage, and before they had joined the family. She had an instinctive consciousness that her husband was in danger of relapsing into his usual state.

The warning was just in time.

"Thank you for the words!" said he. "I will not forget them."

And he did not, but at once rallied himself, and to the glad surprise of Jenny, Will and

Mary met them with a new face, covered with fatherly smiles, and with pleasant questions in pleasant tones of their day's employments. The feelings of children move in quick transitions. They had not expected a greeting like this, but the response was instant. Little Jenny climbed into her father's arms; Will came and stood by his father's chair, answering in lively tones his questions; while Mary, older by a few years than the rest, leaned against her father's shoulder and laid her white hand softly upon his head, smoothing back the dark hair, just showing a little frost, from his broad, manly temples.

A pleasant group was this for the eyes of Mrs. Lewis as she came into the sitting-room from her chamber, where she had gone to lay off her bonnet and shawl and change her dress. Well did her husband understand the meaning look she gave him, and warmly did her heart respond to the smile he threw back upon her.

"Words fitly spoken are like apples of gold in pictures of silver," said Mr. Lewis, speaking to her as she came in.

"What do you mean by that?" asked Mary looking curiously into her father's face.

"Mother understands," replied Mr. Lewis, smiling tenderly upon his wife.

"Something pleasant must have happened," said Mary.

"Something pleasant? Why do you say that?" asked Mr. Lewis.

"You and mother look so happy," replied the child.

"And we have cause to be happy," answered the father as he drew his arm tightly around her, "in having three such good children."

Mary laid her cheek to his and whispered: "If you are always smiling and happy, dear father, home will be like heaven."

Mr. Lewis kissed her, but did not reply. He felt a rebuke in her words. But the rebuke did not throw a chill over his feelings; it only gave new strength to his purposes.

"Don't distribute all your smiles. Keep a few of the warmest and brightest for home," said Mrs. Lewis as she parted with her husband on the next morning. He kissed her, but did not promise. The smiles were kept, however, and evening saw them. Other and many evenings saw the same cheerful smiles and the same happy home. And was not Mr. Lewis a better and happier man? Of course he was. And so would all men be if they would take home with them the smiling aspect they so often exhibit as they meet their fellow-men in business intercourse or exchange words in passing compliments. Take your smiles and cheerful words home with you, husbands, fathers and brothers. Your hearths are cold and dark without them.

XVI.

THE FOILED TEMPTER.

"DON'T urge me, Henry," said Mrs. Hewling to her young, intelligent, good-looking husband; "I cannot go. With me, as you well know, all such gay pleasures are at an end."

"I urge you, Anna dear," said Mr. Hewling, speaking very tenderly and smoothing with his hand, as he spoke, the dark glossy hair from which she had removed every sign of a curl and parted smoothly away toward the white temple, "for two reasons. One, because I think this continued seclusion of yourself wrong and injurious to your state of mind, and the other, because I do not wish to go alone to General Malcolm's. More than half my pleasure is lost, in any company, by your absence."

"It is impossible!" Mrs. Hewling answered, and there was just a sign of impatience in her voice as she spoke, "and I wonder that you can so urge me. Am I not still in black?"

"Lay aside your black, dear." Mr. Hewling's tone lost not a single shade of affection. "You have worn it too long already. Nay, it should never have gathered like a gloomy death-curtain around you, shadowing both mind and body as it has done. Lay your black aside."

"Never!" said Mrs. Hewling, almost indignantly. "When we buried our little Flora the light of joy died in my heart and the darkness of a perpetual mourning gathered around my spirit. I shall never lay it aside."

The hand of Mr. Hewling was removed from the glossy hair of his wife, and with a suppressed sigh he stepped back from her a pace or two.

"Don't let my remaining at home keep you from General Malcolm's," said Mrs. Hewling, in a cold way. "I have no wish to deprive you of any enjoyment."

"If I had not promised to meet an old friend there I would not go," replied Mr. Hewling. "As it is, my word binds me."

He did not say, as he might have done, that the person he had engaged to see was a lady friend, and one to whom he wished to present his wife.

"Go, by all means. I would be selfish to wish to deprive you of a single pleasure," Mrs. Hewling said, in a sad kind of way.

And Mr. Hewling did go—not, however, with any pleasurable anticipations. It was now over a year since death claimed their youngest born, a babe whose life had numbered only a few months. This was the mother's first grief, her first experience in sorrow, and she bowed her head, refusing to be comforted. Ever since that time she had been sitting in darkness, and she would suffer no one—not even her husband—to lead her forth into the cheerful sunlight.

Mr. Hewling was a man of social feeling, and one who took pleasure in friendly intercourse. His wife's gloomy state of mind and her entire seclusion of herself deprived him of one of his life's truest enjoyments, for he never cared to gc into company unless she were with him. On the present occasion he went with more than his usual reluctance. He not only loved his wife, but was proud of her, and as she was a handsome woman, of refined tastes and cultivated intellect, he naturally felt desirous to see her in comparison with other women—that comparison being always so favorable to her, at least in his estimation. Such fond pride in a husband may be classed with virtues instead of weaknesses. Wives, at least, will approve the sentiment, while others may smile, and say, good-humoredly, "An amiable weakness."

To the lady friend—an old favorite of Mr. Hewling's, and one who, ere his choice was made, came near winning the highest place in his affections—he felt particularly desirous of presenting his wife. But he was forced to go to the entertainment at General Malcolm's alone.

It was over three years since Mr. Hewling had seen Miss Lightner, the old friend to whom we have referred, and the meeting was one of pleasure on both sides. The lady had gained womanly attractions during that period, and now met her former friend and almost lover in the beauty of maturer charms. The girlish lightness of her character had given way to a dignified bearing that imparted something noble to her manners, and the ripeness of a cultivated intellect, added to personal graces of no common order, threw around her a web of fascinations that made her a centre of attraction in all companies.

Ere Mr. Hewling was aware of it, he was so drawn within the circle of her influence as to be an admirer. "How wonderfully she has improved! Into what a charming woman she has grown!" he said to himself almost enthusiastically.

And then his thoughts ran back to the time when, in contrast with the sweet maiden he had chosen for wife, her charms failed in power over him and all the wealth of his pure love was given to another. Alas that the contrast left a different impression now!

"Is Mrs. Hewling present?" asked Miss Lightner soon after their meeting. "I have not had the pleasure, you know, of making her acquaintance."

The eyes of Miss Lightner were on the face of her old friend, reading every shade of ex pression. She saw an instant change.

"She is not here," replied Mr. Hewling, almost sighing as he spoke.

"Not sick, I hope?" Miss Lightner's gaze was most penetrating. A suspicion had flashed across her mind that the marriage of her old friend had not proved congenial, and she was looking for the signs of disappointment. Of all the men with whom she had enjoyed an intimate acquaintance, she had admired Mr. Hewling most, and had he chosen her from among the maidens, and asked her to stand beside him at the altar, she would have linked unhesitatingly her fortunes with his. As it was, she had declined many offers, because those who sought her love fell below the manly ideal up to which her perceptions had been raised.

"Sick in mind," replied Mr. Hewling. "It is over a year since we lost a babe, and ever since that time my wife has been sitting in darkness. I cannot dispel the gloom that surrounds her, nor win her from her shadowed seclusion into the cheerful sunlight. I did hope that she would accompany me here this evening, so that you might meet and be friends. But I am disappointed."

The tones of Mr. Hewling expressed even more regret than his words.

"How much I should have been pleased to make her acquaintance!" said the young lady with something of her old warmth and familiarity of manner, and in a tone that gave a pleasant motion to the feelings of her old acquaintance. Then she gradually led the conversation into another channel, and so charmed him with the graces of a rarely-cultivated intellect that the hours flew by on such light pinions that he scarcely noted their passage. Almost through the entire evening they were together. Once Miss Lightner danced, and then Mr. Hewling was her partner. She pleaded fatigue in declining the invitation of another gentleman to join in a subsequent quadrille. So interested were they in each other as to occasion remark.

"How long will you remain in the city?" inquired Mr. Hewling, as he noticed that more than half the company had retired, and saw by his watch that swift-footed time had carried them far past the hour of midnight.

"For some weeks," was answered.

"Have you been to the opera yet?"

"No."

"Then you must hear Gazzaniga," said Mr. Hewling.

"That is one of the pleasures in reserve for me. And it will be a high pleasure, as I am passionately fond of music," said Miss Lightner.

"Are you engaged for to-morrow evening?"

"No."

There was a brief pause. "How will it look for me to be seen at the opera with Miss Lightner and my wife at home hiding herself from the world in a grief that will not admit of consolation?" He did not wait to answer the question to his own satisfaction, but obeying impulse instead of reason, said,

"May I have the pleasure of your company? She sings in Il Trovatore."

"The temptation is too great for me to answer no," replied the lady, throwing into her smile a fascination that gave to her countenance a new beauty in the eyes of Mr. Hewling.

"I have promised an old friend whom I met at General Malcolm's to take her to the opera this evening," said Mr. Hewling to his wife on the next day.

"Have you?" Mrs. Hewling glanced toward her husband with a look of surprise. "Who is she?"

"The lady of whom I have already spoken. Her name is Miss Lightner. I so much regretted your absence from General Malcolm's last evening! I wanted you to meet each other."

Mrs. Hewling sighed, and the light of an

awakening interest which had come into her face lost itself among the old shadows.

"Won't you go with us this evening? Say yes, Anna! It will be such a pleasure to me." The husband spoke with ardor.

"How strange it is that you will urge me in this way!" answered Mrs. Hewling, with enough of fretfulness in voice and manner to give her an unlovely aspect in the eyes of her husband. In the same instant the more attractive face of Miss Lightner intruded itself in contrast, and with the distinctness of a living presence.

Mr. Hewling said nothing more. The case seemed hopeless. Something of coldness and something of alienation were so distinctly perceived that he turned with an involuntary movement partly away from his wife.

There was in the heart of Mrs. Hewling a new, strange and uncomfortable feeling after her husband left her on that evening to attend the opera with Miss Lightner, a lady whom she had never seen, and of whose person and character she had no distinct image or perception. It was something unusual for her husband to be away from home for two evenings in succession, and his absence left her so lonely and her spirit so restless that she wandered uneasily from room to room, or sat still and wept, unable to trace the cause of tears. More unhappy hours than these she had never spent, and when, long after midnight, her husband came home, she threw herself sobbing upon his bosom. With loving words, that had in them a tone of reproof, he sought to calm this turbulence of feeling. To him the transition was unpleasing, and tended to increase the slight coldness and alienation of which we have spoken. He had just parted from one of the most fascinating women he had ever met—from one who, either from weak pride or evil design, had sought to snare him with her beauty—and had returned to his wife, who, instead of wisely seeking to adapt herself to the social necessities of his nature, had in a weak and selfish grief veiled from him the loveliness of her true character, and let him go forth alone into the world to have his eyes dazzled by the glare of false attractions. We make no justification in his case. He was human, and humanity is weak. It is with things as they are that we now deal, and let the reader take them as they are.

Before parting with Miss Lightner, on attending her home from the opera, Mr. Hewling made an engagement to go with her to hear Linda on the next evening but one. He did not mention the engagement to his wife, for he had a feeling as if it were hardly right for him to go a second time to so public a place as the opera with this charming young lady.

Mrs. Malcolm, the wife of General Malcolm, was an old friend of Mrs. Hewling's mother. She was a clear-seeing, true-hearted woman, and much attached to Mrs. Hewling, whom she had often sought to win from her self-imposed seclusion. On the day following this first visit to the opera she called upon Mrs. Hewling, whom she found in a more than usually depressed state of mind. She had a duty to perform, and she had come with that end, and meant to do it faithfully. What little she had seen of the brilliant Miss Lightner impressed her unfavorably, and when she learned Mr. Hewling was with her at the opera on the night following the party at her house, and that they seemed more attentive to each other than to the music, she at once decided as to her own action in the case. To the young mother's "lost darling" she first turned her thoughts. That was a theme on which Mrs. Hewling most loved to dwell, and in contemplating which she always indulged in the luxury of tears.

"Your precious babe is not lost, only saved, and for ever safe in the mansions of our heavenly Father," said Mrs. Malcolm. "But there is a loss which you may suffer, Anna, that will be without hope here or hereafter."

"If the soul is lost, then—"

"I mean not that," said Mrs. Malcolm, interrupting the speaker. There was a pause, and then she added:

"What if you were to lose your husband's love?"

The face of Mrs. Hewling turned instantly pallid, for there was a tone prophetic of evil in the voice of her friend.

"How did you win his love?" Calmly yet very earnestly did Mrs. Malcolm speak. "By sighs and tears, and a sorrowful hiding of yourself away? By the gathering of mourning weeds around you, and sitting down among the ashes of grief, refusing to be comforted? Was it in this way that you won his love? If so, then in this way may you hope to retain the priceless treasure! If not, look to it that you become not unlovely in his eyes! I marvel, and have long marveled, Anna, at your folly, and I now utter a cry of warning in your ears ere it be too late!"

With lips apart, eager eyes and face like ashes, Mrs. Hewling gazed with a frightened look upon her monitor.

"What do you mean? Speak plainly!" she gasped. "Is anything wrong? Your words are like sharp arrows piercing to the very life-fountains!"

"Yes, something is wrong, very wrong!" answered Mrs. Malcolm. "For more than a year you have held your social, cheerful-minded husband away from congenial life, because you cherished a selfish and rebellious grief in your heart, instead of being thankful to your Father in heaven for having given your sweet babe an eternal home among the angels. In that you have wronged him. And now, hopeless of any change in you, he has stepped again into the outer world, and at once his attractive qualities have drawn to his side those who, were you with him in the beauty and charm of your real character, could gain no power over him, but who—"

Mrs. Malcolm did not finish the sentence, for a more death-like pallor was overspreading the face of Mrs. Hewling.

"Anna"—she spoke in a gentler way and with less of fearful portent in her voice—"Anna, my dear young friend, it is not too late. You possess the love of as true and noble a heart as ever beat in manly bosom—a love long tried and—forgive me for saying it—sadly wronged. But the time has come when that love is to be severely tempted. Do you know Miss Lightner?"

"I never met her," replied Mrs. Hewling, in a husky voice.

"If rumor be true, there was a time when she bore to you the relation of rival, but, as the issue proved, an unsuccessful one. Rumor also says that she has refused many offers since, and that she has been heard to remark that when she meets another man like your husband she will marry. Now, Anna, when I tell you that she is a woman of remarkable beauty and of most winning manners, and that, as I read her, is using her utmost power to fascinate your husband, I need not add that there is danger in your path, but a danger that your own hand can sweep aside now as a thing lighter than gossamer. Let it remain, make no effort to be to your husband what you once were, and a giant's strength may not remove it."

Much more in the same earnest spirit did this true friend urge upon Mrs. Hewling, and she was successful in her effort to make her comprehend in its broadest sense the error into which a mere selfish grief had led her, and the fearful peril of all that was dearest in life.

The day to Mr. Hewling was one of the most restless he had spent for a long time. He felt dissatisfied with himself, and when thought turned toward his wife, old, tender emotions did not stir in his bosom. There seemed to be a darker shadow upon his home, while all the world, from which he was held back, seemed garmented in sunshine. Sober reflection had presented to his mind certain aspects of his relation to Miss Lightner that were not agreeable to contemplate, and he regretted his hasty engagement with her for a second evening at the opera.

Mr. Hewling returned home almost an hour earlier than usual. As he ascended the steps of his dwelling he caught a momentary glimpse of a lady near one of the parlor windows dressed in brown silk and wearing a tasteful lace cap. There was something familiar in her appearance, yet he had failed to recognize her, as only a portion of her features was seen. Opening the street door, he passed through the vestibule, and was going by the parlors when the brown silk dress and lace cap intercepted him, and a face no longer draped in sadness and a pair of eyes from which the veil was removed looked lovingly, as of old, into his own.

"Anna!" he exclaimed, with such a tone of surprise and pleasure in his voice that the heart of his wife leaped for joy—"dear Anna, is it you?"

And he kissed her with a new and lover-like ardor.

"Ah," he added, his face alive with smiles as he gazed fondly upon her still beautiful countenance, "how the old times and the old feelings come rushing back upon me! I have found my wife again!"

And he gathered his arms around her and drew her in a strong pressure to his bosom.

"With so much to be thankful for," he said as with his arm around her waist Mr. Hewling moved with his wife to a sofa in the parlor, and sat down by her side—"with so beautiful and bright a world around us, why should we mourn for that which is lost? Why should one sorrow quench the light of a thousand stars—nay, even of the sun itself?"

"Selfish sorrow is always wrong," answered Mrs. Hewling, "and mine has been a selfish one. In mourning for the happy dead I have forgotten my duty to the living. Forgive me, dear Henry! I should have gone with you to General Malcolm's, and doubled your pleasures by sharing them!"

"You would have more than doubled them," said Mr. Hewling, with unusual warmth of manner. "And now," he added, "I must put your new-born purpose to the test. Will you go with me to the opera on to-morrow night?"

"I will," was the unhesitating answer.

"All right!" was the response of Mr. Hewling, made in a tone that half surprised his wife. She did not know, and never knew, that he had only an hour before received from Miss Lightner a note preferring a request by no means indecorous in itself, and seeming naturally to grow out of the brief renewal of their old acquaintance, yet really meant as a link in the chain she was forging with all a woman's art to bind him to her will. Suddenly the true meaning of that familiarly-worded note became clear. He saw the wicked wile, and shuddered at the danger to which he had been exposed.

On the next morning Miss Lightner received from Mr. Hewling this note—the one she had written was returned to her in the same envelope—

"An unexpected occurrence will prevent my keeping my engagement with Miss Lightner this evening."

"Who is the lady sitting next to Mr. Hewling in the box directly opposite?" It was Miss Lightner who asked the question. Her companion, after gazing at the lady for a moment or two, said:

"That is his wife, I believe."

"I presume not. His wife dresses in black, I am told, and has for a long time rigidly secluded herself."

"She has laid aside her black for to-night, then, and come forth from her seclusion," was answered, "for that is Mrs. Hewling herself. What a beautiful woman she is!"

Miss Lightner did not answer, but in her

thought she said "yea" to the last sentence. Mrs. Hewling was indeed beautiful, and her beauty had in it so much of a chastened, almost angelic, purity that she felt it to be an all-powerful spell for the heart of her husband.

Little of the music, little of the fine acting, did the foiled tempter hear or see during the progress of the opera on that evening. She could not keep her eyes away from the lovely being who sat with such a womanly grace by the side of her husband, and ever and anon leaned toward him lovingly as he spoke a few brief sentences in the pauses of the music. What were her spells in comparison but silken strands on the limbs of a Samson?

XVII.

DRIFTING AWAY.

"MY good Bertha joins me in the invitation," wrote an old friend who lived the easy life of a self-indulgent country gentleman some fifty miles away from the noisy city, amidst the work and din and cares of which I often grew weary. "Come, and come now, when the trees are greenest, the earth in richest attire and the air like stainless crystal," he added. "We will ride, and sail—I have the fairiest of pleasure-boats—and spend the days as merrily as if the world had never a care or sorrow. Come! I will take no refusal. You are wearing yourself out too fast in that toiling city."

The invitation came at the right moment. I was drooping over my work with slow hands and failing ardor.

"I will be at Fern Dale," I wrote, "in a week. Many thanks for your kind invitation."

And in a week I stood face to face with my old friend. It was twice twelve months since I had seen him. He had gained liberally in flesh during the time, and his face, though rounder and larger, was fresher and younger in appearance than when I last saw him. The years had not dealt so kindly with Bertha, his sweet wife, I was grieved to see. Her face had grown thinner, though not less beautiful. It was not the beauty of old that caused your eyes to linger on her countenance, for the delicately-rounded outline and warm tinting were gone. But there was more thought and feeling there, and a depth and mystery in her eyes which I had never seen before. How singularly in contrast was the broad, radiant smile that lit up his whole face with the glow of sunbeams, and the flickering light that played now and then so feebly, yet so full of angel sweetness, just around her mouth! She was sitting with a baby on her lap when I entered. Instead of laying it down or calling an attendant, she received me with the nursling in her arms, and her eyes passed every now and then from mine to the cherub face that lay against her bosom.

"Another baby," said I as I touched the peachy cheek with my finger.

"And the dearest darling of them all," she answered, looking down upon it tenderly.

"She's perfectly bewitched by that baby," said my friend as he laid his hand in a fond way upon her shoulder. "You would think, to see her, that she'd never seen a baby in her life before. But come into the library; I've got a hundred things to talk with you about."

And he drew me away ere I had been five minutes in the company of his wife. I saw that her eyes followed us, and I fancied that a look of disappointment was in them.

"I'm sorry to see that Bertha is not looking so well as when I was at Fern Dale last time," said I as we sat down in the handsome library.

"Not looking so well!" My friend seemed a little surprised at the remark. "You have forgotten. In my eyes she never looked better. She was always slight and delicate, you know, and rarely had much color."

"Perhaps my memory is at fault, but I have

a vision of Bertha with rounder, ruddier cheeks than I see to-day."

"That great baby in her arms will suggest a reason for the change. It does not come from failing health."

My friend seemed so entirely at ease on the subject that I said no more, but I did not feel satisfied. We talked for an hour in the library, when dinner was announced and we joined his wife at the table. She had on a white lawn dress, dotted over with small blue forget-me-nots, and plain lace cap. A slight warmth was visible in her cheeks, and her eyes as she lifted them to mine were full of smiling welcomes. She looked pure and beautiful as a consecrated vestal. I saw my friend's eyes rest proudly and lovingly upon her for a few moments ere he gave himself up to the agreeable work that lay before him.

I noticed that while my friend's wife did with a pleased alacrity the honors of the table, urging one dish after another upon her guest and her husband, she ate very little herself. The fact must have escaped the observation of my friend or he would certainly have remonstrated; but it was so apparent to me that I could not help saying, as I saw her playing with instead of eating her dessert:

"Don't you eat anything, Bertha?" I had known her many years—even before her marriage—and always addressed her with the old familiarity.

"Oh, she lives on air!" spoke up my friend, smiling, "so don't imitate her example while at Fern Dale. I am made of grosser stuff, and can't get on without the substantial things that make up what are called creature comforts."

Bertha smiled in return, and looked beautiful, but too ethereal in my eyes.

After dinner we drove out, leaving Bertha at home with her children and domestic duties. Not a word was said about her going with us. Our drive was over breezy hills and amidst scenery of the most charming character. I felt new life in all my pulses as we went rushing through the exhilarating air. It was sundown when we returned, both of us as keen for supper as though a hearty meal had not been taken only a few hours before.

The warmer glow that mantled Bertha's cheeks at dinner-time had faded, and as I looked at her across the tea-table I noticed an expression of weariness about her eyes and a languid falling of the lips that made me feel uncomfortable. She asked if I had enjoyed the ride, and listened with much apparent interest to my descriptions of many points in the fine scenery through which we had driven. I was a little surprised, however, to learn from a remark she made that she had never looked upon it herself.

After supper my friend and I retired to the library, where we spent the evening alone, talking of old times, discussing the merit of new books or lingering over the current topics of the day. Bertha did not join us. Once I asked for her. I had pleasant recollections of hours spent in her company.

"Oh, she's buried with the children or closeted with her cook," answered my friend, smiling, in his easy, good-natured way. "Bertha has become a famous housewife."

"She has too good a mind for burial after this fashion," said I. "Bertha was born for something more than a simple housewife."

"I know it—I know it," replied my friend, with a slight closing of his brows. "But women will take their way. Her children and her household have completely absorbed her."

"Do you think this absorption of her life a good one—a healthy one—for either mind or body?" I asked.

"Perhaps not. But there is a wonderful power of adaptation in nature, as you are aware. I guess it will all work out right. I often wish it were different; yet, as wishing does no good, I never permit myself to get worried over what can't be helped. I am something of a philosopher, you know, and manage under all circumstances to keep a quiet mind. If Bertha likes her way best, why so be it; she's a good, loving, over-indulgent wife to me, and I won't force her out of the world she seems most pleased to dwell in, though our tastes do run parallel in so many things, and we might enjoy so much together."

My friend's feelings lay close to the surface, and I saw his eyes glisten as he turned them away from me. He loved his wife as tenderly as any man who loved his own ease and pleasures as well as he did, could love anything out of himself. She was in his eyes all that could be wished for or expected, the paragon among women. He was proud of her, very proud of her.

On the next morning, when I met Bertha at breakfast and looked narrowly into her face, I saw more of the work of exhaustion than I had noticed on the day before. The pearly skin lay in flat surfaces on her cheeks, forehead and shrunken nostrils, instead of showing rounded undulations. Her lips were very thin and white. Her eyes, large, dark and lustrous, shone out upon you from a farther distance in their shadowy orbits. She had no appetite, and only made a feint of eating, as I could see, while her husband piled away the steak, muffins and omelet in a most liberal fashion, and kept himself so busy at this pleasant work as to permit his wife's abstemiousness to escape observation.

"You don't look very well this morning," said I, feeling really concerned.

Bertha smiled faintly as her husband turned a look of inquiry upon her face, and answered:

"My head aches a little;" and then added, "I hope my fretting baby didn't keep you awake. I don't know what ailed him. He didn't sleep for an hour at a time all night.

Husband had to go into another room. He can't bear loss of rest."

"No," said he, "I must have my regular sleep. How these women manage to worry night after night with their babies, up and down at all hours, is more than I can understand. It would kill me."

Bertha coughed slightly, cleared her throat, and coughed again two or three times. There was a sound in the cough that was unpleasant to my ears. I glanced toward my friend to see how it affected him, but he had not appeared to notice it.

"And kills the mothers sometimes," I ventured to remark.

My friend looked at me for a moment or two, as if I had disturbed him slightly, and then went on with his breakfast. I noticed the cough again once or twice during the meal.

After breakfast my friend and I retired alone to the library, leaving Bertha to her maternal and household cares. A sail on the river which ran along one side of my friend's estate, and in that "fairiest of pleasure-boats" about which he had written to me, was to be our forenoon's occupation. After spending an hour or two in the library, talking and reading, we went down to the river, my friend carrying a lunch-basket which Bertha had placed in his hand.

"Why can't you go with us?" I asked as I looked into her fading face.

She shook her head, and half turned it toward the door from which she had stepped into the portico to give her husband the basket, thus indicating that duty must go before pleasure.

"It's no use to invite her," said my friend, in what struck me as a light and careless manner. "She never goes anywhere. Leave her with her babies and her servants; she is happiest among them."

I stood nearest to Bertha when this was said, and could not have been mistaken in the sound that reached me: it was a faint sigh.

"There's something wrong here," said I to myself as we walked toward the river. "A life is wasting rapidly away, and no suspicion of the fact seems to have been awakened. My friend is either very selfish or very blind. How can he look into his own ruddy face, as it stands each day reflected to him in his mirror, and then look upon that pale, shadowy, fleeting countenance, and not feel the truth?"

A week at Fern Dale confirmed all my first impressions as to the rapidly-failing condition of Bertha. And yet my friend showed no anxiety, no dim consciousness even, of the peril in which his wife stood. "How can he gaze into that pale, thin face," I would ask myself over and over again, "and not take the warning that nature gives? Was his own enjoyment of mere sensuous life so great that he could not understand a condition like Bertha's? He loved her, nay, almost idolized her, and when I would hint occasionally in a concerned way my fears touching her health, he would regard me with a vague, bewildered countenance, as if I were troubling him with the shadow of some far-off evil. It never seemed to occur to him that the evil was at his door.

One morning Bertha did not make her appearance as usual at the breakfast-table. On asking for her, my friend answered that she had been up most of the night with her baby, and was too much indisposed to rise.

"Nothing serious?" I remarked.

"Oh no," he answered. "She often has such spells. We shall see her at dinner-time, as usual, only looking a little paler, perhaps."

"Only a little paler! That must be a death-like pallor," I said to myself.

This morning we were to have a sail on the river. Soon after breakfast we went to the boat-house and unmoored the fairy bark in which we had already spent so many pleasant hours together. As she glided gently out, like a bird floating on the buoyant water, through some mishap the light cord by which my friend held her slipped from his hand, and she passed from his reach in a moment out into the current, and commenced drifting away. My friend became instantly excited, and showed great anxiety about the boat. His face flushed, his eyes dilated, all his movements were hurried and disturbed. He ran here and there in an incoherent manner, and appeared for some moments to lose all self-possession. At last, catching at a small coil of rope, he tied a stone to one end of it and gave me the other end to hold, then throwing the stone with all his strength it fell into the boat. Eagerly taking the rope from my hand, he drew on it until the slack was in. Now came the moment of suspense. The boat was moving steadily with the current; should the stone not obtain a firm anchorage inside, but release itself and draw over the gunwale, the little vessel would float beyond our present means of rescue. But the expedient proved successful. The stone held with sufficient tenacity to overcome the pressure of the current, and soon the pleasure-boat came floating to our outstretched hands.

"Safe!" exclaimed my friend as he grasped the side of his pet with eager fondness. "How careless I was!" he added as he stepped over the side and commenced adjusting the sail.

"You could easily have recovered her again," said I, "even if she had drifted away a mile or so before a row-boat could be procured in which to go after her."

"Oh yes," he replied, "but I didn't think of that. I was only conscious that my beauty was drifting away beyond my reach. Don't laugh at me, but I have a real affection for this boat."

Soon we were moving away over the rippling water under the pressure of a gentle breeze, my friend every now and then referring to the little incident I have mentioned.

"You don't know," he said as we floated

into a sheltered cove where the wind no longer laid its soft cheek against our snowy sail that hung loosely against the reed-like mast, "how that little peril of my boat disturbed me," again alluding to the circumstance.

I looked at him without answering.

"You are sober," he remarked. "What thoughts are shadowing your mind?"

"Thoughts that concern you. Shall I let them come into speech?" I said, after a moment of silence.

"By all means, my friend. Don't hesitate."

He leaned forward and looked at me anxiously.

"I was thinking," said I, "of a far more precious thing that is drifting from you, steadily drifting, and getting more distant every day, and yet you heed it not."

"I don't understand you." He looked bewildered.

"Bertha." I merely uttered the name.

He grew pale instantly.

"Bertha is drifting from you," said I, "and unless you stretch forth a hand to save her right speedily, she will pass out of your reach."

He let the rudder, which he had been holding, slip from his grasp, and leaned with a frightened look toward me.

"Why do you say this?" he asked, in a breathless manner.

"Because it so appears to my eyes. Bertha has failed sadly since I saw her last. All her color has departed, and all the fine roundness of face and limbs has wasted away. She eats nothing, comparatively, yet is taxed with duties that would wear out a strong man. You, with your vigorous health, could not endure them."

"But what can I do?" asked my friend, with pale alarm in his face. My few sentences had startled him from a pleasant life-dream. "She will bury herself, as you see. What can I do?" he repeated.

"You can stretch out your hand and save her before the current that is now floating her away bears her beyond your reach," said I, confidently, "and I take the privilege of a friend to warn you in time. Not once since I have been here has she shared our recreating drives or refreshing hours on the river. She does not sit with us in the library, flowing in with our pleasant talks and making thought more beautiful, as in other days, and when we meet her at meal-times, looking so pale and spirituelle, it is plain to be seen that mind and body are feeble from excessive weariness. Can this go on long and her delicate organism not give way? Be assured not, for the strain is too great."

"But what can I do?" asked my friend again, looking still more alarmed. "She is wedded to these household cares and enslaved to her children."

"I have not seen," said I, "any attempt on your part to win her away from them. There has been no remonstrance against her self-sacrificing course; no manifested concern; no urgent invitations to join us in our rides and rambles—I speak plainly, for there is a life at stake—but a dull kind of acquiescence. Now, if you wish to keep her long, all this must be changed. You must, at any cost of effort, see that she no longer violates the plainest laws of health."

"You have awakened me from a dream—a dream which needed a wakening from," said my friend as he grasped the rudder again and headed the boat homeward. "Drifting away! drifting away!" he added, in a subdued tone, a few moments afterward. "Yes, it is even so. But I will catch at her receding garments and hold her back."

At dinner-time we met Bertha, looking worse than I had seen her since my arrival. I noticed that my friend's eyes wandered every little while to her face, and that he did not eat with his usual appetite. After the dessert, and before we left the table, he leaned toward her and said, with a tenderness in his voice that no wife's heart could resist,

"I am sorry to see you looking so worn out, Bertha. Last night was a severe tax on you. Have you been lying down this morning?"

"Part of the time," she answered, looking at her husband gratefully. It was plain to be seen that she was not used to such tender inquiries.

"This way of life won't do, Bertha," he went on. "It is destroying you. I see you drifting away from me"—his voice failed a little—"and I must put forth a hand to draw you back. Nature will not bear the burdens you are laying upon her."

I saw light coming into her pale face and love beaming out from her eyes upon her husband. His interest and concern were genuine, and she felt it.

"We are going to take an easy ride this afternoon," he added, "and want you to go with us. Now, don't say no!"

I saw objection in her face, and her lips moved as if she were about putting her objection in words. But her husband's "Now don't say no!" coming as it did on his warmly-expressed interest and concern, changed her purpose, and she said:

"If it will give you pleasure."

"Nothing in the world would give me more pleasure," replied my friend, with almost lover-like warmth.

There was visible already a new life in the countenance of Bertha. A soft glow was faintly dyeing her cheeks and a mellow light tempering the unnatural brilliance of her eyes.

"When do you wish me to be ready?" she asked.

"At four o'clock. We will ride until six. That will be long enough for you."

It was the Bertha of other days who talked so pleasantly and looked so cheerful during that ride. At tea-time she was another being from what she appeared on the evening before, or indeed on any evening since my arrival at Fern Dale. The ride had quickened in her mind a new and healthier impulse. She was a lover of all things beautiful in nature, and this had given her a pure enjoyment which could not soon die out. During the evening my friend by a little management drew her away from her nursery into the library, where we enjoyed her company for over an hour. How solicitous my friend was to keep her mind interested, to give her thoughts a new direction, to call back old themes in art and literature that once gratified her taste or charmed her imagination! She felt the change in him, and was, I could see, half surprised yet touched thereby.

On the next day she accompanied us in our morning drive, and in the afternoon was induced, after a little persuasion, to take a sail on the river. There was an unmistakable glow on her cheeks as she came back from this excursion in fine spirits, and I noticed that she took a relish of tongue and ate two biscuits at supper-time—an appropriation of food quite beyond anything I had seen in her case since my visit to Fern Dale.

"You have caught her garments ere she drifted quite away," said I to my friend as we sat together that evening in the library.

"Yes," he answered with feeling; "and I will cling to them as a man clings to his life! She shall not get free upon the waters again through any fault of mine. Was ever a man so thoughtless and stupid as I have been?"

"Many, very many, are just as thoughtless, just as blind, as you were," said I; "and hundreds of overtasked wives—self-tasked, it may be, as in Bertha's case—are drifting steadily away from mortal shores upon the sea of eternity, and in a few weeks, or months, or years, they will be out of the reach of hands that will clutch after them in agony when it is too late!"

XVIII.

CAN YOU AFFORD IT?

THE question was answered by a look of surprise.

"Afford it? I'm not sure that I take your meaning."

The questioner, a lady in middle life, smiled as she responded in the query:

"Can you afford the possession of so costly an ornament?"

"Still in the dark," said the young man with whom she was conversing. "Costly?"

"Expensive is the better word, Thomas. I should have said expensive. The original cost won't be much, for the article is cheap in our market. It is the expense of maintenance afterward that should be taken into consideration."

"Ah!" Light glinted upon the young man's dull perceptions.

"You apprehend me?"

"Not clearly."

"In plain words, then, can you afford to take Miss Araminta Brown for a wife?"

"Why not?"

"Have you counted the cost?"

"I believe so."

"May I see your estimate, Thomas? Don't think me officious or over-curious. I'm an old friend, as you are aware, and old, true friends stretch their privilege sometimes when they feel more than usually interested, as I do now. You've made no proposal yet?"

"None."

"Ah! I'm glad of that. So you can retire from the field without dishonor."

"Retire! I've not thought of retiring, Mrs. Hardy."

"A prudent soldier will retire and save his forces for successful encounter in another field if he sees the odds too strongly against him."

"Still enigmatical! Am I pressing forward to so dangerous a conflict?"

"In my judgment, you are."

"Puzzled still."

"The encounter, Thomas, to which I refer is

your world's battle. Marriage makes or mars most men, and I think I have studied your character closely enough to be satisfied that it will make or mar you. You don't want a pretty doll, a bundle of useless accomplishments, a vain, showy girl, a dainty butterfly in the world of fashion, but a woman, for a wife. It may be all very pleasant to dance and flirt, to sit by the seaside in pale moonlight, to time the music while your charmer sings, to talk of love and poetry, but, my friend, these are only as the bloom on the grape. The essential of life is all below, and the grape must come to the wine-press. Think of that, Thomas! Is there rich juice in the heart of Araminta Brown?"

A sober hue of thought crept into the face of Thomas Wilder. He began to comprehend something of what was in the lady's mind.

"Life is not all a holiday," continued the lady. "The play is short, and when the curtain falls we go back into sober and often hard reality. The summer's airs, in which the butterfly and dainty humming-bird enchant us with their grace and beauty, continue only for a brief season. The winters are long and cold. What of the butterfly and humming-bird then? Gone to warmer climes or dead! My friend, there is no hope in the butterfly or the humming-bird."

"I do not hold the comparison good," said the young man in reply. "Araminta is not a mere butterfly. She is a girl of mind and feeling."

"Not much mind, Thomas; and as to feeling, that may be in the right or wrong direction. But let us go back to my first suggestion. There is a practical dollar-and-cent side of the question which it would be folly to ignore. What will be the cost of this alliance? That determined, the next query comes in order: 'Can you afford it?' I think not. But this is for your decision. What is your salary?"

"Fifteen hundred."

"Liberal, as the times go?"

"Yes."

"Do you look for an increase?"

"No, but there have been intimations which lead me to believe that an interest in the business will be offered at no very distant period."

"Ah! I'm glad to hear you say so. But that is a thing on which no reliance can be placed?"

"None at all."

"So that in estimating the expense of marriage the salary alone must be taken into account?"

"That alone."

"Very well. Now, what do you suppose it will cost you to dress Araminta according to her present style?"

The young man shook his head.

"Give an estimate," said the lady.

"Two hundred dollars a year?" He put the sum large, so as to be sure of including the outside penny.

"Six hundred."

"You're jesting!" answered the young man.

"No."

"Six hundred dollars!"

"Or seven, maybe. The safer estimate is seven. Shall I give you some of the figures?"

"If you please."

"Take your pencil and follow me. I happen to know the young lady's milliner and dressmaker, and am posted in a few items. She is fashionable. Do you know just what that means?"

"I presume so."

"Let us see. The fashions change twice a

year at least. Sometimes three or four times--four times with the ultras, and Araminta is a little inclined to be ultra-fashionable in dress. It is spring, we will say. Well, the wardrobe of your wife—you have married Araminta—needs replenishing. And first, there is a bonnet. Of course the winter bonnet won't do for spring; and besides, she has worn it so long that she hates to be seen in the street. Now, what is your idea in regard to the cost of a spring bonnet? Let me see."

"I pay five dollars for a hat."

"And gentlemen's wear costs more than ladies', you think?"

"Yes."

"Which shows how well you are posted. Put down twenty-five dollars for the bonnet."

"You're jesting!" Thomas Wilder looked blank.

"Just the cost of her bonnet this spring, as I happen to know. So put down twenty-five dollars, and twenty-five more for a spring mantilla. Add forty dollars for a full-trimmed silk dress—"

"Forty dollars!" interrupted Wilder, in a tone of great surprise.

"And thirty for a plainer one. She must have two."

"Well, I've got the items down," said the young man, but in a tone of incredulity, as if his friend were making sport.

"Perhaps you think the price of these silk dresses high. Your mother wore black lustring at a dollar a yard, and ten yards were a full pattern," said Mrs. Hardy.

"Just my thought."

"So I inferred. You met Araminta at Mrs. Blanchard's last week. We were both there. Did you notice the elegant dress she wore?"

"Not particularly. But I remember that she looked charming. I feel the whole effect, but have no eye for detail."

"That dress cost forty-five dollars. You can figure it out yourself. Fifteen yards of silk at two dollars and twenty-five cents a yard. How much?"

"Thirty-three seventy-five," answered the young man, who was quick at figures.

"Trimming and making, twelve dollars."

"Over forty-five!" Look and voice expressed astonishment.

"Just so. Fashion plays into the hand of

trade. Wide skirts, flouncing and trimming cut deeply into dress goods of all kinds, and swell the mantua-making bills enormously in the eyes of those who have to pay them. Let us see: you have provided two silk dresses, a bonnet and a spring mantle. What is the cost?"

"One hundred and twenty dollars." There was an unmistakable depression in Wilder's voice. The thermometer of his feelings was running down.

"Valenciennes collar and sleeves, twenty dollars more. Lace-bordered handkerchief, eight dollars. A Chantilly veil, twelve; lace parasol, eight. Bracelet, pin and earrings, new style—"

"There, there, there! No more!" and the young man crumpled the piece of paper on which he had been figuring, and thrust his gold pencil into his pocket with an air of desperation.

"You think me trifling?" said Mrs. Hardy.

"If you are in earnest, I am all at sea," was answered.

"Better be at sea in a tight ship than too near the breakers on a coast like this, my friend. It is just as I say. The cost of maintaining the luxury of a fashionably-dressed wife, however desirable the article may be, is not within the range of your ability. Another item which must be considered is the summer-tour item. Araminta goes to Saratoga and Newport, as you are aware. The cost of an extra outfit will not fall below one hundred dollars, and the expense of the thing—you will have to join her for a part of the season at least—cannot safely be entered under one hundred and fifty dollars."

"It doesn't follow," answered Wilder, making a feeble attempt to rally from the effects of these astounding intimations which came marshaling their forces under the guise of hard facts, "that my wife must go to Newport and Saratoga and sport the wardrobe of a duchess. The woman who marries me must adapt herself to my circumstances. Again, if the cost of furnishing Araminta is so great, how does her father maintain himself? His business is only of moderate range, and he has four daughters in society. I think there must be some exaggeration in your estimates."

"Mr. Brown has failed in business twice, to

my certain knowledge, within the past fifteen years," said Mrs. Hardy.

"I remember, now, that he was in trouble about five years ago," returned Wilder.

"When he got a settlement with creditors at forty cents on the dollar, as I had certain information at the time."

"Hu-m-m." The young man dropped his eyes to the floor and sat musing for some time. "Failed twice?" He looked up at Mrs. Hardy.

"Yes, twice, and may have to do it once or twice more ere getting these four expensive daughters off his hands, who are fitly educated for taking their husband, if they succeed in capturing foolish young men who have their own way in the world to make—your case, Thomas—along the hard road of anxious care, incessant toil and sharp humiliation which their father has trod and is still treading. He never goes to Saratoga or Newport. You did not find him there last year?"

"No."

"Nor the year before?"

Wilder shook his head.

"He must stay at home and 'financier,' as you men call it, through all the dull, hot sum mer months, in order to keep off the disaster of failure which hangs ever over his head like the naked sword of Damocles."

Wilder looked down at the floor again and sat without replying.

"Can you afford the expense?" inquired his maternal friend.

"I'm afraid not." There was a depressed air about the young man. Araminta Brown, arrayed in the fine feathers that make a fine bird, had captivated his fancy—nay, more, she had qualities which, under better training and influences, would have given a preponderating side to her character, and these Wilder had recognized.

After leaving Mrs. Hardy, he went home and in sober communion with himself reconsidered the whole question. To advance or recede—that must be decided now. For a time he argued against his friend, Mrs. Hardy, and doubted the fairness of her estimate touching the cost of dressing a lady who followed in the wake of fashion; then her character for sincerity and truth weighed on the other side, and certain considerations which she had presented loomed up into grave importance.

Still in doubt and perplexity, still undecided,

was our young friend when tired nature bore him away into dreamland, but did not remove from thought the subject on which it dwelt so intently. He was with Araminta, and more charmed by his charmer than ever. They were walking in a garden among flowers, she in colors decked as gayly as the children of spring and summer, and with breath, to her lover, as perfume laden as theirs. Then they were passing down the city's crowded streets, and ever and anon paused to admire the beautiful things displayed in windows. A splendid bracelet attracted Araminta's attention, and she uttered a desire to become its possessor. They entered the store, and soon the brilliant thing was glittering on her wrist. Fifty dollars was the price. As Wilder took the money from his purse and was handing it to the jeweler, a pair of stern eyes looked into his. The jeweler was transformed into one of his employers, and the expression of his eyes made his heart sink.

"She is your wife?" said the employer.

In one of the usual kaleidoscope changes that accompany dreams, our friend found himself a moment afterward at his desk deep in the mysteries of accounts and business. He was aware of voices near him in conversation, and understood that he was the subject of discourse.

"Shall we take him into the firm?"

Almost breathlessly he waited for the answer. It came in these words:

"No, that would be imprudent. His marriage with an extravagant girl will involve him in expenses beyond the dividend his interest would yield. Debt and temptation must follow, and we know where they lead. I'm sorry, but the step cannot be taken."

"His salary will not support him now," remarked the first speaker.

"Of course it will not."

"What then? Will it be debt and temptation?"

"Can it be anything else?" was the response.

"Then is it safe to retain him as clerk?"

"I think not."

The answer came with such a shock upon the dreamer that he awoke. Starting to his feet, he crossed the room two or three times before his bewildered thoughts were clear.

"Only a dream," he murmured, in a tone of relief, as he sat down again at the table from which he had arisen and recalled in each minute particular the vision which had haunted his imagination. "Only a dream," he repeated, "but how full of warning!"

Did he marry Araminta Brown? The question now put in sober earnest, "Can I afford it?" received such an emphatic "No" that the argument closed and was never opened again. Araminta has been consoled by another lover, who may become her husband, but we pity the husband unless his coffers are deep, and even then, should he happen to possess a heart, he will find that he has given gold for tinsel.

XIX.

THE MEREST TRIFLE.

 BRIEF passage at arms—half in sport, half in earnest—then the young husband went away to his office forgetful of the parting kiss. The heightened color of Mrs. Orton's face gradually toned down until the usual warmth was lost.

"I'm sorry to see this," said Aunt Jane, speaking frankly. She was on a visit to her niece. Both look and voice were serious.

"To see what, aunty?" A flush of surprise lit up the countenance of Mrs. Orton, that had been faintly shadowed a moment before.

"Little disagreements between you and your husband—petty disputes, fault-findings, cavilings over unimportant things."

"Why, aunty!" The color came back to Mrs. Orton's face.

"Yesterday morning I noticed that Henry

kissed you before he went away. That little tenderness was omitted this morning. Why?"

The niece did not answer.

"Words are things, my dear," resumed Aunt Jane, "and if there is any hardness in them, they hurt. Love doesn't try to hurt unless in defence of its object—no, not even in sport."

"Why, aunty! You are making a great deal out of nothing," said Mrs. Orton, almost inclined to be offended. "We often talk so to each other, but don't mean anything. It's our way."

"I'm sorry that you have fallen into so bad a way, Helen. The error is a serious one, and may lead to the most unhappy consequences. You lost love's tender sign this morning just because of this way, and I think, if you look down into your consciousness, you will find some unpleasant things there which but for this way could not have existed. Henry made one or two rather sharp accusations, at which I saw your cheeks redden and your eyes flash."

"All fancy, Aunt Jane."

"No. When he said that self-will made you blind, either his accusation or his manner touched the quick of your feelings, and the keenness of voice with which you answered, 'All men are tyrants at heart, and have a name for whatever opposes them; in my case it is self-will,' showed that you meant to hurt him in return. And you did hurt him. In consequence, you lost a kiss."

"That's a trifle!" said Mrs. Orton, with forced indifference.

"Your heart and tongue do not accord in this declaration, Helen. No, it is not a trifle, it is a serious thing: it is the beginning of alienation."

The ear of Helen detected a disturbed thrill in the tones of Aunt Jane's voice which seemed rather a response to some memory than the effect of any present cause. She did not reply. It seemed as if a shadow were creeping into the room. Aunt Jane, on closing the last sentence, had dropped her eyes, and she was losing herself in thought—not pleasant thought, as could be seen.

"Don't think anything more about it, aunty," said Mrs. Orton, with affected cheerfulness. "It isn't just right, I will acknowledge. A bad habit, of which we must break ourselves; but you must make a great deal of allowance for us, as we are only children yet, you know, and children are willful sometimes."

"No, dear, not children, but of rational age. The substance of your mind is hard enough to take enduring impressions, and I warn you solemnly to take care what kind of impressions are suffered to be made."

"Oh, why will you be so serious, aunty! It's the most trifling thing in the world. Henry and I understand each other perfectly. The fact is, we enjoy these little tête-à-têtes now and then. They make a pleasant variety. We must have things spicy and pungent occasionally, or we would lose our taste for common good."

"So I thought once, but—" Aunt Jane checked herself. A little while afterward she looked up at her niece and said:

"Helen, did you never hear from your mother about my early life?"

"Mother has never spoken of it," replied Mrs. Orton.

"She was always considerate, always prudent, a wiser and better woman than your aunt, Helen, and, more than that, happier. The currents of her life have run smoothly, and why? Chiefly because she was not, like too many others, all the while casting obstructions therein. You resemble me in more things than you resemble your mother. I wish it were not so. Next to my good wish must come my good deed. I will tell you of my early life—I will unveil the skeleton in my house that you may see it and take warning.

"At twenty I was married—a light-hearted, self-willed, thoughtless girl, in almost everything unfitted for the position of a wife. My husband was older by six years, but not superior in mental discipline. An only son, he had been indulged, mother and sisters yielding to him for so long a time that he had come to expect others to give way when he asserted his will. Apart from this, he was affectionate, kind, honorable and intelligent, possessing rare intellectual powers and considerable force of character. He was worthy of a woman's love: he had my love. Ah, if I had been wise in my love, what sorrows might have been escaped! But I was not wise—no wiser than you are, Helen. Very soon after our marriage, as trifling differences of opinion arose, we commenced to wrangle in a half-earnest way, and in doing so often hurt each other. The faults and peculiarities mutually observed were mutually declared. I was often seriously hurt or annoyed by what my husband said in these frequent contests, and he as frequently showed anger or pain. We were not always careful in our speech to each other before people, but oftener, then, took occasion to say the hardest things. The way in which you spoke to Henry this morning startled me, it was so like what I had done to my cost many sorrowful years ago.

"We had been married just one year. The period had not been the happiest of my life. I was disappointed in my husband. His conduct toward me was far from being what I had anticipated. He was not tender, and conciliating, and forbearing, as in the beginning. He lost temper with me easily, and when I found fault with him, as was too often the case, rarely failed to answer sharply. There was danger in my path, but I did not see it. Blindly I moved to my fate, and there was no one to warn me as I am now warning you. If I had been gentle and conciliatory, if I had ruled my own spirit, denied myself the indulgence of self-will and unwomanly fretfulness toward my husband when his conduct did not suit my temper, this desolation of my life would have been avoided.

"One morning we sat down together at the breakfast-table. We had been to a large party on the previous night. My nerves were a little unstrung, the effect of late hours and a late supper, but I did not feel particularly out of humor. The party was referred to, and my husband, speaking of a lady who was present, said that she was the best dressed woman there. 'Not very complimentary to your taste,' I answered. I suppose that my look and tone were both contemptuous, for I was not guarded toward my husband. I saw his eyes flash and the color deepen on his face. A keen retort fluttered on his lips, but did not fly off against me. This was unusual, for he was generally quick to lift the gage of battle when I threw it down. I felt that under this repression there was strongly excited feeling. Instead of being warned, I was piqued at his silence. It stood as a sort of defiance, and without giving thought or consideration as to the result I said sharply. 'She was the worst dressed woman in the company.' 'She was a lady in her behavior to her husband,' was the answer I received in a tone that left me in no doubt touching the application of his words.

"Dear Helen, if in that moment I had lost the gift of speech, it had been well, for I did not know the art of using it aright. I became very angry. 'Her husband is a gen—' But I caught the word ere it dropped into full expression. It might almost as well have been uttered. 'There are some things that I will not take from man or woman,' came slowly from his lips. I noticed that his face had grown pale. 'Guard your own lips if you expect others to be especially guarded,' was my cold retort. There was silence for a little while. My husband laid down his knife and fork, and sat in a strange brooding way for almost a minute. 'Some people are free enough to give, but they can't take,' said I, breaking this silence. He looked up at me with a new expression in his eyes that gave me a chill, but I did not restrain myself. 'I'm about tired of this way of living.' This sentence I threw at him almost roughly. 'And so am I,' he answered, rising from the table. 'It doesn't suit me, and never has suited me. I can't say a word but I'm taken up; I can't advance an opinion but it is controverted.

It's wrangle, wrangle, all the while! Love may lie at the bottom of it all, but it's another kind of love from what I bargained for.' 'I'm sorry,' said I, hurt and offended by language that sent a conviction of unwifely conduct to my heart, 'that you've been so disappointed. I, too, bargained for something very different from what I have obtained.' There was hardness in my voice and accusation in my eyes.

"The look he then gave me I shall never forget. It was not an angry look, but full of rebuke, of regret and of pain. He turned and went away, taking up his hat and leaving the house without once glancing back to where I stood in the dining-room door gazing after him as he moved down the hall. Repentance came quickly when I found myself alone. What a poor, insignificant thing had risen up into a mountain barrier between us! The lady about whose style of dress we had wrangled was nothing to either of us. If my husband admired her evening toilette, why should I object? Tastes differ. It was certainly his right to say what he thought in so unimportant a matter. I grew angry with myself as I looked more soberly at my conduct. I saw that I had been weak, petty unamiable. I cried for an hour, and in my grief and repentance resolved to confess my error and entirely reform my conduct toward my husband.

"I was not easy in mind all day. An unusual weight rested on my feelings. I seemed to be in the shadow of an approaching trouble. At the hour when I expected my husband's return I sat waiting for him, still in the better state my repentance had wrought. Love had unfolded all her sweetest flowers, and I would delight him with their odors. But I waited for him in vain. He did not come. He never came back!"

"Oh, Aunt Jane!" exclaimed Helen, grasping the old lady's arm. The shock of this declaration had driven the color from her face. After a few moments the aunt resumed:

"Days, weeks, months passed, but no word nor sign came from him. After leaving home he went to the store where he was employed as a clerk, and asked for the amount of salary that was due him. Taking this, he went away, and beyond that there was no trace of him. I will not attempt a description of what I suffered. Reason was nearly lost. Others blamed him, but I did not, for after it was too late to profit by clearness of vision, I saw the hereditary and acquired peculiarities of his character, which were as a second nature, and in regard to which I had conceded nothing, but instead, chafed and pricked him in the tenderest places. The foundations of his character were good, and I might have built upon them a temple of happiness wherein to dwell secure amid the fiercest storms of life. But I failed to build, and so have been out in the storms for these many years.

"For two years I lived in suspense. No word came in all that time from my absent husband. One day a letter arrived from a city far in the West. The address was in a woman's hand. The writer was a stranger. She said that a man was lying sick in her father's house. He had come over with a party across the plains from the Pacific coast. She thought him very ill, and that he might not recover. They had asked him about his friends, and if there was any one to whom he would like word sent. At first he said there was no one, but afterward, as he grew worse, said she might write to me these words: 'May God pardon us both,

Jane. We were equally at fault. There is no anger left in my heart. It died out long and long ago. Forgive me, as I forgive you.'

"In less than a week I was in that far-off Western city—not too late, thank God! to find my long-lost husband alive; to take his dying head upon my breast; to warm his lips with burning kisses; to see love in his eyes ere the veil of night dropped over them."

For a little while the old floods of feeling swept across the heart of Aunt Jane.

"I have uncovered my life for you, Helen," she said, on growing calm again. "You have seen the skeleton in my house. Be warned by the sad experience I have known. Keep love's lamp ever trimmed and brightly burning. Let all these little wranglings cease. They mar the present enjoyment and gravely threaten the future. Trifles light as air may give occasion for disagreements of the saddest character. The cloud no bigger than a man's hand may quickly cover the sky and breed a desolating tempest."

As the day drew to a close, Mrs. Orton felt a shadow of apprehension creeping over her. What if her husband, offended by the sharp things she had uttered at breakfast-time, should have determined to go away.' More than once, in a half-serious manner, he had threatened to do this very thing, and she had answered, secure in her confidence, "Go!"

Prompt to the usual hour his step was in the hall, and swifter than ever she had gone down the stairs did Helen fly to meet him. The young husband noted as a pleasant thing this overflow of love, but never knew the cause.

As it takes two to wrangle, all petty strife ceased at once between Helen and her husband. If he was captious, or said sharp words, or criticised her acts or speech, she answered pleasantly, and he was disarmed. No long time passed before they were as tender of each other's feelings and as considerate in their conduct as during Love's golden morning hours. And why should not this always be so? Love has better signs than sharp words, fault-findings and unamiable banter.

XX.

MARRYING A BEAUTY.

ON'T do it," said the old gentleman, speaking with unwonted fervor. "Take my advice, and don't do it."

The fine ardor which had flushed my soul was chilled. Uncle Marion saw the change.

"Beauty is too often a false signal," he added. "If all things were in the first order of creation, beauty would be the outward sign of goodness, but evil has wrought many sad changes in our world, and beauty may not be trusted."

"The beauty of Florence Ware may be trusted," I answered, confidently. "There is a very heaven of innocence in her face."

"Love is blind, my boy—Love is blind!" said Uncle Marion, with oracular positiveness. "As for beauty, it is only a veil, not a representation."

"Cannot a beautiful person be good?" I asked, my tones expressing surprise at the implied negation of his remarks.

"All things are possible," he answered, soberly; "but he who trusts to beauty as the sign of goodness will find himself many, many times bitterly mistaken. Goodness has her signs, but they are not in pure Grecian profiles, nor in white, queenly necks; they are not in brown eyes or pinky cheeks. The face may be lovely as a poet's or painter's dream, while the heart beneath may be full of pride, ambition, selfishness and impurity. I am an old man, George, and from the experience, observation and suffering of many years I warn you against putting faith in beauty, and above all, in the beauty of Florence Ware."

I had known my Uncle Marion as a cheerful old man—quiet and reflective for the most part, but cheerful. The ordinary disturbing influences that continually jostle most people's equanimity of mind had scarcely any effect upon him. He lived in a region above their influence. It was not, therefore, without surprise that I observed an agitation of manner altogether unusual.

Now, as to Florence Ware, a young lady who had recently come into our neighborhood from a distant city to spend a few months with a school friend, her beauty had bewitched me. Of all lovely creatures in human shape, she was, in my eyes, the loveliest. Not only were her form and features perfect, but there was a grace in every movement, and an indescribable charm and sweetness in her countenance, that in my eyes expressed more than human perfection. It had never entered into my heart to conceive of her as anything less than the embodiment of all that was pure and true and good. To be warned, therefore, almost solemnly, not to put faith in her beauty, hurt as well as surprised me.

"Don't do it, my boy!" said Uncle Marion, after a pause, repeating the injunction made a little while before in answer to something more than a jesting remark that I thought of offering my hand to Florence. "The poorest of all recommendations that a young lady has to offer is her beauty. Ten chances to one if its very possession has not spoiled her for a good man's wife. It will be a miracle almost if she be not vain and fond of admiration. The quiet of home will be irksome, and its common duties distasteful. Having feasted on homage, admiration, flattery, how can she live on the plain fare that succeeds her withdrawal from that brilliant outer sphere, where her charms were perpetually reflected back upon her from hundreds of admiring eyes?"

All this did not satisfy me. There might be truth in the general proposition as to the dangerous influence of beauty on a weak mind, but the idea of ignoring beauty in a wife struck me as absurd.

"I will endorse Florence Ware," said I, half desperately, setting myself wholly against my uncle.

The effect of this surprised me. For a little while Uncle Marion seemed like one who had been stunned. His eyes were fixed on the floor, his brows drawn heavily together, his lips shut firmly. After a while he drew a long breath and looked up into my face. There was a change in him. The old quiet look was gone.

"Endorse no one on mere appearance," he said, "for nothing is more deceptive. I do not assert that the face always lies, but I will say that it oftener hides than reveals a person's true quality. Don't trust it, my boy! There are given more unerring signs than the face ever reveals, except when the soul is off guard. All that a man or woman is will, under certain circumstances, betray itself in the eyes and coun tenance, but you are rarely admitted to the view. The face you meet in company, when every outlet of the mind is guarded, is not the face by which you may judge of character. You must see the person at home, on the street, in business or domestic life. You must take the view from many stand-points, and study and compare. A prudent person will do this before entering into the most ordinary business relations with a man, and yet I find you actually meditating an offer of marriage to a girl simply on the credit of her pretty face! You had not even so much as heard of her six weeks ago. As to who and what are her father and mother you rest in complete ignorance, and are just as ignorant of the girl's disposition and character. The bright eye and beautiful face are accepted as credentials for everything. But only 'handsome is that handsome does,' and my word for it, the chances are all against the 'handsome does,' in the case of Florence Ware."

"If we judge harshly without evidence, Uncle Marion, we will in almost every case judge wrongly. I am sure that you are unjust to Florence. I doubt if you have met her twice since she came into the neighborhood," said I, with feeling.

"I have seen her, perhaps, as often as you have, George," he answered, "and under circumstances more favorable to observation. She is very beautiful, I will own—bewitchingly so. Her countenance, when lighted, almost bewilders. I never saw but one face just like it—"

The old man's voice suddenly faltered. His eyes were shadowed by a new and strange expression. Some long-buried memory had quickened into life. He arose in a slightly-agitated way, crossed the room to a bookcase, and opening it, appeared to be searching for a volume. It was only a feint to draw my attention from his unusually disturbed manner. I understood this at the time. He came back after a little while with a book in his hand, which he laid on a table without opening. I was watching him closely.

"George!" He faced round upon me in a quick, nervous way. "Don't trust in beauty!

Don't let it bewilder you! Don't let it betray you as it once betrayed me!"

He stopped, cast his eyes down and sat silent for a few moments, then looking up, he forced to his lips a feeble smile that hid their sadness, and told me this story of his past life.

When about your age, he said, an advantageous business offer took me to New York. I became the junior partner in a flourishing silk-house, and soon found myself introduced to a pleasant circle of acquaintances. One evening, a few months after my arrival in the city, I was at a party where nearly all the guests were strangers. In consequence, I was left mostly to myself, and was beginning to feel rather dull, when a lady whom I knew came to me and said,

"I have a charming young friend here to whom I must introduce you. I know you will like her."

A few moments afterward I found myself standing before the loveliest being my gaze had ever rested upon. Her beauty was faultless. The tenderest, sweetest, brightest of eyes looked up into mine. I saw before me a countenance in which seemed blended all things pure and good. Every line of every feature seemed a perfect line of beauty, and there was not a tint, or light, or shade in the whole complexion that an artist would have criticised. You smile, but, soberly speaking, and at this distance of time, I mean just what I say. Her beauty came up to my best ideal.

Of course I was charmed—nay, more, fascinated—for I stood in the presence of an enchantress. She read her power over me in the admiring eyes that looked into hers. I was too fresh and young to hide or dissimulate. She overcame me on the instant, and knew that I was entangled in the web of her beauty. I say "of her beauty," meaning just that.

She was a blonde, with large, dark blue eyes and full, dark lashes; hair of a soft chestnut brown or golden hue, as the light happened to fall on it; skin of that semi-transparent texture rarely found, but always so like a veil behind which the spiritual body seems hiding from mortal eyes its enchanting loveliness. She was just a little above the medium height in woman, and being slender, looked tall. Every motion was grace. I say it now, after nearly thirty years have passed since that first meeting. And I repeat now, looking back through those thirty years, that she was of almost faultless beauty. I was captivated. From the instant I looked at her I was a worshiper. She was sweet and gracious in her manner, my undisguised admiration having proved the passport to her favor.

"If her hand is yet free it shall be mine," I said, as I lay awake that night feasting my inward eye on the charms that still shaped themselves to my imagination. I asked no question as to her hereditary or acquired character, but took everything for granted. She must be good, pure, loving, for were not all these written in beauty on her face?

I had asked the privilege of calling upon her, and she had graciously consented. On the very next evening I was in her presence. She welcomed my coming in the sweetest manner, and threw over me a deeper and more bewildering fascination. It was only by the exercise of perpetual self-restraint that I held myself back from a foolishly precipitate offer of marriage. Twice in the week that followed I sought her presence, and was as blind to any danger as is the moth while circling round a blazing candle.

With an art the most perfect in its simulation of artlessness she drew me on and on, until within little more than two months after our first meeting I laid my destiny at her feet, and she accepted the trust and became the evil genius of my life.

I was very happy. Heaven had no conceivable bliss higher than mine. I dwelt in light and beauty. And yet the door of this charmer's heart had never really been opened to me; and if it had been opened, there would have been no room in its crowded chambers for me to enter, for they were already full of pride, vanity, self-love and love of pleasure. I might have known all this. If I had been wise, prudent, clear-seeing, as a man ought always to be when he contemplates marriage, I might have seen that below the gilding all was common and poor. But beauty had blinded me.

For causes which need not be stated our marriage was deferred for a year, and the date fixed. In that time some of the gilding fell off, and I had glimpses of things which often made me very sober. But I was so proud of her, so fascinated by her personal charms, that I came quickly out of these passing shadows into the pleasant sunshine. If she did love admiration, if she were fond of social pleasures and public assemblies, if her eyes were continually looking out and inviting homage, if she had winning smiles for all the attractive men who sought her notice, I had still many reasons and excuses for my own satisfaction. Her heart, for all this, I said, was mine; we were betrothed, were all the world to each other, and would soon be united in the holiest bonds.

We were married at last. Twice at her desire the appointed time was changed and the wedding deferred. It did not really take place until four months after the period first agreed upon. In each of these intervals of time, as it has since been very plain to me, she meditated a breach of the engagement, and only remained true because ardent admirers did not press their claims to favor in formal declarations of love.

Yes, we were married at last. The wedding was a brilliant affair. All that art could give to nature was lavished upon the bride. She was more like the creation of a dream or a poet's imaginings than one of flesh and blood. And all this wonderful beauty was mine—mine!

Vows were given, hands clasped, kisses exchanged, the benediction spoken, and we twain were bound together. The long suspense was over. What a moment of bliss!

I had been during all this year and a half living out of the sphere of my own true life and dwelling in a region of enchantment, and all this time I had been longing to get down into the real things in which I was to find true enjoyment. My prize gained, I wished to leave the open field, and bear it away to the sanctuary of a home, there to enjoy the blessing I had won. My beauty was to be my own delight--my treasure sacred to myself! Alas! the time for awakening was not far distant.

How largely I had counted on the pleasures of companionship when the sweet maiden became my wife! and yet, strange to say, I had never in a single instance been able to draw her into the expression of an intelligent opinion about a work of art, or a book in any of the higher branches of literature. If a reader of history, she did not betray the fact. She never referred to the leading poets, and if their names or best productions were mentioned, she smiled, but offered no appreciative response. But she was enthusiastic over opera singers and theatrical stars, and her conversation was always more of persons than acts, opinions or principles. She was a hero-worshiper, with little or no sympathy for heroism. Actions were dead, unsympathetic of the past, but the man and woman were centres of admiration. She could understand the glory of position, but not the grandeur of achievement.

During all the year and a half that intervened from the time of our engagement until we were married, I failed in every effort to draw her thoughts into the region of interest where mine dwelt. I was the lover, the wooer, the worshiper, and so bent down to the region where she dwelt. But I could not live there for ever. I was organized spiritually for life in another sphere of mind. My soul craved food of another and more substantial quality. For a year and a half I had lived a kind of artificial life; had put aside old habits of thinking and feeling; had left my real tastes hungering for appropriate food; had given up nearly everything essentially my own; had deferred on almost all occasions to the preferences and pleasures of a beauty so much enamored of herself that she rarely if ever thought of con sulting my wants or feelings. Could this last after marriage? No.

It did not take a very long time to reach the period of awakening. I soon found that my company no more sufficed for my wife than it had sufficed for my betrothed—that the home of her husband was scarcely more attractive than the home of her aunt had been. Her life was in the world—in pleasures, admiration, excitement. Take these away, and you robbed her of almost everything. During a few months after our marriage I yielded with a gradually diminishing grace. After that, seeing how absorbed she still remained, and how little interest she manifested in her home, both duty and feeling prompted me to lay upon her the hand of restraint. I did this as gently as possible—as lovingly as possible. But it made a strong ripple in the current of her life. I saw a veil fall instantly over her beauty. The soft eyes hardened and the sweet face grew cold.

A chill went inward to the very centre of my being, for I understood something of what this meant. I had been studying her from a closer point of view since our marriage, and was gradually arriving at a truer knowledge of her character. Day by day there had come to me new and painful revelations touching the quality of her mind. I had put aside the veil of beauty and looked into the soul, searching for the real things that beauty represented, but had not found them. Still I hoped they might be there —some of them at least—and kept on searching.

The hard eyes and the cold face were too strong for me in the beginning. I took off the restraining hand: the ripple was gone, and the current ran on smoothly again, but in the old channels. This could not last. I am firm and strong when I see clearly. I had not seen clearly for a great while, for beauty had deceived me into the faith that it was the sign of all perfection. I knew, now, that it only concealed weaknesses of character which must be guarded; a poverty of mind that must ever leave me hungry in companionship; an unkindness of spirit, when all was not yielded, that must hurt me deeply in every contact. But the way of duty grew plainer and plainer before me at every step. The hand of restraint was put forth again, and again the current of her life was agitated. She struggled against the im pediment. I did not yield. Then the foundations of a separating wall, to rise up between us, were laid. To me she was beautiful no longer. Her countenance, so lovely to every one, so full of all sweetnesses, so bewitching and so bewildering, was only a transparent veil to my eyes, and I looked through it, gazing sadly and in continually increasing alienation on the deformity and incompleteness that lay hidden below. She was so worldly, so absorbed in gayety and pleasure, so fond of admiration! Even as before marriage, she was in all large companies a centre of attraction. A light class of young men were continually fluttering around her, and by her manner she as continually invited their attentions.

This annoyed, fretted, even angered me at times. If I had really loved her, I would have grown jealous. But I was only annoyed. Pride, not jealousy, was aroused. I felt that my honor was touched. I was humiliated, through my wife's weakness, before the world. Men for whom I cared nothing—nay, disliked—became visitors at my house, dropping in at all hours, day and evening, whether I was at home or not. In public assemblies I was continually chafed by the observation she attracted. Men would recognize and point her out to their companions. In the intervals between acts or parts they would leave their seats and make their way to where we were sitting, to be graciously received by my wife.

Human nature endures to a certain point, and then rebels. I saw myself approaching this point, and not without serious apprehension. As a husband, it was but meet that I should object to certain associations and familiarities that were hardly reputable—even if not dangerous—for a young wife. The gentle hand put forth to restrain would not do. This had already been attempted.

Earlier, by two hours, than usual, I came home one pleasant summer afternoon, suffering from an attack of nervous headache. I was almost blind with the pain that pierced one of my temples. Entering, I passed to the sitting-room, then to our chamber, but did not find my wife. I called her name, but there was no answer.

"She's gone out riding," said a servant, who had heard me call.

"Out riding? With whom?" I spoke too quickly to hide my astonishment

"With a gentleman."

"What gentleman?"

"The one that comes 'most every afternoon, sir. I don't know his name."

"Oh, very well," I answered, endeavoring to put on an air of indifference, and turning from the servant, re-entered our chamber and shut the door.

My whole being was in a tremor of confused excitement. Some time elapsed before I grew calm. My headache was gone.

"Out riding with a gentleman almost every afternoon!" I said to myself when the rush of feeling and confusion were over. "What does this mean? Who is the gentleman? Out riding, and not a hint of the fact to me!"

It did not look well. There was room for suspicion. I could do nothing but wait for my wife's return, and I waited in self-tormenting impatience for more than two hours, listening to the sound of every approaching vehicle, disappointed a hundred times as the rattle of wheels went by. At last the hour came at which I usually returned home, but my wife was still away. Strange doubts and fears began creeping into my soul. For a little while I was in most painful suspense. Still I hearkened for the pausing of wheels, but no carriage stopped. At last I heard the bell ring. Standing in the hall above, I listened while the servant went to the door.

"Has Mr. Marion come home?" It was my wife's voice. I did not wait to hear the answer, but stepped back to our sleeping-room and dropped down on the bed. She came lightly up stairs, and seeing me, asked, in surprise, if I were sick.

"I came home two hours ago with one of my bad headaches," I made answer, speaking heavily, as though I were still in pain.

"Oh, I'm very sorry," she answered. "How unfortunate that I happened to be out! I promised Mrs. Grant that I would call on her this afternoon and go over some new music which she has just received from Paris."

"Subterfuge! Falsehood!" I said in my heart bitterly. I groaned in pain, turning my face away. She naturally mistook the seat of pain. It was not in my head.

"What can I do for you?" she asked, bending over me.

"Nothing!" I perceived that my voice was

repellant, and I noticed that she lifted herself suddenly and stepped back from the bed.

"Julia!" said I, rising up quickly. I was moved by an irrepressible impulse to speak. She was already half across the room. It was still light, and I could see her face distinctly as she turned with a start. Her look was surprised, and the hot blood was already mounting to her forehead. "You were out riding this afternoon. May I ask with whom?" I had dropped my voice so as to control it, and spoke calmly, but with seriousness.

"Who said I was out riding?" She was off her guard and showed confusion.

"Margaret," I replied, still speaking calmly. "I asked for you when I came home, and she answered that you were out riding with a gentleman. It is only natural that I should desire to know the gentleman's name."

"It was Mr. Harbaugh." She rallied herself with a strong effort, threw the deeper stains of crimson from her face and tried to smile with an innocent air. She was far from being successful. My eyes were too keen. I had learned to look through all the veils in her power to lift between me and her real self.

Mr. Harbaugh! Why, this was an old admirer, for whose smiles and favor, months before we were married, she had turned half indifferent from mine! I was jealous then, surprised, startled, alarmed, now! Mr. Harbaugh! And he had been taking her out riding almost every afternoon! I was stunned for a little while.

"If you have any objection—" she began, reading surprise and displeasure in my countenance. I waved my hand for her to keep silent. Objection! And was that all she had to say? Objection! Did her perception of the case reach no farther than this? I was dumb.

She now had time to recover herself, and she made all haste to gather around her the rent garments of self-control, and to assume an attitude of injured innocence. The hurt look, the sad, tear-filled eye, the quivering mouth,—all these were arrayed in accusation against me. But they had no effect. I was not to be influenced against the logic of facts by feints like these.

The wall of separation that was slowly rising between us grew higher in the evening that followed. She spent the hours alone, affecting to be deeply hurt with me; I alone, also, brooding, accusing, repenting, foreboding. In the morning, as I was going out, I said to her:

"Julia, if Mr. Harbaugh asks you to ride with him to-day, it is my will that you decline."

Her eyes flashed. Crimson stains burned on her cheeks instantly.

"Take care, sir!" she answered, in a warning voice.

"Take care! Of what?" I felt an angry spirit rising within me.

"I am not yours to command. Be pleased to keep that in mind, sir! I am your wife, yet still a free woman—as free as you are." Her eyes were like darts, her face imperious. She drew herself up in a queenly way, beautiful, but dangerous.

"As the guardian of your honor," I made answer, "I must stand in the way of its attaint. Your good name is too precious. I cannot, I will not, see it shadowed!"

"Honor! Good name! Is the man sleeping or awake?" She affected to laugh. But the light died quickly out of her face.

"The young wife who, in the absence of her husband during business-hours, rides out almost daily with a man of leisure, is in danger of having light words spoken against her, and your good fame is too precious a thing to be left to any risks."

I emphasized the words "almost daily," and looked keenly at her as I uttered them. The color, so high a moment before, dropped away from her face; her eyes wavered under my steady glance; she turned partly from me and sat down. I did not feel angry. Pity was at this moment the stronger sentiment—pity for the humiliation with which she seemed overcome.

"Remember, Julia," I said, with as much tenderness as I could throw into my voice, "that I am wholly in earnest. You have been thoughtless, that is all. But public opinion will judge of you more harshly."

She sat with her face still partly averted, quite immovable, and without any response. I stood for a little while in doubt as to her real state of mind, and then went away very much oppressed in feeling.

On returning home at dinner-time she received me with a pleasant face. I could detect scarcely a line of the hardness and passion which had disfigured it on the evening before.

"You are indeed very, very beautiful!" I found myself saying, mentally, as I dropped my gaze, suppressing an involuntary sigh, from her almost radiant countenance. Of course, no word bearing the remotest allusion to the unhappy incidents of the previous day escaped our lips. With a lighter heart I returned to my business, but instead of going direct, I turned aside from my usual course to see a gentleman with whom certain negotiations were pending. I spent half an hour with him. As I was leaving his office, Mr. Harbaugh went dashing past in a buggy. He did not observe me. I kept him in sight until he turned a corner three or four blocks distant. He was going in the direction of my house! The danger I had thought passing away, was at my door! I did not hesitate. An omnibus that went within a block of my residence was going by, and I jumped in. Happening to be the only passenger, the horses trotted on briskly. In twenty minutes I pulled the check-string and leaped to the pavement. A few rods more and I would be in sight of my house, which stood just past the next corner. Only two or three steps had been taken when, sweeping gayly around the corner came the buggy of Mr. Harbaugh. Julia was sitting by his side, her face covered with smiles. She saw me, and clutching after her veil, drew it closely over her face. My first impulse was to stop the vehicle and invite her to come down. There was a moment or two of hesitation about acting on the impulse, and in this brief lapse of time the opportunity was gone. They went by me like a flash.

I stood still in a weak, indeterminate state of mind for almost a minute. Then fearing lest some one had observed me and the passing of my wife, I started on. There was no use in returning home. The bird I had been so anxious to guard had opened the cage in my absence, and was gone. So I went to my place of business. A hundred things were thought of and conjectured during that unhappy afternoon—a hundred expedients for saving my wife from the danger that hung over her determined on, and then set aside as doubtful. I grew more bewildered, felt more impotent, with every passing hour.

I made it a point not to return home until my usual time, so that Julia might have an opportunity to get back before that period if she wished to do so. I found her in the parlor with her bonnet thrown off and lying on one of the chairs. She came toward the hall quickly to meet me. There was a half-troubled, half-assured look in her face, over which she flung a wreath of smiles.

"Now, don't be angry!" she said, in a coaxing, deprecating voice. "I couldn't help myself! The engagement had to be kept. But indeed, indeed, there shall be no more of it! It is too bad that you should have seen me, when I was not in heart going against your wishes! I said to Mr. Harbaugh that it was the last time he must call for me."

The serious look did not die on my face. I was too deeply hurt and troubled—the more hurt and troubled that I saw through Julia's poor disguise. That wife must needs be a good actor who would deceive a husband startled into suspicion as suddenly as I had been.

"My strongly expressed wishes—nay, my positive injunction—should have had more weight with you than a light and injudicious promise," I answered with perhaps more severity of tone than I intended using.

She stepped back from me as though I had pushed her away. But I did not relax in my severity of manner. The affair was too serious to be lightly passed over. Then came the wet eyes, the hurt look, the down-curved and quivering lips, the air of injured innocence.

"You should have said that you were under promise to ride out again this afternoon. The wife who conceals from her husband anything that he has a right to know acts unwisely. Her happiness is in peril. She is in danger of misjudgment. She opens the door for suspicion."

She turned from me, even while I was speaking, with the air of one wrongly accused, and walked slowly from the room. I did not follow her; but sat down to think. An hour afterward the tea-bell rung. I sat still waiting for Julia to come down. Nearly five minutes passed, and I heard no movement. The bell was rung again. I went up stairs and found her sitting by the bed in our chamber, with her face bowed down and hidden on a pillow. I touched her, and she started as one rousing from sleep.

"It is the tea-bell," I said.

"Oh, is it? I didn't hear."

She looked at me for some moments with real or affected bewilderment, then arose and accompanied me down to the breakfast-room. There was no conversation during the meal. I think each was so much in doubt as to the other's true state of mind as to be afraid to touch on any theme lest there should be a jar from some discordant string.

I remember that evening as the most unhappy one of my life—I mean, of my life up to that period. Julia sat for most of the time with a novel in her hand, but from stealthy observations of her face from time to time I was satisfied that she was taking little or no interest in the pages that were turned at very irregular intervals. I also had sought refuge in a book, but there was only the pretence of reading on either side. During that memorable evening I took the calmest and soberest possible review of the whole ground on which I was standing, and the result was a most painful conviction that I had brought a thirsty soul unto dry wells, that I had built up hastily a beautiful palace, the foundations whereof rested on sand.

The Julia of my imagination, the pure, tender,

wise, perfect being, reflected in grace of form and transcendent beauty of countenance, I had loved with a sentiment akin to worship. But the real Julia, who had come to me so radiant, so angelic in form and feature, from the marriage altar, I did not, could not, love. For one of my thought and feeling there was nothing in her to love. Day by day one disguise after another had fallen, and on that day the last veil to her real quality had been given to the winds. I saw her stripped of even womanly innocence! So young, so beautiful, and yet of so mean a quality! Could my soul mate with a soul like this? Was there any hope of conjunction? I saw the wall rise higher between us. I looked at her across a gulf that widened every moment.

I was always poor at disguises. As I feel, so I usually appear. If I simulate, it is with an effort that is of short duration. In my bearing toward Julia from that day she could not help seeing an altered state of mind. She made no effort to win back my failing love, but rather hid her sweetness when we were alone. In company she shone out with a flash and brilliancy that often astonished me by its contrast with her home exterior, and I often saw the eyes of men whose character I knew too well resting on her face. There is a beauty so full of all pure intimations that it repels such eyes. It blinds, confuses and rebukes them. But such was not, alas! my wife's beauty.

She soon grew self-willed and assumed a more independent line of conduct, in a measure defying me. She knew that I strongly disliked Mr. Harbaugh, and yet would always receive him in the most gracious manner when he happened to be in any company where we were present. He had ventured to call and spend an evening with us two or three times, but I treated him with such a frigidly polite air that he gave up these intrusions. I saw that in doing so I was adding stones to the wall that was growing up between Julia and myself, but to act otherwise was impossible.

Coldness, constraint and a constant sense of disapproval at home, warmth, freedom, admiration and flattery abroad. I do not wonder that a creature wrought of such elements as made up the character of my wife should dislike her home and get out into the world and amid other associations as frequently as possible. I do not wonder that, not really loving her husband, she should be fonder of some men's society than of his, nor that, having neither prudence nor principle, she should act in such unbecoming ways as to provoke scandal.

I could not play the spy upon my wife. A sense of honor, of good faith with myself, prevented this. And yet I had reason to fear that in my absence from home during business-hours she received calls from gentlemen, or, it might be, went out with them riding or walking. A few times I had met her on one of the fashionable streets, where business happened to take me, and she always had an attendant. Once I saw her riding, but did not make out her companion. As she had not seen me, I did not question her on the subject.

I was becoming more unhappy every day. This partition wall, this widening gulf, must in time effect a complete separation. The beautiful temple I had builded must ere long fall into hopeless ruin, and what then? I shuddered often as this hard question struck upon my soul with a painful jar.

It was a warm October day, which, coming after a cold spell of weather, was an invitation to the open air.

"Shall we ride out this afternoon, Julia?" I said as we sat at the dinner-table.

"My head aches," she answered, in a dull voice.

"The ride may do it good," I suggested.

"No; riding never helps me when I have the headache. My remedy is to keep quiet."

I said no more. She had not spoken of a headache until I proposed riding. I thought of this at the time.

On coming home at six o'clock in the evening it was almost dark. I did not find my wife.

"Where is Mrs. Marion?" I asked of one of our servants.

"She hasn't returned yet," was answered.

"Where did she go?"

"Out riding."

"With whom?"

There was hesitation. I saw by the servant's manner that she did not think my wife had gone away in the right company.

"With Mr. Harbaugh," she said, rather falteringly, dropping her eyes from mine.

I turned from her quickly and went up stairs The shadows of approaching evil sometimes fall heavily upon us, but too late to serve as warnings. I felt night closing round me—a dark and starless night. After this could I receive my wife home again? Could I open the door and let her pass in over the threshold? These questions crowded themselves into my mind, and I was in too much confusion of thought to answer them clearly. Between my soul and her soul the gulf had so widened in an instant that henceforth we must dwell at an almost inconceivable distance from each other.

Blind as I had been during the long period that intervened before our marriage, weakly as I had taken purity and truth for granted, I yet held the marriage relation to be the holiest and most sacred of all relations. I therefore not only blamed my wife, but, faithful and true myself in thought as well as deed, my nature rose in antagonism and disgust against her. A sense of loathing crept into my soul as I sat and meditated. She had lied to me, feigning headache, and yet I was scarcely away from my home ere she accepted the companionship of a man without principle—one whom I had actually forbidden her to be seen with in public. Could I take her into my bosom as before? Could we ever walk side by side again, or dwell together in one house? I give you my state of mind—confused, distressed and without decision.

At our usual tea-hour Julia was still absent. New and alarming suggestions came into my thoughts. She had been weak, vain, imprudent, false to the spirit of her marriage vows, lacking in those virtuous instincts that are the beauty and crown of womanhood, but I had not believed her vile. I had felt that she was in danger, but dreamed not that in its worst form it was ready to sweep her away. The suspense of mind which I now suffered was agonizing.

"Shall I serve tea?" I started, and then repressed all signs of disturbance.

"Not yet. Something has detained Mrs. Marion. She'll be here very soon."

The servant went down stairs. I got up and walked the floor. Five, ten, twenty minutes, half an hour, and still Julia was absent. What was to be done? I stood still, trying to reach some conclusion—trying to decide upon some line of conduct. There came to my ears the sound of carriage wheels. I moved to the window, listening. It approached—seemed passing; no, the rattle stopped suddenly. The carriage was at my door. I drew back from the window and stood waiting. The bell was rung hard. The jangling noise startled me. I came out of the room where I had been sitting, and stood in the upper passage, while a servant went to the door. It was opened. I heard myself inquired for in a man's voice. The tones were familiar. It was our physician. I ran down stairs and met him as he stood in the vestibule. He took my hand and looked at me with troubled eyes.

"I have bad news for you," he said.

"What is it?" I asked, quickly, drawing him, by the hand I had taken, out of the vestibule toward the parlor door. He did not reply until we were in the parlor.

"An accident has happened," he then said.

"To my wife?"

"Yes. She was thrown from a vehicle, and has one arm broken. I fear there are internal injuries besides."

"Where is she?"

"At her aunt's."

"Why there? Why was she not brought home?"

"She was taken there, as I undetstand it, by her own request," replied the doctor.

"Where did the accident occur?"

"A mile from the city, on the Briartown road."

It would have been nearest for her to come directly home, and yet, at her own desire, she was taken to her aunt's!

"Have you seen her?" I asked.

"Yes. I was sent for the moment she arrived."

"Who called for you?" I put the question very abruptly.

"A Mr. Harbaugh." The doctor's voice betrayed his reluctance to pronounce the name. He then added, "Her arm has a compound fracture."

"And there are internal injuries, you think?"

"I fear so, but they may not be serious. When I left her she was more comfortable."

"You will visit her again to-night?" I said.

"Oh yes." The doctor arose. I did not seek to detain him, and he went away. I could see from his manner that he was not satisfied with my state of mind.

"What is the matter, sir?" Our two servants confronted me in the hall, putting this question, as I turned from the departing physician. "Is she much hurt? How did it happen?" they added before I was able to collect my thoughts to answer.

"Mrs. Marion was thrown from a carriage, and has an arm broken," I replied.

"Where is she?" was the next eagerly-put inquiry.

"At her aunt's."

"Indeed! And why didn't they bring her home?"

I did not answer the query, for any answer, save what I felt to be the true one, would have been subterfuge.

"I shall not want any tea," said I, passing the servants and going up stairs. I glanced back from the first landing. They were looking after me with a half-dazed, half-wondering air. I found myself panting, as I sat down to think, like one who had been pursued.

To think! When thought increased my pain and bewilderment. To think! If I could have ceased to think, to feel, to comprehend! There was no impulse prompting me to fly to the bedside of my injured wife. I was not attracted toward her, but repelled. I did not even feel pity for her bodily suffering, it seemed so light in comparison with the agony she had caused me to endure, with the sorrow and shame she was opening her heart to receive. The broken bone would knit in time, the bruised flesh heal, but there was no medicine for my heart. She might, and no doubt would, come out into the sunshine again, but I must dwell in perpetual shadow. I could not shut away the future and narrow down all considerations to the simple present, forgiving and forgetting everything because of an accident and its absorbing shock and suffering. It was not hardness in me, not want of feeling, but the too clear apprehension of all the sad things that were involved.

Deliberately, after a short interrogation of every changing state of mind, of every argument pro and con, of every consequence near and remote, I resolved not to visit my wife at her aunt's unless she sent for me. The decision looks hard, wrong, cruel, seen only from the outside, but it was not the dictate of either hardness or cruelty. Right or wrong, I believed the decision best. In fact, except through the humiliation of that true manhood which none can violate without self-hurt, it was impossible for me to follow my wife in what I felt to be her voluntary departure from the home of her husband. She had gone away, in a secret and clandestine manner, so far as I was concerned, with a person against whom I had spoken in the most decided way. A serious accident had betrayed the fact. Then, instead of having herself conveyed back to the home of her husband, she was taken, at her own instance, past his home, to that of the relative with whom she resided before marriage. You say, in her favor, to explain this last fact, that it was not so much against her that she preferred a removal to her aunt, in her injured, helpless condition, to being committed to the care of servants. Let it go in her favor, if you will. But it did not satisfy me. Why was I not sent for immediately? Why was I not informed of the accident until the doctor had been there and set the fractured bone, and then only through his courtesy? I was not a dolt, a blind child. I could see, I could feel, I could read, the meaning of things.

After deliberation, as I have said, I resolved not to visit my wife at her aunt's unless she sent for me, or in some plain way signified her desire to have me come. All the evening I waited at home for her messenger, but none appeared. In the morning I received a note from her aunt briefly stating the accident and asking to see me.

"There are reasons why, as things now stand, I cannot see you at your own house," I wrote back in answer. "Will you not call and see me? I will remain at home until ten o'clock. Come, if you please. I very much desire an interview."

Her aunt came, as requested. She was the sister of Julia's mother, was a handsome, middle-aged woman, was fond of dress and company, vain and superficial. I had never liked her. She passed for a widow, but common report had it that her husband was living somewhere at the South. This report afterward proved true, the husband appearing just in time to save a rich, weak old man from marrying her.

The aunt came. She was in great trouble, and volunteered to censure Julia for not going to her own house. I did not think the censure wholly sincere. In fact, I never put faith in her for anything. She was a fluent talker and protester of feeling. All her expressions were ardent and in the style superlative. It was meet for me to be on my guard, and so I was guarded. My reception of her was grave, my manner very serious.

"How is Julia this morning?" I asked, coldly.

"She is not in so much pain. It was a frightful affair! I wonder she had not been dashed to pieces!" And then she went into a wordy account of the accident. After she had talked herself out of breath, I said:

"It would have been nearer for her to come home. Why did she not do so?"

"Mr. Harbaugh—" She checked herself. I knitted my brows sternly.

"It was her own act. She went past her husband's home voluntarily," I said, "and I am not pleased, not satisfied, touching the motives by which she was influenced. All the circumstances taken into account, her conduct has a questionable look, and I ask for explanations. Why was I not sent for immediately on her arrival at your house? Why was I not sent for last evening?"

"Oh, the doctor said he would call here as he went home," interposed the aunt.

"The doctor!" I spoke with indignation. "I, her husband, could be notified informally through courtesy of the doctor as he returned homeward on his round of visits! Quite a diversion in my favor! I tell you, madam, this whole thing is out of the true order, and has a bad look! I am not satisfied with it as it now stands."

My visitor's face grew red suddenly, her mouth jerked and quivered, tears filled her eyes.

"Poor child!" she sobbed. "Hurt, suffering, distressed, and to have this added! It is cruel in you, Mr. Marion! If you really loved her—"

"Stop!" I said, with angry sternness. "I will have nothing of this! And let me warn you, madam, against the folly of lending any countenance to the wrong step my wife has taken. If you value her peace of mind, her good name, her future well-being, seek by all means in your power to draw her back to the right path, from which her feet have clearly diverged. There are two ways in life, one leading to honor and happiness, the other to shame and misery. She has been hesitating for some time at the point where these two ways diverge. I have observed it with fear and trembling. Alas for her! the wrong road has been chosen. If she goes onward, she parts from her husband, blights her good name, raises to her lips a cup the wine whereof is bitter. By all that is good and holy, lead her back, lead her back!"

I was strongly excited, spoke almost vehemently and with no guarded choice of words. The aunt was offended, not drawn to my side. Her pride took flame. The evil in her went over to the side of her beautiful niece. I was unreasonable, a brute, a tyrant, cruel. She said this in plain words, with hot cheeks and flashing eyes.

"I warn you, madam!" My answer was stern and threatening. "If you trifle with a solemn issue like this, you are throwing happiness like chaff to the winds. You see that I am deeply moved, sadly in earnest—that to me, think as you may, this matter is one of infinite concern. I know just where I stand, what I can yield and what I can withhold, what I can and what I cannot do, what I have to suffer if the worst comes to the worst. Take, madam, this into account. I am as inflexible as iron when my course is once taken. And in this thing I have taken my course. If Julia ever sees me at your house, she must send for me, and I must be sure that she has sent!"

The word I had not at first intended speaking

was beyond recall. The hard decision, not clearly made in my own judgment, was precipitated under the power of excitement, and so fixed in a strong will. Having spoken, I would endure.

I saw by the aunt's face that she was not on my side—that no good was to be expected from her influence.

"I will report your ultimatum," she said, stiffly, then adding a stately "Good-morning!" withdrew.

When alone, I sat down, with an effort to calm my feelings, and to look at the situation in its new and perilous aspect—to examine my relation to my wife, and to determine whether I was right or wrong in the line of conduct to which I had committed myself. As I grew calmer, I did not see quite so clearly the wisdom or prudence of the course I had declared. It was an "ultimatum," as Julia's aunt had said, and "ultimatums" are not always safe things. "But it shall abide!" I confirmed the decision mentally, clenching my nervous fingers until the nails hurt the sensitive palms.

In kind, gentle and yielding natures we often find an element of inflexibility that comes suddenly into force, changing the pliant willows of character into unbending oak. I had been kind, gentle and yielding: naturally my disposition leans to this side; but I was so no longer toward my weak, erring wife. For months I had been gradually coming to a nearer and nearer view of her true quality of soul, and the more disguises my hands removed, the less beautiful she appeared, the less pure, true, loving, until I found a mean deformity that disgusted, instead of that womanly truth, tenderness, sweetness and beauty which I had so worshiped, but only, as it proved, in the unsubstantial ideal.

I was changed even in my own eyes. I hardly knew the kind-feeling, gently-deferring man of former times to be the inflexible one of to-day. This almost death-grapple with a fate, of all fates, for a man of my interior constitution, the most fearful to contemplate, had turned the fibres of my soul into brass, and given it strength for any conflict. It seemed as if I had grown older in will, power of thought and strength to bear by twenty years in a day.

"We shall see what will come of this!" So I said in a self-sustaining spirit as I went out and took my steps business-ward. I did not return home until evening. Had my wife come to better reason? Had she sent for me, as love and duty would prompt, when she understood the peculiar view I had taken of her conduct? My mind was in suspense with these questions. I grew eager and oppressed with heavier heart-beats as I came near home. But no message awaited me.

"Has any word been left?" I asked of a servant.

She shook her head and said no.

"A letter?"

"None."

I passed her, and went up to the desolate rooms that mocked me with a chilly silence. I sat down in the chambers which had been dedicated to purity and abiding love—chambers where once everything had worn a halo of golden light, caught as it seemed from the inner heavens, and felt my heart shudder as in a cold, blank, dreary void. "But the end is not yet!" I said, aloud, uttering an inner conviction that flashed into light as if a spirit had spoken in the adytum of my soul. "The end is not yet."

Early in the evening I had a call from the doctor. His manner, as we met, was serious and constrained.

"How is my wife?" I asked, repressing all signs of interest.

"Not so well. She has considerable fever, and pain in the fractured arm."

I dropped my eyes from his intent gaze, and made no farther inquiry about Julia. I understood why he had called, and was neither pleased nor displeased at his intrusion. He was a sincere, right-meaning man, and therefore I could hear him even on a subject the most sacred to myself without being offended.

"I was deeply pained, Mr. Marion," he said, after a pause, "to learn, on visiting your wife this afternoon, that you had not seen her since the accident."

I looked at him while he was speaking, and then, without answering, dropped my eyes again. There was nothing in my manner that was meant to repel him, nor was there invitation to proceed. He was silent for a little while, then resumed:

"Too much is involved to let feeling rule your conduct. There are certain steps in life which, once taken, lead away from happiness, and are never retraced. It is because I fear you are about venturing these steps that I have called on you to-night. Will you confer with me as with a true friend?"

I gave him my hand spontaneously. I said, "You are a true man, and honorable, doctor! Your motive in calling has my highest respect. Speak without hesitation; I will listen and weigh your words."

He reflected, as if in doubt where to begin the work of intervention.

"I do not like your wife's aunt. She is not, in my estimation, either a wise or a prudent woman."

"Just my own opinion," I answered.

"Then can you think it safe to leave Mrs. Marion for even a little while, as things now are, entirely under her aunt's influence?"

I had no brief response to this question that could satisfy the doctor, and so did not attempt to meet the interrogation in any direct form. I only said:

"There are evils which cannot be escaped. Once in motion, they are as irresistible as the down-rushing avalanche. When truth and honor are cast upon the winds, where are we to reap the harvest of virtue and happiness? I ask myself this solemn question, and hearken in vain for the answer. It does not come, and I sit in the shadow of a great fear that appalls and paralyzes me."

This was so vague that the doctor was thrown at fault. He came back, however, to the subject he wished to impress on my mind.

"It is a great pity that she was ever taken to her aunt's," he said.

"The act was her own," I answered.

"Perhaps not entirely her own," remarked the doctor.

I understood him. His words kindled a fire in my heart—a great fire of indignation that burned up the last filament of love. Not her own act! Whose then? By what influence was she moved to go past the home of her husband? The doctor's suggestion was unfortunate. It took my thought into the very core, the rotten core, of my dishonor and her shame. Better that I should have considered the act wholly hers than as instigated by this man Harbaugh. He influence my wife to avoid her husband's home! He, whom I loathed as unprincipled and impure, whose very touch would have made me shudder as if it were a snake's touch!

"So much the worse, doctor—so much the

worse!" I answered, all my external calmness giving way. "This makes the sin against her husband deeper and more unpardonable—this gives the measure of her alienation. You have touched me in the tenderest place!"

"There are considerations of prudence," he said, appealing to my reason, "that no man should disregard. Admit that your wife is in danger. Then is it not your duty to spring at once to the point of protection and rescue?"

My wife in danger! Of what? I answered the question to myself, and grew hard as iron.

"The enemy to her peace and mine dwells in her own heart," I replied. "She must of her own will and effort cast out the demon. If not, the worst comes. While the demon remains I am thrust to the outside, and have no power to protect or defend."

The doctor was perplexed by the case. He saw it but obscurely, yet comprehended enough to understand the calamity that hung suspended like a sharp sword above our heads. He would save us, but the power of rescue was not in his hands. I was not to be influenced by any mere outside considerations, by worldly prudence, by fear of opinion, by dread of pain. Pain! there was no pain possible beyond the present anguish, no humiliation of soul deeper than what I then experienced, in that my wife—that being I had so loved as the embodiment of all that was pure, sweet, chaste, tender, loving—should turn in spirit from me and find congenial companionship with one whose very breath must poison a virtuous woman's soul! Herein lay the impediment: I felt her to be unworthy.

"She went from me of her own election"—I spoke resolutely—"and until she repents of this act and gives me true signs of repentance, I shall not go to her. When she is able to return she will find the door open. If she enter, well; if not, the responsibility of all that follows rests alone with her. The matter is one of the gravest moment, and I shall treat it gravely. If she prefer other men's society to mine, we cannot live together as man and wife. The thing, to one of my feelings, is simply impossible. Another's duty might lie in another direction, but mine does not. Marriage, in my regard, is too holy for this kind of profanation. I speak plainly, doctor, and in a degree of confidence, that you may understand my position in this painful affair. If you can help my wife to see that she is standing on the brink of a precipice, she may be frightened and move back. Disgrace may be avoided. But it is too late to restore peace of mind."

He left me with a shadow of trouble on his fine countenance. He was my friend, and desired to save me from an impending calamity, but could not perceive the way.

Days went by, and I held to my resolution. I neither visited my wife nor sent to inquire after her.

"She has turned herself from me," I said, "and she must turn to me again. The first act was hers, and the second must be hers also. If she have any love for me, she will turn again; if not, we dwell for ever apart."

She did not turn to me. Days were added to days, until the period of separation was lengthened to weeks. Except for an occasional meeting with the doctor, I should have remained as ignorant of her condition as if an ocean rolled between us. From him I learned that she was safely recovering from the effects of her injury. Concerning her state of mind I asked nothing, and he ventured no communication. I understood from his reserved manner and the real concern which was not hidden that her mental condition was not satisfactory. He had, it was plain, seen enough to satisfy him that she did not possess the qualities which go to make the true wife, and in the delicate and doubtful position she occupied was not exhibiting either a right spirit or right conduct. So much I inferred, right or wrong, and it helped to sustain me in the course I had adopted.

The weeks lengthened into months. Julia made no sign, and I waited on. The anguish which I had felt in the beginning was giving place to a dull aching of the heart. I had the strength to bear this internal pain without much change in exterior. I kept my life calm at the surface, and intermitted nothing in business.

One day, nearly three months after the unhappy event described, as I was returning to my desolate home late in the afternoon, a carriage drove rapidly past me. I lifted my eyes from the pavement in time to see Julia sitting beside Mr. Harbaugh. She did not show any shrinking or shame, but looked at me coldly and placidly. Exteriorly, I was as calm as my wife. Inwardly, the last wild struggle was begun. It was brief. That evening I gave my servants notice that I should not want them after the week's close. On the next day I directed an auctioneer to make an inventory of my furniture, preparatory to a sale.

My last and hardest trial came. Up to this time Julia had sent for none of her clothing, and I had not seen it best to supply her, voluntarily, with any portion of her wardrobe. But now that I was going to destroy the fair home I had builded for love to dwell in because there was no love, it was but fitting that what was hers, even to the minutest thing, should be formally transferred. I shrank from the task, but it had to be done. At first, the articles, as I looked at and touched them, gave a sense of disgust, as if associated with something impure. But this passed, and I soon found my eyes full of tears, my hands trembling and my heart melting with softness.

In her jewel-case was her miniature. She had given it to me before our marriage. The clear, sweet eyes looked up into mine from the setting of pearls with which I had had it encircled—looked up into mine tenderly, lovingly, full of all pure suggestions, drawing my soul with an intense attraction.

"So sweet, so beautiful, so like an angel, and yet so unworthy," I said, putting the pictured face aside with a quiet movement that was only a veil to the agitation within. But I could not shut the image from my sight. The lovely countenance was still before me in all its radiance, the eyes were resting peacefully, innocently, tenderly, in mine, and holding me by a spell. I must break this spell, it was a false charm, luring only to disappointment. So pushing aside the image, I called back Julia's face as I had seen it on that day—cold, shameless, almost taunting. By this I had power over myself once more. Through the mingling of indignation and disgust with pain, I found strength of will to go on with the work in which I was engaged.

I did not venture to look at the miniature again. It was laid aside in the jewel-case with many souvenirs of love that I had bestowed upon my wife. It was hard to let some of these go from me, because they had meant so much in the giving. But the question of retaining any of them had only brief debate. I saw that it was best to keep nothing, for the smallest thing would only be a painful reminder.

It was, perhaps, well that in the beginning of

this sad evening's work I came so early upon the miniature. Other things had less power to disturb me. The gold-tipped ivory fan I had bought for her; the costly laces; the India shawl; the silver card-case; the rich dresses in which she had looked so entrancingly beautiful,—one after the other was taken from drawer and wardrobe, and consigned to trunks and boxes, with all things to which she had any personal claim. I moved through these tasks in a dull, heavy way, more like an automaton than a sensitive being. I seemed to myself like a man grinding in a dark prison-house, with chest constricted for lack of air. At last it was over. Everything to which Julia had the smallest claim was assigned to her, the trunks locked, and the boxes closed with nail and hammer. This was as a coping to the wall of separation which had for months been steadily rising between us.

I cannot find language that will convey to you any just idea of what I suffered that night. I did not falter for a moment—never once looked back—never questioned as to the right or wrong of what I was doing. If Julia had come to me, in the midst of that unhappy work, tearful, repentant and asking to be forgiven, I could not have received her gladly. I would have received her in all kindness, yet soberly and sorrowfully, as one not worthy of my love. I would have done all in my power to make her life pleasant and peaceful—would have been true to her, just to her, patient and kind. But as for love, that would have been impossible, because my soul could not find in her soul the quality for which it sought. As to what the future might give under the reforming and re-creating power of a new life, all was of course in the future. I speak only of that present. But she did not return to me.

On the next day I sent Julia everything to which she had a personal right, but without communication of any description. On the day following I saw her riding out with Mr. Harbaugh.

"No heart, no conscience, no shame!" I said to myself, bitterly, as I recognized her. Yet mingled with this bitterness was a sense of relief, for her acts justified my course and made it plain that separation was inevitable.

Many scandals were soon abroad, of which intrusive friends gave me intimations. The aunt told her story, seriously to my injury. I was represented as a jealous domestic tyrant whose abuse finally reached to such a climax of outrage that my wife was compelled to leave me. Too sad and heart-sick to care about denying anything, I let all pass without an explanatory sentence or a word of vindication. "Let me suffer what I may," I said to myself, "she must always have the worst of it."

Into the gay world, young, beautiful, fascinating, she went as before, while I shrank from society and lived almost alone. Right-thinking people lose respect for a man who is seen often in public with a woman living separate from her husband, especially if the circumstances attendant on the separation have given rise to scandals, as in this case. The consequence was that men who felt that they had a good reputation to sustain avoided the society of my wife, and the same result followed with ladies who were duly careful in regard to the kind of people who were invited to their social entertainments. In consequence, the circle in which my wife moved gradually narrowed itself, and she fell more exclusively into the company of a class of men and women who represent a low standard of honor and virtue. With these she was in high favor, her beauty her wit and her vivacious spirits throwing a charm around her wherever she appeared.

A year dragged heavily away. During the period I saw Julia a few times on the street, a few times in public assemblies and a few times driving out, always in company with some male attendant; only twice with Mr. Harbaugh. That individual, for all his lack of principle, had his own reasons for desiring to stand fair with right-minded people, and so prudently dropped my wife's company when the separation from her husband made her notorious. I did not always know the men I saw with her, and never inquired about them. Those I did know were not of unblemished reputation.

At the end of a year I was notified that an application for divorce had been made. I did not employ counsel, nor in any manner respond to the notice. A time for hearing the case was appointed. It was heard and decided on the evidence produced, which was made to bear unfavorably on me. The divorce was granted, with alimony. I was ordered to pay her the sum of twelve hundred dollars a year, dating from the time of separation, so long as she refrained from marriage.

I was not displeased or annoyed at the allowance of alimony. If she had made application to me for money, even in liberal amounts, I would have met the application favorably. Legally she was my wife, and all legal claims on me for her support I was willing to pay. But I did not wish to communicate with her, or make what might seem overtures. So I had held myself passive. The award of alimony met my state of mind, and was coincident with my view of our relation. I held to the word of Scripture, and did not believe that any civil authority had power to break the bond of marriage. For myself, while she lived, I could not, except at peril of my soul, contract another marriage, and I had resolved to stand to my integrity.

For six months only was the allowance paid. I took up a newspaper one morning, and as I was opening it my eyes fell upon her name. It was in the marriage department. An ardent young Southerner had met her, and in the first warmth of admiration laid his heart and fortune at her feet, and she did not hesitate about accepting the offer.

"Better this than worse," I said to myself, sighing deeply, for it made my heart feel very heavy. She went away, and I saw her but once more. Two years afterward I read in an extract from a Southern paper that her husband had been shot in a duel with a man whom he had challenged for alleged improper familiarity with his wife, and a year later it came to my knowledge that she had married the murderer of her husband.

One incident more, and I will end this sad history. It was a little over ten years later. My health had given way through too close application to business, and I was spending a couple of weeks at the seashore. The season being at its height, there were arrivals and departures every day, and a constant succession of new visitors. One morning, on taking my seat at the table, I found myself opposite a little girl whose face startled me with its faultless beauty and strange familiarity. She was Julia's miniature image! Her companion was a tall, sallow, dark-eyed, unhappy-looking man, every line of whose countenance gave token of self-indulgence and unbridled passion. Toward the little girl I noticed that he bore himself with a kindness and gentleness of manner that only a fond father could manifest. I only toyed with my food on that morning. Appetite left me with the recognition of this child as Julia's daughter. I had no question touching the fact. Her husband and child were before me, but where was she? Dead, or living separate?

My fixed stare at the child attracted her notice; observing this, I turned my gaze away. When I looked again the sombre black eyes of her father were scanning my countenance. There was an evil look in them, a cold, cruel antagonism, a lurking ill-nature, a serpent-like instinct to wound. I dropped my eyes away from his. There was a kind of dagger-thrust in them that hurt me. But to the child's face I turned again and again. More and more perfect grew its likeness to Julia's. I was deeply disturbed. Time had laid a smooth surface over my heart, but it was broken into ripples and fragments in a moment. Was Julia in the house? Should I meet her face to face? The thought had power to disturb me seriously. I felt that I could not stand in her presence without betrayal of feeling.

For the next two hours I moved about the parlors, piazzas and grounds of the hotel in an uneasy, expectant state of mind. Several times

I encountered the child, accompanied by a colored servant-woman. Her beauty was faultless, but it was marred by self-will, fretfulness and ill-nature toward the servant, on whom she exercised various petty tyrannies. She was possessed of an unquiet, dissatisfied spirit, was always seeking for new pleasures, but never finding. Twice I saw her lift her hand and strike the servant in passion. Each time the blow hurt me as if I had been struck over a half-healed and still sensitive wound.

About ten o'clock the city morning papers came in. I had retired to one of the parlors, which happened to be nearly deserted, and was unfolding my newspaper, when there came in, through the door opposite to where I was sitting, the tall, dark, gaunt man who sat opposite me at breakfast. Leaning heavily on his arm with both hands, one clasped within the other, was a showily-dressed woman whose thin, sallow face and sunken orbits marked her as a wasted and wasting invalid. But there was a gleam in her eyes and a dullness of expression in her countenance that told a sadder story still.

They moved slowly down the long apartment,

the man always a step in advance, and the woman dragging, as it were, weakly after him. His countenance expressed little interest in and no tenderness for his companion. Plainly, she was a care and a burden. Forward they came, nearing the place where I sat. On first seeing them I had raised my open newspaper, so as to more than half conceal my face, and was looking at them over the top. As they stood fronting me I let the newspaper fall and looked full at them. The act was without a motive on my part—done without conscious volition. Slowly, and without interest of manner, the woman lifted her eyes and looked at me. In an instant all was changed. Electric excitement leaped along every nerve. Out of the leaden dullness of her face flashed the glow of startled feeling. Her hands were withdrawn from the man's arm, clasped and reached forward in a wild, theatric way. Her lips drew apart; her eyes, widely distended and fearful to look upon, burned into mine. Surprise, fear, terror, swept alternately over her countenance. Then a low, sad, heart-searching cry or wail broke from her lips. She would have fallen had not the man caught her in his arms. I saw her eyes close and her face grow ashen, but I did not move. I shrank from touching her. There were others in the room, and two or three of them came to the man's assistance. The woman was by this time unconscious. They wished to lay her on a sofa, but the man said, "No, to her own room." And so they bore her away, and I sat immovable.

"Can I have a word with you, sir?" Something over two hours had elapsed. My trunk was packed, and I was turning from the office after having paid my bill. The tones were severe, almost threatening, the sinister eyes, into which I looked calmly, full of accusation and cruelty. The tall, dark Southerner confronted me with a scowl.

"Certainly, if you desire it," I answered, and we walked together out of the office and along one of the piazzas until we reached a point where we were entirely alone. The man pointed, in a kind of peremptory way, to a chair, which I took. He sat down in front of me. His manner was excited, and to some extent offensive. But I was never calmer in my life.

"Who are you?" he demanded.

"Is that woman your wife?" My response was in this interrogation.

"Yes, sir! She is my wife!" He was emphatic.

"And the child I saw with her this morning is her child?"

"Yes, and my child," he answered.

My coolness was subduing him. His manner changed visibly.

"But who are you? That is the question I wish to have answered." This time his manner was without offence.

"Pardon me," I said, "for delaying an answer. First, let me inquire how long your wife has been in such poor health, and how long it has been since her mind broke down."

I saw in him a brief struggle with angry impatience, which he overcame, and replied,

"Her health broke down a year ago, and her mind has been failing ever since."

"May I ask the cause?"

This was pressing him too far. His eyes flashed. Almost fiercely he answered, "No!"

There followed a pause, in which we sat looking at each other. I watched his face until I saw the angry wave subsiding. Then I said:

"You ask who I am. Do you still desire an answer?"

"That is the very thing I want. Speak! Who are you?"

"Once"—I lowered my voice to keep it steady—"Once I was the husband of your wife."

He started up as if an adder had stung him. His sallow face changed to a dull white, and then grew darkly crimson with the returning flood. A little while he stood like one in a labyrinth of thought, blank surprise taking the place on his countenance of imperious demand. A few moments more and he left me without a word or a sign.

An hour later and I was on my way back to the city. A few days afterward I read in a gossiping letter from the seashore about the wife of a Southern gentleman who had become so violently insane as to make her removal to an asylum necessary. Certain particular statements in this letter left me in no doubt touching the person to whom reference had been made. It was Julia!

My uncle paused and sat silent and sober for a considerable time. He then resumed:

"I should not have thus uncovered the past

had not the motive been strong. Julia had a daughter beautiful as herself—the one I saw as a child at the seashore. That daughter has grown to womanhood. She is still beautiful—beautiful as was her mother at her age—but her beauty may not be trusted. I have seen her. I have observed her closely. Neither mother nor father has given her that hereditary basis of character to which a true man may conjoin himself. Her name is Florence Ware!"

If I had been insane enough to marry my beauty after this, I would have deserved disappointment and misery. But my uncle's experience was a sufficient warning, and I scarcely deemed it prudent to venture on an experiment that threatened a life-long disaster.

XXI.

JOHN ARMOR'S SCARE.

MAN would never snap me up after that fashion more than once," said Miss Blair, sharply, as Mr. Armor left the breakfast-room and she saw the tears coming into Mrs. Armor's eyes. "What right had John to speak to you so?"

The young wife's lips quivered, and a tear or two dropped over her cheeks.

"Unless you're the spiritless thing I never dreamed you were, Jenny Armor," added Miss Blair, warming with indignation, "you'll teach John the lesson he needs to learn, and that at once. The sooner you make him understand that in marrying you did not give yourself over to a master, the better for you both."

Now, quick-tempered, good-hearted John Armor felt sorry for his unguarded speech the moment it passed his lips, and ashamed of having spoken unkindly to his wife before a third person. As he was closing the door he heard the first indignant sentence uttered by Miss Blair, and pausing with the door ajar, got the benefit of her farther utterances.

Anger, regret and mortification were the disturbing elements that made our young husband feel anything but comfortable as he left the house.

The hardest thing in the world for some people is to acknowledge themselves in the wrong, and of this class was John Armor. He might have gone back and made it all up with Jenny, after a little struggle with his pride, if she had been alone, but to confess his fault before Miss Blair was not to be thought of for a moment. So he went off to his store feeling mean, miserable and angry by turns.

"Teach me a lesson!" dropped from his lips as he strode along. The accuser and self-justifier was at his ear trying to work evil between him and his Jenny.

"Teach me a lesson! She had best not try any experiments of that sort."

Then his good angel got audience and said: "Is this the gentle husband, the strong, true man, who was to love and cherish? Who gave you the right to speak unkindly?—to rebuke and reprove?"

But the evil counselor made angry speech, saying: "Has a man no right to complain when met with discomfort in consequence of his wife's neglect? If he toil early and late while she sits in ease at home, shall he not dare to speak a word of remonstrance, though everything goes wrong? There may be spiritless husbands who will meekly submit, but John Armor is not one of them!"

And now, coming, it seemed, from a distance, far inward or upward, sounded a gentle but pleading voice, and it said:

"This is not well, John Armor."

And at the words a figure grew into distinctness in his mind. He saw his Jenny—his true and pure and loving young wife—sitting with bowed head and sorrowful face and wet eyes, the picture of suffering, and all because of his harsh, unkindly speech.

Almost instantly this picture faded, and a new one grew out of the confused images that remained. The form of Jenny became distinct once more, but her attitude and countenance were changed. She stood erect, with a cold, unloving face, and looked into his eyes with angry defiance, and at the same time out of his memory into his thoughts came these words:

> "A woman moved is like a fountain troubled;
> Dark, unseemly, thick, bereft of beauty."

But his better angel pressed near again, and turning another leaf, brought out from his memory into his thought these lines:

> "Oh, woman! in our hours of ease
> Uncertain, coy and hard to please:
> When pain and anguish wring the brow,
> A ministering angel thou!"

And then another page of memory was turned, on which a never-to-be-erased picture was painted in strongest outlines and deepest colors—the picture of a sick bed, and a dear, loving, self-denying, patient, ministering angel bending over it.

"John Armor," he exclaimed, half aloud, as this picture held him like the spell of a magician, "you are a wretch to hurt that loving heart!"

The accuser and self-justifier—the evil spirit that loved only to work alienation and give pain to human hearts—pressed in again and tried to obscure the picture, but in vain. John Armor held to his better feelings, and repented of his unkindness. Still, the words of Miss Blair were a power in the hands of the evil spirit, who kept perpetually thrusting them in unguarded moments into the thoughts of John Armor.

"John is not my master," answered Jenny Armor, with a flash in her wet eyes as she heard her husband shut the street door with a heavy jar.

"Of course he is not, and the sooner he is made conscious of the fact, the better for you both, as I have said. No man has a right to speak to his wife in the way he spoke to you just now. If you bear it tamely, he will be master and you slave: there will be a husband and wife only in name."

A hard, half-angry expression grew slowly in the face of Jenny Armor. She did not answer, but an evil counselor within was seconding the evil counselor without. She began writing bitter things on the tablet of thought against her repentant husband.

"Better grapple with the enemy now while

you are young and strong and free," said the false friend.

"My enemy!" replied Jenny, turning quickly upon Miss Blair. The word startled her. "My enemy!"

"Yes, your enemy. I call things by the right name. Is the man or woman who seeks to make you a slave a friend or an enemy?"

"John Armor my enemy!" A dazed kind of look came into Jenny's face. It flushed and paled by turns, then grew fiery red, while flashes leaped from her eyes.

"Nancy Blair!"—Jenny's voice trembled with suppressed feeling—"this has gone far enough."

"Oh, just as you please!" answered Miss Blair, in a tone that was meant to annoy. "You are like the rest of them;" and she tossed her head with as much contempt of manner as she felt it safe to assume. "John will come home at dinner-time and snub you as he did this morning, and you will drop a tear meekly and bear it all with wifely submission. It is woman's lot. Oh dear! Don't I wish, sometimes, that I had one of these top-lofty fellows to deal with! Wouldn't I take him down!"

Jenny kept silent. She felt that she was in dangerous company—that a person like Miss Blair, if permitted to influence her, would lead her into trouble.

Miss Blair tried to pursue the subject, but Jenny turned it aside, and at last resolutely ignored it. Miss Blair was disgusted with her friend, and went home early in the day, much to Jenny's relief of mind.

"Have you heard about the trouble between Carman and his wife?" said a friend of John Armor that morning.

"No. What is it?" asked the latter.

"She was a Miss Lewis."

"Yes; I knew her very well. A beautiful, spirited girl."

"High-strung, as we say. Well, her husband undertook to be a little stiff on the marital prerogative question, assumed the rôle of head and master of the household, and set himself to fault-finding when things were not just to his fancy. One morning—so the story goes—he was particularly sharp on his wife at the breakfast-table in presence of a lady visitor, one of that class not greatly troubled with the man-fearing, man-pleasing spirit. After he had gone away, this lady—so the story continues—took occasion to animadvert pretty strongly on the tyranny of husbands, and the duty of wives to protect themselves against their oppressions and exactions, and succeeded in so exasperating Mrs. Carman that in a fit of blind passion she left her home and has not since returned."

"A most unfortunate affair," said Armor as a low shiver of concern went down to his heart. "A meddlesome, mischief-making woman like that ought to be hung!"

"Hanging is rather severe," answered the friend, smiling at Armor's almost savage warmth.

The young man's peace of mind was gone. How nearly parallel were the cases! He had been sharp on his wife at breakfast-time, and in presence of a visitor, and this visitor had, as he knew, advised Jenny to set herself against him, to teach him a lesson. What if, in a moment of anger, she had gone off as Mrs. Carman had done? The thought stunned him. He was filled with pain, alarm and anxiety.

"If she has done this, it will be the saddest day in her life and mine," he said to himself, a bitter realization of the truth of what he uttered in his heart. He was proud and not given to concession. For a crisis in life like this he was peculiarily unfitted. There was nothing so hard for him as to acknowledge a wrong. He could render sevenfold of reparation if he might withhold confession. Feeling how impossible it would be for him to go after and seek a reconciliation with Jenny if she should try the mad experiment of going away, he saw that such a step on her part would be the shipwreck of happiness to both.

Slowly the hours went by. It seemed to John Armor as if the time for going to dinner would never come. A quarter of an hour earlier than usual he left his store and took his way homeward. How still the house seemed as he entered! A shadow of evil portent fell upon him as he opened the door of their cozy sitting-room and found no one there. Everything was in order, not a book nor a chair out of place, nothing to show that Jenny had used the room that morning. He stood still, hearkening, but only the strong, heavy beat of his heart was audible in his ears.

With quick steps he went over to the chamber. Jenny was not there! He did not call her. He shrunk in strange dread and reluctance from that. To send her name into the oppressive stillness and get back only an echo was more than he felt that he could bear.

"Where is Mrs. Armor?" he asked. He had gone down to the dining-room and spoke to a servant who was setting the table.

The girl started as she looked into his scared face.

"Isn't she in her room?" she inquired.

"No."

"Nor in the sitting-room?"

"No."

The girl's face now reflected the anxious expression that Armor was not able to conceal. But suddenly he saw it change, and a queer smile dimple about the corners of her mouth. At the same moment a hand was laid on his arm. Turning quickly, he looked into the bright, loving eyes and smiling face of Jenny.

"Oh, darling!" he exclaimed, with a tenderness and fervor that was like an old love-passage, and he kissed her half wildly, not heeding the presence of a servant.

There were no explanations. John's pride would not let him make confession of all he had heard, thought and suffered, but the lesson he had received needed not to be learned over again.

Miss Blair would have wrought an evil work between Jenny and her husband if she could have done so, but instead of an agent of evil she had been made an instrument of good.

It was a long time before John Armor got well over the scare of that day, and its memory is a perpetual restraint on his quick temper and readiness for overbearing speech.

XXII.

NOBODY BUT JOHN.

OME one is coming," said I as the click of the shutting gate fell on my ears, and I looked at Maggy's soiled, untidy dress and tumbled hair.

Maggy started, and glanced hastily from the window, then sat down again in a careless way, remarking, as she did so:

"It's nobody but John."

Nobody but John! And who do you think that nobody was? Only her husband.

Nobody but John!

A few moments afterward John Fairburn came intc the room where we were sitting, and gave me one of his frank, cordial greetings. I had known him for many years, and long before his marriage. I noticed that he gave an annoyed glance at his wife, but did not speak to her. The meaning of this annoyance and indifference was plain to me, for John had come of a neat and tidy family. His mother's housekeeping had always been notable. She was poor, but as "time and water are to be had for nothing"—this was one of her sayings—she always managed to have things about clean and orderly.

Maggy Lee had a pretty face, bright eyes and charming little ways that were very taking with the young men, and so was quite a belle before she got out of her teens. She had a knack of fixing her ribbons, or tying her scarf, or arranging her hair, shawl or dress in a way to give grace and charm to her person. None but her most intimate friends knew of the untidiness that pervaded her room and person when at home and away from common observation.

Poor John Fairburn was taken in when he married Maggy Lee. He thought that he was getting the tidiest, neatest, sweetest and most orderly girl in town, but discovered too soon that he was united to a careless slattern. She would dress for other people's eyes because she had a natural love of admiration, but at home and for her husband she put on any old dud, and went looking often "like the Old Scratch," as the saying is.

On the particular occasion of which I am speaking—it was after she and John had been married over a year—her appearance was almost disgusting. She did not have on even a morning-dress, only a faded and tumbled chintz sack above a soiled skirt, no collar, slippers down at the heels and dirty stockings. Her hair looked like a hurrah's nest, if any one knows what that is. I don't, but I suppose it is the perfection of disorder. No one could love such a looking creature. That was simply impossible.

"Nobody but John!" I looked at the bright, handsome young man, and wondered. He ate his dinner almost in silence, and then went back to his work. I had never seen him so moody.

"What's come over John?" I asked as he went out.

"Oh, I don't know!" his wife answered. "Something wrong at the shop, I suppose. He's had trouble with one of the men. He's foreman, you know."

"Are you sure it's only that?" I asked, looking serious.

"That, or something about his work. There's nothing else to worry him."

I was silent for a while, debating with myself whether good or harm would come of a little plain talk with John's wife. She was rather quick-tempered, I knew, and easy to take offence. At last I ventured the remark:

"Maybe things are not just to his liking at home?"

"At home!" Maggy turned on me with a flash of surprise in her face. "What do you mean?"

"Men like beauty and taste and neatness in their wives as well as in their sweethearts," I said.

The crimson mounted to her hair. At the same moment I saw her glance at a looking-glass that hung opposite to her on the wall. She sat very still, yet with a startled look in her eyes, until the flush faded and her face became almost pale.

"Maggy," said I, rising and drawing my arm around her, "come up stairs. I have something very serious to say to you."

We walked from the little dining-room and up to her chamber in silence. I then said,

"Maggy, I want to tell you about a dear friend of mine who made shipwreck of happi ness and life. It is a sad story, but I am sure it will interest you deeply. She was my cousin, and her name was—"

Maggy bent forward, listening attentively. "What?" she asked as I hesitated on the name.

"Helen."

"Not Helen White, who married John Harding, and was afterward deserted by her husband?"

"Yes, my poor dear cousin Helen. It is of her I am going to tell you."

"I never knew why her husband went off as he did," said Maggy. "Some said he was to blame, and some put all the fault on her. How was it?"

"Both were to blame, but she most," I replied. "John Harding was, like your husband, one of the neatest and most orderly of men. Anything untidy in his home or in the person of his wife annoyed and often put him out of humor, but he did not, as he should have done, speak plainly to his wife, and let her see exactly how he felt and in what he would like a change. If he had done so, Helen would have tried—as every good wife should—to conform herself more to his tastes and wishes. But he was a silent, moody sort of a man when things did not go just to suit him, and instead of speaking out plainly, brooded over Helen's faults and worried himself into fits of ill-humor, and what was worse than all, grew at length indifferent to his home and wife, and sought pleasanter surroundings and more attractive company abroad.

"Every man thus estranged from his home is in danger, and Harding was no exception to the rule. Temptation lay about his feet, and that commonest temptation of all, the elegantly fitted up billiard and drinking saloon.

"They had been married just about as long as you and John have been when the sad catastrophe of their lives took place. I had called to spend the day with Helen, and found her in her usual condition of personal untidiness and disorder. When her husband came home at dinner-time I noticed with painful concern that he had been drinking—not very freely, but just enough to show itself in captious ill-humor. Helen had not dressed for dinner, but presented herself at the table without even a clean collar, and with an old faded shawl drawn about her shoulders. She looked anything but attractive.

"I saw her husband's eyes glance toward her across the table with an expression that chilled me. It was a hard, angry, determined expression. He was scarcely civil to me, and snapped his wife sharply two or three times during the meal. At its close he left the table without a word, and went up stairs.

"'What's the matter with John?' I asked.

"'Dear above knows!' replied Helen. 'He's been acting queer for a good while. I can't imagine what's come over him.'

"'Does he come home in this way often?' I asked.

"'Yes, he's moody and disagreeable as he can be most of the time. I'm getting dreadfully worried about it.'

"As we talked we heard John moving about with heavy footfalls in the rooms above. Presently he came down, and stood for a little while in the hall at the foot of the stairs, as if in hesitation. Then he went to the street door, passed out and shut it hard after him.

"Helen caught her breath with a start, and turned a little pale.

"'What's the matter?' I asked, seeing the strangeness of her look.

"'I don't know,' she replied, in a choking voice, laying her hand at the same time on her breast, 'but I feel as if something dreadful were going to happen.'

"She got up from the table, and I drew my arm around her. I too felt a sudden depression of spirits. We went slowly up to her chamber, where we spent the afternoon, and I then took upon myself the office of a friend, and talked seriously to my cousin about her neglect of personal neatness, hinting that the cause of her husband's estrangement from his home and altered manner toward herself might all spring from this cause. She was a little angry with me at first, but I pressed the subject home with a tender seriousness that did the work of conviction, and as evening drew on she dressed herself with care and neatness. With a fresh ribbon tied in her hair and color a little raised from mental excitement, she looked charming and lovable. I waited with interest to see the impression she would make on her husband. He could not help being charmed back into the lover, I was sure. But he did not come home to tea. We waited for him a whole hour after the usual time, and then sat down to the table alone, but neither of us could do more than sip a little tea.

"I went home soon after with a pressure of concern at my heart for which I could not account. All night I dreamed uncomfortable dreams. In the morning, soon after breakfast, I ran over to see Helen. I found her in her room, sitting in her night-dress, the picture of despair.

"'What is it?' I asked, eagerly. 'What has happened?'

"She looked at me heavily, like one not yet recovered from the shock of a stunning blow.

"'Dear cousin, what is the matter?' I said.

"I now saw by a motion of her hand that it held tightly clutched a piece of paper. She reached it to me. It was a letter, and read:

"'We cannot live happily together, Helen. You are not what I believed myself getting when we were married—not the sweet, lovely, lovable girl that charmed my fancy and won me from all others. Alas for us both that it is so! There has been a shipwreck of two lives. Farewell! I shall never return.'

"And this was all, but it broke the heart of my poor cousin. To this day, though nearly three years have passed, she has never heard from her husband.

"I saw her last week in the country home to which she has been taken by her friends—a wreck both in mind and body. She was sitting in an upper room, from the windows of which could be seen a beautiful landscape. She was neatly attired, and a locket containing her husband's picture hung at her throat. Her head was drooped and her eyes on the floor when I entered, but she raised herself quickly and with a kind of start. I saw a momentary eager flush in her face, dying out quickly and leaving it inexpressibly sad.

"'I thought it was John,' she said mournfully. Why don't he come?'"

I had to stop here, for Maggy broke out suddenly into a wild fit of sobbing and crying which lasted for some time.

"What ails you, dear?" I asked as she began to be a little composed.

"Oh, you have frightened me so! If John should—"

She cut short the sentence, but her frightened face left me in no doubt as to what was in her thoughts.

She arose and walked about the room in an uncertain way for some moments, and then sat down again, drawing in her breath heavily.

"If young wives," I remarked, believing that in her present state the truth was the best thing to say, "would take half the pains in making themselves personally attractive to their husbands that they did to charm their lovers, more of them would find the lover continued in the husband. Is a man, think you, less an admirer of womanly grace and beauty after he becomes a husband than he was before?"

"Hush! hush!" she said, in a choking voice. "I see it all! I comprehend it all." And she glanced down at herself. "I look hateful and disgusting."

After a plain, earnest talk with Maggy, I went home. I give her own words as to what happened afterward.

"I was wretched all the afternoon. John had acted worse than usual at dinner-time, and what you told me about poor Helen set my fears in motion and worried me half to death. Long before the time he usually came home I dressed myself with care, selecting the very things I had heard him admire. As I looked at myself in the glass I saw that I was attractive; I felt as I had never felt before that there was a power in dress that no woman can disregard without loss of influence, no matter what her position or sphere of life.

"Supper-time came. I had made something that I knew John liked, and was waiting for him with a nervous eagerness it was impossible to repress. But the hour passed, and his well-known tread along the little garden-walk did not reach my anxious ears. Five, ten, twenty minutes beyond his hour for returning, and still I was alone. Oh, I shiver as I recall the wild fears that began to crowd upon me. I was standing at the window, behind the curtain, waiting and watching. All at once I saw him a little distance from the house, but not in the direction from which he usually came. He was walking slowly, and with his eyes upon the ground. His whole manner was that of one depressed or suffering. I dropped the curtain, and went back into our little breakfast-room to see that supper was put quickly on the table. John came in, and went up stairs, as he usually did, to change his coat before tea. In a few minutes I rang the tea-bell, and then seated myself at the table to wait for him. He was longer than usual in making himself ready, and then I heard him coming down slowly and heavily, as if there were no spirit in him.

"My heart beat strongly, but I tried to look bright and smiling. There was, oh, so dreary a look on John's face as I first saw it in the door. He stood still just a moment with his eyes fixed on me; then the dreary look faded out; a flash of light passed over it as he stepped forward quickly, and coming to where I sat, stooped down and kissed me. Never before was his kiss so sweet to my lips.

"'I have found my little wife once more,' he said, softly and tenderly and with a quiver in his voice. I laid my head back upon his bosom, and looking up into his face, answered, 'And you shall never lose her again.'"

And I think he will not. The sweetness of that hour, and the lesson it taught, can never be forgotten by my friend Maggy.

XXIII.

LOVE, A GIVER.

YOU'RE a selfish man!"

The words leaped out with a quick, angry impulse. There was a frown on the beautiful face and a flame that was not of love in the bright eyes.

If the soft hand laid so trustingly in his scarcely three months before had struck him a stunning blow, Alfred Williston could not have been more surprised or hurt. "Selfish!" It was the first time that sin had been laid at his door. "He's a generous fellow, the most unselfish man alive," "There's not a mean trait in his character,"—such things had been said of him over and over again, and repeated in his ears by partial or interested friends, until he almost believed himself the personification of unselfishness. And now to be called "a selfish man" by the sweet little rosebud mouth that looked as if only made for kisses—to be called "a selfish man" by her to whom he had given all he had in the world, and himself in the bargain! No wonder that Alfred Williston stood dumb before his pretty wife.

The accusation was made, and for good or for evil it must stand. No taking back of the words can take back their meaning. "You're a selfish man!" had been cut by sharply-uttered tones deep into his memory, and there the sentence would remain. He did not attempt to meet the charge. To have done so would have been felt as a degradation.

"Good-morning!" dropped coldly from his lips, and he went away without offering the usual parting kiss. It was showery at home and cloudy at the office for the greater part of that forenoon.

"What's the matter, my friend? You look as sober as a judge on sentence day!" remarked an acquaintance who called upon Williston.

"Look about as I feel," was moodily answered.

"Heigh-ho! wind in the wrong direction and moon in the rainy quarter already?" rejoined the visitor, familiarly, with a sly, provoking laugh.

Williston turned his face partly aside that its expression might be concealed.

"Sunshine and shower, summer and winter, you will have these alternations like the rest of mankind, and learn to bear them with philosophy."

"Do you think me a very selfish man, Edward?" asked Williston, turning upon his friend a serious face.

"Selfish? Oh dear! No, not very selfish. I've heard you called the most generous fellow alive. But we're all more or less selfish, you know—born so, and can't help it, unless we try harder than is agreeable to most people. There was a time when I had a very good opinion of myself as touching this thing, but I grow less and less satisfied every day, and am settling down into the conclusion that I'm no better than my neighbors."

"Well, I despise a selfish man. He's the meanest creature alive!" Williston spoke with a glow of indignation.

"He's mean just in the degree that he's selfish," replied the friend. "And as we are all more or less selfish, we are all more or less mean. I don't see how we are to get away from that conclusion."

Williston knit his brows like one annoyed or perplexed.

"Has anybody called you selfish?" asked the friend.

"Yes."

"Who? The little darling at home? Ha! I see! That's the trouble!"

The young husband's deepening color betrayed the fact.

"She called you selfish? Ha! Good for Margy! Not afraid to give things their right name. I always knew she was a girl of spirit. Selfish! That's interesting. And did you really fancy that you were unselfish?"

This half-in-sport, half-in-earnest speech had the effect intended. A slight glimpse of himself as seen by another's eye gave Williston a new impression, and let in a doubt as to his being altogether perfect.

"And you think me selfish?" he said, in a tone of surprise. "Well! I guess there's been a new dictionary published of late."

"As far as this word is concerned, the heart

is the most reliable dictionary. If you wish to get the true definition, look down into your heart," replied the friend.

"My eyes are not, perhaps, as sharp as yours," said Williston. "I don't find the definition there."

"Maybe I can help you to a clearer vision. Why did you marry Margy?"

"Because I loved her."

"Are you quite sure?" said the friend, with provoking calmness.

"Take care, Fred! I shall get angry."

"Oh no! You're too sensible and too well poised for that. Answer my question. Are you quite sure?"

"As sure as death!"

"It's my opinion that you married because you loved yourself more than you did Margy."

"Now, this goes beyond all endurance!" exclaimed Williston. "Is there a conspiracy against me?"

"Gently, gently, my friend. The mind is never clear when disturbed. You loved Margy—there is no doubt in the world of that—loved her and do love her very dearly. But is your love unselfish? That is the great question now at issue. A boy loves a ripe peach, and climbs after it that he may enjoy its flavor. In what did your love of Margy differ from this boy's love of the peach? Was it to bless the sweet maiden—to give her yourself—that you sought her with a lover's ardor? Or was it to bless yourself? Did you think how much she would enjoy your love — how much happiness you would give her—or did you think chiefly of your own joy? Don't frown so! Put away that injured look. Go down, like a man, into your consciousness, and see how it really is. If you find all right, then you stand firm in serene self-approval; if all is not right, then you will know what to do. Love seeks to bless its object—is all the while endeavoring to minister delight—is a perpetual giver."

The hot flushes began to die out of Williston's face. He was looking down into his heart and getting some new revelations of himself, and they were not satisfactory. How had he loved Margy? What had been the quality of his love? Never before had such questions intruded themselves—never before had he found queries so difficult to answer. A troubled, anxious countenance and a deep sigh attested his disappointment in this self-investigation.

"I don't know whether to be angry or grateful," he said, knitting his brows. "Is it a true or a false mirror that you are holding up before me? Is the spectrum growing more and more distinct, an image of myself? I am in doubt and confusion."

"Love is a giver," answered his friend—"does not think of itself—desires only to bless. If you have so loved Margy, then has she wronged you. But if you have thought mainly of yourself, of your own delight, then, I trow, the dear little woman was not so far wrong when she called you selfish."

"One thing is certain," said Williston, speaking soberly: "I take pleasure in giving her pleasure. Any want that she might express I would gratify, if in my power. I could not deny her anything."

"Except the denial of yourself," remarked the friend.

Their eyes met, and they looked intently at each other for some moments.

"I am not sure that I understand you," said Williston.

"If Margy wanted a set of Amoor sables costing a thousand dollars, and you had the money with which to buy them, her desire would be gratified."

"Undoubtedly. I would find pleasure in meeting her wishes," was promptly answered.

"If she had a fancy for diamonds or India shawls—for elegant furniture and pictures—and you had the means to gratify her tastes, you would find delight in giving her the possession of these things. You would let her have her own sweet will in everything."

"You have said it, my friend. Nothing pleases me so much as to see her gratified."

"No great self-denial in all this, however. In the cases supposed you are entirely able to give what Margy asks for, and no special love of money comes in to chill your ardor. It is the easiest thing in the world to meet her wishes. But let us take some other case There is to be a musical party at your friend Watson's. You care but little for music, and less for musical people. The case is different with Margy. With music and musical people she is in her element. You come home with a new book from a favorite author, promising yourself an evening of enjoyment in reading aloud to your wife. She meets you with face all aglow, and in her hand a note of invitation from the Watsons. 'It will be such a delightful time!' she exclaims, in her enthusiasm. Now comes the true test of your love—now its quality must stand revealed. If she had known about the new book and the pleasure you had promised yourself in reading aloud to her through the evening, I am very sure she would have sent a note of excuse to the Watsons, and cheerfully denied herself, for your sake, the delights of a musical evening. But knowing nothing of this, she lets fancy revel in anticipated enjoyment, and does not think, perhaps, of your defective musical taste. Thus stands the case, my friend, and how will you meet it? In the other case, it was the generous hand that gave of its abundance. Now, it is sheer self-denial."

Williston drew a heavy sigh, moved himself restlessly and looked down upon the floor.

"This love that we talk so much about," resumed the friend, "is a very subtle thing, and very apt to hide from us its true quality. It is much oftener love of self than love of the object sought. Hence we have so much unhappiness in the state of marriage, which, on the theory of mutual love, ought to be full of bliss. But I am using time that cannot well be spared to-day, so, good-morning. If Margy has done you a wrong, help her to see it, and she will not only apologize for calling you selfish, but cover your lips with penitent kisses."

The case supposed, touched the difficulty at its very core. Since Williston's marriage he had shown himself gifted with but a feeble spirit of self-denial. He enjoyed his home and his wife, but not in a generous spirit. She was more social, and her tastes had received a better cultivation. She enjoyed music and art intensely. Her soul responded lovingly to all things beautiful. After his friend left him, Williston, in the new light which had penetrated his mind, began to see the relation existing between himself and his wife in some different aspects. One little incident after another was called up from memory and reviewed, and he saw in them, as in a mirror, an image of himself so different from any before presented that he was filled with pain and surprise. Such a thing as self-denial had scarcely come within the range of his virtues. Self-denial he had exacted often It had been no unusual thing for Margy to defer her tastes and wishes to his, and he could think of many cases in which she must have done so at considerable sacrifice of feeling.

A new sentiment began to pervade the mind of Williston—a deeper and tenderer feeling for his young wife—and in this new sentiment he had a perception of something purer and fuller of joy than anything hitherto experienced—the joy of giving up even his very life's love for another.

"Dear Margy!" he said, speaking to himself in this new state. "The tramp of my heedless foot must have been very crushing, to have extorted that cry of pain, for your charge of selfishness was but the voice of suffering that could not be repressed. Many times had I trampled upon, many times wounded, the love given to me so lavishly, but never before did the bruised heart reveal its anguish."

The tears that gushed from the eyes of Margy Williston as her husband turned so coldly from her and left the house rained on for over an hour; for the greater part of this time she indulged in accusing thoughts. She went over instance after instance of his selfish disregard of her pleasure, and recounted the many times she had given up her desires to gratify his demands. But this state of feeling in time changed, or wore itself out. A calm succeeded in which her better nature had an opportunity to speak. The hand of pain folded away many coverings that had been laid over her heart, and she could see into some of the hidden places never before revealed. She did not find everything in the order and beauty imagined to exist. She was not so loving and unselfish as she had fancied herself to be. There came a new gush of tears, but the rain was gentler, and, instead of desolating, refreshed the earth of her mind.

"I have thought more of my own gratification than of his," she began to say within herself. "His tastes differ in many things from mine. What I enjoy may be irksome to him. If I insist upon having my own enjoyments, regardless of how they may affect him, must not a degree of separation take place? Can he love me as much as before—will I love him as much as before—if I exact what he cannot give willingly? And if our love grow less, what is there in all the world to compensate for its decline? Losing that, we lose all. Take away that light, and all else will lie in shadow. Disturb that harmony, and every chord of life is out of tune."

So she thought, gaining a clearer sight and firmer will to act in the line of self-rejection whenever self interposed to hinder love. As the hours went by and the time drew near when her husband would return, a dead weight began to settle down upon Margy's heart. They had parted in anger. For the first time the lightning of a summer storm had flashed in their sky. There had been a quick descent of the tempest, hurting and blinding them. How much of wreck and ruin had been wrought in that brief war of inner elements it was yet impossible to know.

At last the time of return was at hand. A few minutes beyond the hour, and a vague fear began creeping into the soul of Margy. Shadowy forms of evil seemed hovering around her, the weight on her bosom grew more oppressive, her heart labored so heavily that its motions were painful.

Suspense was not very long. She heard the

door open, and the music of a well-known step in the hall. Restraint became impossible: her temperament was too ardent for repression in moments of deep feeling. Springing down the stairs, Margy had her arms about her husband's neck ere he had time to put his thoughts in order, and was crying on his bosom. The fervent kisses laid as peace-offerings on her lips were sweeter to her taste than honey or the honeycomb.

"Can you forgive me?" she asked, in the calmness of spirit that ensued. "I am very weak sometimes, and feeling is so strong."

"If there had been no provocation to feeling," Williston answered, frankly, "it would never have broken the bands of restraint. The fault was mine, not yours. It was selfish in me, and you said only the truth, but the truth is sometimes the most unpleasant thing we can hear. It sounded very harsh in my ears. I felt angry, and rejected it. Not so now. I have seen myself as in a mirror."

Margy laid her fingers on his mouth, and then they were silent. After a few moments, she said, gently,

"We are human, and, of consequence, weak

and selfish by nature. Let Love teach us a better law than Nature has written on our hearts. Then we shall draw nearer and nearer together, and the pulses of our lives, that sometimes beat unevenly, take the same sweet measure."

And it was so. But not at once, nor until after many seasons of mutual self-repression.

XXIV.

FIVE YEARS AFTERWARD.

"SHE'S a little fool!" was the impatient exclamation of Cousin Flora.

"I don't know about that," said Flora's father. "John is a fine young man, and if Kate loves him—"

"Loves him! Pshaw!"

And Flora tossed her head and curled her pretty lip. "Who is he, and what is he? Just a poor clerk, and nothing else. It's a disgrace to us all! And she might have had Harry Layard or Grant Armon. They would have given their eyes for her."

"John Lyon's father was an honest, true man," replied Mr. Perkins, "and his son has so far led an upright, blameless life. He is not fast like Harry Layard, nor an idler like Grant Armon. In my view he is worth a dozen of them. Kate's a sensible girl, and if she marries John Lyon for love, her chances of happiness will be a thousandfold better than if she married either of the young men to gain position, for as to loving them, that is out of the question."

"Love!" There was a tone of contempt in Flora's voice. "All very well in poetry and novels, but she can't live on love alone. A poor clerk for a husband! Oh dear! To pinch and screw, and count every penny, to be shut up in a mean little house, to be cut by your friends and left out of society, and all for love! Ugh!" And the young lady shivered.

Mr. Perkins did not argue the point with his daughter. He knew that it would be of no avail. A false social sentiment had perverted her feelings and lowered her views of marriage. But he was glad in his heart that his lovely niece had accepted the hand of John Lyon.

Two weddings took place a year afterward, one a brilliant sensational affair, fully reported in the newspapers, the other making not a ripple on the surface of society.

Harry Layard, who had been refused by Kate because the pure-minded, true-hearted girl could not love him, could not trust him with her happiness, offered himself to Flora and was accepted. Mr. Perkins yielded a reluctant consent, and gave away the hand of his daughter with many painful misgivings. Theirs was the brilliant wedding, and the quiet, unostentatious, sweet home ceremonial, of which society took no note, that of John Lyon and Kate.

Three years afterward Mr. Perkins died, leaving a bankrupt estate. His son-in-law had by this time got well through the moderate fortune left him by his father. Only a few months before this event he had given up his elegant house for lack of means to support the establishment, and Flora had gone back to her father's house disappointed and humiliated. Long before this had come the sad discovery that her husband possessed few qualities that she could respect or admire. He was selfish and self-indulgent. His moral tone was low. He had no worthy aims in life. He was fashionably indifferent to her, and gayly attentive to other ladies. This she had thought very fine and Frenchy in the beginning, and had indulged in little flirtations of her own that were very exciting and enjoyable in their way. But they led to light talk, and scandals associated with her name, which came near involving her husband in a quarrel with a "man-about-town." Flora was innocent, but the affair left a blemish on her good name. Society is quick to credit an evil report against one of its members, for Society knows but too well how bad the heart is.

On the very day that Harry Layard, the fashionable spendthrift, gave up his fine house and became a poor dependent on his father-in-law, John Lyon, now partner in the well-established mercantile firm where he had served faithfully as clerk, took his happy wife and child into a pleasant home bought with careful savings. Over this home Peace spread her wings, and in it Contentment had her dwelling-place. Love, regarded almost as a myth in certain circles, was a beautiful personation here, sweet and pure. The husband was still the lover, and the wife as tender and responsive as when the kiss of betrothal touched her fervent lips.

A year after the death of Mr. Perkins, Mr. Layard, for some mean service to a rising politician, got a consul's appointment in a South American port, and took his broken-spirited young wife away from the scenes of her fashionable follies and bitter disappointments. She had never noticed Kate after her marriage with the poor young clerk, and the cousins had become as strangers to each other.

A day was going out in chill December. The wind was gusty and cold, roaring down chimneys, whistling through bare tree-tops and moaning about the corners of houses. A sense of comfort had all who sat by ruddy fires and felt the warmth and protection of homes.

In one home, by an open grate, in a handsomely-furnished room, was a young mother with a child in her arms. They made a picture of contentment. The curtains were drawn back from the windows, and as the twilight fell, the red glow from burning coals made the room and its inmates visible upon the street. Many who passed stopped for an instant to glance at this living picture and take it away in their memories, ever to be a thing of beauty.

Among those who paused to look at the mother and her child was a young woman whose pale sad face and garments too thin for the chilly air were in marked contrast with the comfort on which she gazed. As she looked, a man passed her quickly, sprang up the steps of the house, and opening the door, went in. At the sound of his key in the lock she saw the face of the woman light up with sudden joy, and a moment afterward a manly form bent over her and a kiss warm as any lover's was laid upon her lips.

Who was the poor, lonely one in the street, and who the happy one within? They were the cousins — one a widow, homeless in the city of her girlish pride and social triumph; homeless, and well-nigh heartbroken; landed only a few hours before from the ship that brought for burial to his native land the dead body of her husband; the other crowned with motherhood, and drinking from the cup of life its richest nectar.

A hand was lifted to the curtain while yet the fascinated gaze of Flora rested on the picture, and in another instant it was shut from her view.

A cry of pain rose suddenly on the air. It penetrated the room.

"Hark! what was that?"

The color went out of Mrs. Lyon's face. A woman's low cry in strangely familiar tones reached her ears and went with an electric quiver of pain to her heart.

She drew back the curtain, and saw in the fading light a woman's form on the pavement. The instinct of humanity was quick in the heart of John Lyon and his wife. They did not stop for doubt or question—did not wait for some other good Samaritan to go to the rescue—but took the unconscious wanderer in.

It was just five years since Cousin Flora turned her back on Kate, and this was their next meeting! Five years of a true and of a false marriage, and here was the issue thereof, here the fruitage! Ponder the lesson well, young maiden! If you would be happy in marriage, look to personal qualities alone. If the man is not pure and excellent, manly and self-reliant, you run a fearful risk in casting your lot with him. The chances of happiness are all against you. It is the man you marry, not his position, nor his family name, nor his wealth. It is the man of evil or good character to whom you are conjoined in the closest of all imaginable intimacies, and with whom you must dwell in love or in dislike and disgust. He will lift you into honor and safety, or drag you down into wretched humiliation and untold sufferings.

Ay, ponder the lesson well!

XXV.

WHAT WILL THE WORLD SAY?

OT Grace Allen, surely?" said Wilson Maynard, in tones of disappointment and surprise.

"Yes, Grace Allen," replied his friend.

"A milliner! There must be some mistake. She is too sweet, too intelligent, too accomplished a girl for that! I cannot believe it."

"Just as you please, Wilson. But if you have any particular interest in knowing, and will just step down with me to-morrow morning to Mrs. Millinett's, you can see her in all the glory of principal workwoman to that very useful individual."

"Well, it's a shame!"

"What's a shame?"

"Why, that a girl like Grace—for that she is no common girl a single hour spent in her company has convinced me—should have to stoop so low."

"Then, like a true knight, you should fly at once to her relief, and elevate her to what you think her true position in society."

"That I cannot do."

"Why? Do you not think her worthy?"

"Oh, as to that, I should think her in every way worthy, from the little I have seen of her, though if I were to think seriously of marriage, I should wish to see a great deal more of her. But I find that there is one positive objection."

"Indeed! What is that?"

"How can you ask? She is a milliner!"

"Well, what difference does that make?"

"What difference? How strangely you talk!"

"I am sure, Wilson, that I am unable to see the great difference that it would make. For my part, it seems to me a recommendation."

"A recommendation! Really, I am unable to see what you are driving at."

"I will try and enlighten you. The father of Grace Allen, though not rich, was one of those foolish men whose affection for their children shows itself in a disposition to relieve them from all kinds of care and toil. A very industrious man himself, he was able to provide for his family sufficiently well to take away the necessity of labor, even in household affairs, from his daughter. She was provided with the best teachers, and no effort was spared to render her truly accomplished, so far as the storing up of the various branches of knowledge was concerned. Possessing, naturally, a good mind, none of these advantages were lost upon Grace, and her father had the pleasure of seeing her spring up to womanhood an honor to himself and the pride of the social circle in which she moved. But in one of those mysterious dispensations of Providence that meet us at every turn in life, the father of Grace was removed from this world. Having lived fully up to his income, there was nothing left for his wife and fondly-loved child.

"Now came the trial that was to prove her. Mrs. Allen was advanced in years, and in feeble health. Grace was in the freshness and vigor of early womanhood. Upon which do you think should have fallen the burden of supporting the other? It did not take Grace long to answer this question. She entered a milliner's work-room, and has ever since supported her mother."

"That was truly noble!" ejaculated the young man, while a glow of admiration lit up his countenance. "But"—and the glow faded—"why did she choose such an occupation? Surely, with her education, she might have found employment at something far more respectable."

"I am not able to see, Wilson, why a milliner is less respectable than—what shall I say?—a music or French teacher."

"I can, then."

"Enlighten me, if you please."

"Why—why—why you see, a milliner is not half so respectable. Anybody can see that."

"Then, as I cannot see it, of course I am nobody," the friend said, laughing.

"But I am sure," returned Maynard, with a serious look and tone, "the employment is not esteemed respectable. You know that, at least."

"I know so, because it is plainly apparent, Wilson, that you do not think it respectable, and it is probable that there are others who think as you do; but you must excuse me when I say that the employment in which Grace is so honorably engaged is not thus esteemed by the thinking and sensible portion of the community—those who can look beyond the surface, and, seeing, prize true worth wherever it is found. Surely, were Grace to fold her hands in idleness, and suffer her mother to toil for her, when she is far more able to take care of her mother, you would not think her more respectable?"

"Oh no. But then, as I said before, there is a choice of employments, and in that choice a person like Grace Allen should discriminate more wisely than she has done."

"As to that, Wilson, so far as I have been able to learn, in her choice of employment she discriminated with great wisdom. She has naturally a taste for such employments as the one in which she is now engaged. For years before her father's death, from choice she made her own and her mother's bonnets, and I have heard my sisters say that none of their friends wore neater bonnets than Grace. All honest employments being in her eyes, as in the eyes of every sensible person—you must excuse me, Wilson—respectable, she chose that for which she had naturally the greatest predilection. The consequence has been that, from taking an interest and feeling a pleasure in her occupation, she has come to be Mrs. Millinett's most valuable assistant. Indeed, that individual's large custom mainly depends upon the tasteful air that everything has which comes from her establishment, and well she knows whom to credit for this. The consequence is that the compensation received by Grace is far above what persons in her capacity ordinarily receive, and much more than she could hope to obtain at any other employment. And thus is she enabled to provide for her mother every desired comfort."

"Still, she is but a milliner," the young man responded, musingly.

"I cannot see what great difference that can make, Wilson," his friend replied. "It certainly does not take away, in the slightest degree, from the real worth of her character. Her ends of life, which really constitute the true quality of mind, remain the same. As your wife, or the wife of any one, she cannot be considered in the smallest iota less worthy for having filled the station she now does. Indeed, as I before remarked, she is far more worthy than she was formerly. Because the selection, from principle, of her present employment, which she must have known was not looked upon by some prejudiced individuals as 'respectable,' has strengthened her character and given her a degree of independence where right and principle are concerned, that must make her far better qualified to fill the position of a wife."

"That may all be so. But—"

"But what, Wilson?"

"Why, what will the world say if I were to marry a milliner?"

"I don't know that the world has anything to do in the matter," the friend replied. "It is your business, not that of other people."

"Still, they will meddle with it."

"Perhaps they will. But what of that?"

"I'll tell you what of it. It would be my wife that they talked about and sneered at, and I cannot bear that my wife should be alluded to in any such a way. And besides, it would exclude her from good society."

"Not good society, Wilson."

"What do you mean?"

"I mean that any persons who would exclude Grace Allen from their association because she had been a milliner would not be entitled to the name of good society. They might be 'exclusives,' 'elite' or 'fashionables,' or anything else you might choose to call them, but the title of 'good,' as applied to them, would be altogether out of place."

"It wouldn't do to let the world hear you talk in that way."

"I never conceal my sentiments, and never intend to conceal them. And what is more, my friend, I do not feel that there is the slightest necessity for doing so. The world is not so blind to true merit, nor so wonderfully exclusive, as you seem inclined to think. The general opinion is always in favor of real worth, and is ever ready to elevate that worth to its true position. And you may rest assured that if you neglect to pluck this beautiful and fragrant flower now blooming unseen and unknown, there will be found some one ere long who will find it and wear it upon his bosom, the admiration even of the very world from whose imaginary sneer you shrink so sensitively."

"Well, let him risk it that chooses. I am unwilling. Still, she is a charming girl. The hour that I spent in her company last evening—the first time, you know, that I met her—was the pleasantest hour that I have passed for a long time. Intelligent, easy and graceful in her manners, a close and rational observer, combined with high personal attractions, she is one of the most lovely women that I have ever met. I have never seen one whom I would choose for a companion before her."

"You have thought of removing to the South," Maynard's friend said. "Her origin, or rather her present employment, would not be known there."

"True—not at first. But then I should live in daily fear of something occurring to make it known. No, no. I had better run no risks."

"Perhaps not," the friend said, in a changed tone, for he began to feel that Maynard was really unworthy of Grace, and that in endeavoring to remove the difficulties that intervened he was doing wrong.

"It seems to me a little strange," Wilson Maynard remarked, after a few moments' silence, "that Mrs. Carpenter would introduce her into company at her house. It will not only injure her standing when the fact becomes generally known, but it throws young men who visit there into the danger of forming an unpleasant, and perhaps a very undesirable, association.

Suppose, now, that I had permitted myself, after meeting her for a few times, to show her marked attentions. The result would have been unpleasant to both of us so soon as I came to know the truth."

"Of course, for no one thinks of concealing the occupation in which she is engaged. Grace herself would not have hesitated a moment to have given you that information. Indeed, she has told me that she sometimes uses the fact that she is a milliner as a kind of touchstone to try the sincerity of professed good-feeling from certain quarters. It is surprising, she has said to me, how quickly the manner of some changes toward her when it becomes known. But nothing of this moves her."

"There is no doubt of her being an excellent girl. I only pity the misfortune of her lot."

"By her it is esteemed a good fortune. She feels that it protects her from those who cannot discriminate between the real and the fictitious, and she knows that, if ever sought by a man of real intelligence and truth of character, it will be because he finds in her a likeness of his own mind—that he will take her for herself. And then she knows that she will be happy."

"May all the good fortune attend her that she desires is my fervent wish," said Maynard, with something of regret in his tones. "The flower of the wilderness must bloom on another bosom than mine. I dare not risk the certain consequences."

His friend urged him no farther. He felt that it would be wrong to do so—that, as has just been said, Wilson Maynard was unworthy of Grace Allen.

About the same time that this conversation was in progress, a young physician universally esteemed in the community for his superior intelligence and high-toned principles sat in one of the richly-furnished parlors of Mrs. Carpenter, engaged in earnest conversation with that lady. As to this conversation, we will commence at the beginning and go regularly through with it, that the reader may perceive its full import.

"Who is that young lady whom I have met several times at your house, Mrs. Carpenter?" asked Doctor Norton, after he had been seated a few moments with the lady he addressed.

"Which one do you mean, doctor?"

"Why, the most beautiful, interesting and intelligent woman that was in these rooms last evening. Can you designate her by that description?"

"I think I can. But that will depend upon how nearly alike we estimate character and personal attractions."

"Oh, as to that, I think there is but little danger of going wrong. So speak out, if you please, madam."

"Do you mean the young lady dressed in white who sang and played, toward the close of the evening, with so much sweetness and taste?"

"Of course I do."

"Her name, doctor, is Grace Allen."

"Grace! She is truly named, that is certain. And now, who or what is she?"

"What she is you have already said—a beautiful, intelligent and interesting woman."

"Exactly. That is settled. Now, who is she?"

"A poor girl who supports an aged mother in ill health with her needle. In plain terms, a milliner's chief workwoman."

"Surely you jest, Mrs. Carpenter!"

"You know me better, doctor."

"I do. But your information astonishes me. That woman, so superior in every way, a milliner! By what ill fortune has she been compelled to resort to such a means of livelihood?"

"By the death of a father who lavished everything upon his child while living, and left her nothing when he died."

"Have you known her long?"

"Ever since she was a child. And the more I see of her, and the longer I know her, the more I esteem her. Humble as her sphere in life is, I know few, if any, whom I consider her equal."

"Just my opinion, formed from half an hour's conversation with and an hour's observation of her," Doctor Norton said. Then, after musing a few moments, he resumed:

"I believe I may speak out my mind plainly to you as a friend, Mrs. Carpenter?"

"Certainly, doctor."

"Then, is this young lady—this Grace Allen—engaged?"

"I believe not, doctor. But why do you ask? You certainly cannot think of marrying a milliner?"

"No, of course not. I think of marrying an

intelligent, virtuous and accomplished woman, if I can find one who comes up to my ideas. And from the little I have seen and heard of Miss Allen, I think she is just the woman I am in search of. Of course I wish to see more of her. As to her being a milliner, I have no interest in the matter, as I do not want any one in that capacity. Will she make a good wife? That is the question. If so, and she can fancy me, why it will be the easiest thing in the world to lay off the milliner and put on the wife."

"But what will people say, doctor?"

"They will say, I suppose, that I have a very sweet woman for a wife. What else can they say?"

"Why, they'll say, 'But she was only a milliner.'"

"Indeed! Well, suppose they do? It will be very easy to retort."

"How?"

"Why, if they charge her with having been guilty of the crime of making bonnets, she can charge upon them the crime of wearing them. Now, pray, which is the greatest crime? If it is wrong to make bonnets, surely it is wrong for any one not only to pay another for making them, but to wear them after they are made! Is not that sound logic?"

"It seems so. And glad I am to find that my friend, Doctor Norton, can have the manliness and independence to discriminate thus wisely. I am sure he will find in Grace Allen a woman not only to love, but to be proud of. As for myself, I number her among my choicest friends, and though I can in but few instances prevail on her to be present here when I have company, I always esteem her on such occasions to be the chief attraction. Sometimes young men and young women have been present who did not treat her with the right kind of consideration, because they felt themselves above persons in her condition. Such, no matter to what families they belong, I never invite again to my house. I consider them to be unfit companions for myself or my friends. Their false ideas of life, their weak, vain, perverted notions, I wish not intruded upon her. Let them go to their own."

"Yes, let them go to their own," Doctor Norton responded, with warmth. "If not asking too much of a favor of you, shall I be able to see Miss Allen here soon again?"

"I will invite her here on any evening that will be agreeable to you."

"Say to-morrow evening."

"Very well. Let it be to-morrow evening."

After Wilson Maynard had parted from his friend the image of Grace still remained pictured in his imagination, and he felt drawn toward her despite what he was pleased to call his better judgment. But he resisted this inclination, and reasoned against the absurdity of a man of his standing (a young merchant with a borrowed capital of four thousand dollars and a business credit of five times that amount) lowering himself so much as to marry a milliner!

"Good-morning, Wilson," his friend said to him, a few weeks afterward. "Have you made up your mind to marry that milliner yet?"

"Don't talk about it, if you please. If I did feel a little inclination toward that girl before I knew what she was, I can assure you that I am perfectly cured now."

"It's as well, perhaps," was the reply.

"But I have found one who is just the thing," resumed the young man.

"Indeed! And who is she?"

"Not a milliner's girl, I can promise you.'

"Oh, of course not! But who has so fully met your ideas?"

"Her name is Clarissa Howell. Do you know her?"

"Yes, very well."

"What do you think of her?"

"That she is a very good sort of a girl—amiable, and all that."

"You speak indifferently."

"Do I?"

"Yes. And I should like to know what you mean by it."

"Oh, nothing! Only that I never happened to see anything particularly interesting about Miss Howell. Still, I have always found her a pleasant girl, and have passed many agreeable hours in her company. But I think that her education is defective, as are also her views of society."

"How so?"

"In the first place, she has not been raised by her parents to do anything except go to school. Consequently, she might do well enough for a man to dress up and place in his parlor by way of ornament, but certainly she is not fit to govern a household, or to manage the economical affairs of a family."

"I don't see that as any great objection."

"You don't?"

"No. I do not wish to make a slave of my wife."

"Of course not. But you certainly expect your wife not only to take charge of your domestic concerns, but to take pleasure therein."

"Well, I don't know. I am no friend to making slaves of women. Certainly, I do not expect my wife to live in the kitchen."

"Nor does any man of right feeling. Still, there are duties connected with a wife's position that require her to know a good deal about the practical part of housekeeping. An ignorance of how to perform these will cause a derangement in her family that none will feel to be more unpleasant and annoying than her husband."

"As to that, I am sure I am no judge. No doubt Clarissa's mother has taught her all that is necessary. Indeed, I am sure she has, for I have heard her called one of the best of housekeepers."

'You must judge for yourself, of course, Wilson," his friend replied. "But one thing is certain: Clarissa Howell is neither so handsome nor so intelligent as Grace Allen."

"That may be. But then she is a respectable girl, and moves in good society."

"I do not like to hear you talk in that way, Wilson," his friend said. "The inference of course is, that Grace is not respectable and does not move in good society. Now, I know to the contrary, and so ought you. I am sure you met her at Mrs. Carpenter's. As to the amount of respectability attached to industry and idleness, it seems to me that the proportion is largely in favor of the former. And I am sure that if you look at the subject with an unprejudiced eye you will think the same."

"As to all that, I don't pretend to think much about it. But I do know that the world—that is, the genteel class—do not esteem a milliner, or a mantua-maker, or indeed any persons who have to work with their hands for a livelihood, as respectable. They are all classed with mechanics, and should associate together. They are well enough in their places, and useful, but I am not going to connect myself with any of them."

"And yet Mr. Howell was a saddler before he opened the store he now keeps."

"If he was, his daughter is not a saddler, nor a seamstress, and I am thinking about her, not her father. As to his having pursued a trade for a living, that is a fact of past times. He is a merchant now, and Clarissa is the daughter of a merchant!"

"That is, if a man who retails groceries, and has to spend every dollar he makes in the support of four or five idle, expensive daughters, may be called a merchant. Don't look so indignant. I am only telling you the truth in homely language."

"Oh, as to that, talk on. It don't make any impression."

"Then there will be no use in my talking," the friend responded, and so the subject was waived.

The allusions of the friend were pretty true. Clarissa was about as fit to make a man a wife as most girls at the age of fifteen. She was one of five sisters raised in idleness, their heads full of high notions and contempt of everything vulgar. She dressed well, talked pretty well, although there was no great deal of sense in what she said, sang well, danced well and looked pretty well. Indeed, she was just the kind of a girl to captivate such a man as Wilson Maynard. And she did make a conquest of him—not by accident, but from design, for she made herself particularly interesting to him. She studied his tastes and predilections, and modified her actions and the expression of her opinions precisely to suit his notions. The business of her life was to get married, and everything she did looked to that end.

In due time Maynard engaged himself to her, and eventually they were married.

Three days after that event took place, when he was again settling down to business, his friend, before introduced, came into his store to pass a word or two. While sitting and conversing, Maynard, who held a newspaper in his hand, let his eye fall accidentally on a portion of the sheet.

"Ha! what is this?" he said, suddenly.

"What is it?" asked his friend.

"'Married, on Tuesday evening last, Doctor James Norton to Grace, daughter of the late William Allen.'"

"Indeed!" cried the friend, in a delighted

tone, striking his hands together under the impulse of an instantaneous emotion of pleasure. "Really, I am delighted!"

"But that don't mean, certainly, Grace Allen the milliner girl?"

"Yes it does, though! Her father's name was William."

"There must be some mistake, surely," persisted Maynard.

"Why so?"

"Because I don't believe a man of Doctor Norton's standing would stoop so low."

"You can think of that as you please, Wilson, but I can tell you one thing: I have met Doctor Norton several times of late at Mrs. Carpenter's, and Grace was there every time, and what is more, the doctor paid her marked attentions."

"Well, if it is so, he is a great fool. He will never be able to introduce her into good society, that's certain."

"Don't be so sure of that, Wilson. The doctor can introduce her where he pleases, and what is more, her own real worth of character will be her passport."

And now let us hear what the world will say

about these two events, premising, by the way, that the opinions of one or two or three individuals are generally set down as the opinion of "the world."

"What a lovely woman Doctor Norton's wife is!" remarked the lady of a wealthy and "respectable" citizen, a few weeks after the marriage, to the lady of another wealthy and "respectable" citizen.

"Indeed, she is a sweet woman."

"They say," resumed the first speaker, "that she was one of Mrs. Millinett's workwomen when the doctor married her, and that by her industry she supported her aged and invalid mother."

"So I have heard."

"I think the doctor deserves credit for his discrimination. A man of less observation and good sense would never have discovered her."

"No, that is certain! Well, she is a sweet woman, worthy to fill any station. I, for one, feel proud of her acquaintance."

"And so do I," was the sincere response.

"And so Maynard is married!" said one lady to another, about the same time that the last brief conversation occurred, though in a different circle and in a conventional grade below.

"Yes," was the reply, "and a pretty bargain he has made of it! He'd a great deal better have married a woman that knows how to do something—a milliner or a mantua-maker for instance, or some one at least that has a few ideas above mere dress and show."

"So I should think. But that's the way with our young men now-a-days. They must have ladies for their wives. And pretty work they make of it! No wonder they don't get along any better than they do."

"No, indeed, it is not. Why, those Howell girls are no more fit for young men's wives than they are for—for—I don't know what!"

"No matter; but they'll all be picked off by foolish young men because they are ladies—that is, are above working."

Thus the world will talk. And if we study tc conciliate its good opinion, with no other end in view, ten chances to one if we do not take a false step, and fail to secure the good opinion we have been seeking into the bargain. There is a more general common-sense estimation of things in all classes than a few seem willing to believe. The weak ones talk and give out their narrow views as the ruling ones in the social circles. But common sense and common honesty, in the appreciation of character, are far more general than some profess to believe.

XXVI.

WHEN IT WAS OVER.

MR. FULTON was stunned by the shock of his wife's death. He had not expected the event, and was not, therefore, in any way prepared for it. True, Mrs. Fulton had been in feeble health for some years, and for the past twelve or eighteen months her fading face and shadowy form, to all but her husband, had been suggestive of that last time which comes to all. To him she looked pale and wasted, but he had grown so familiar with this aspect that its significance failed. Day by day the wasting went on, the pallor increased, but these progressive changes were imperceptible to his eyes. Only those who saw Mrs. Fulton at intervals of weeks or months were impressed by the warning signs.

"Hearty as a buck." This language gives

the true impression of Mr. Fulton's physical condition. He knew nothing of aching heads, of weary limbs, of nervous exhaustion and depression. The blood that leaped along his veins was full of richness and vitality. Every nerve was in health, every muscle rounded. He enjoyed life. Motion was a pleasure. Such men, resting in the consciousness of their own mental and physical states, are not ready sympathizers with pain. They understand but little of what those suffer in whom vitality is low, or the mechanism of whose bodies are defect and weakness.

Mr. Fulton was not what the world calls a selfish man, and yet he was too self-absorbed to make a true and tender husband to the patient, loving woman whom he left for most of the time in weary loneliness. All day long he was absent under the necessities of business. Could he not give his evenings to the wife who had numbered the hours in waiting for him to come home, and who always had smiles and lovelit eyes to greet him? Not often. His life was too full to be repressed to the sluggish quiet of an invalid's chamber. It made him dull and stupid So he must have his meetings with friends after the day's work was over, his recreations, his social contacts, his enjoyments. Without these, life would grow stagnant in his veins. It was hard on his poor wife, he knew, to be restricted to a few rooms—often to one—to sit lonely at home, to be in pain, but then it was a necessity out of his reach. If he could have given her at a word both health and happiness, with what promptness would that word have been spoken! But he rarely thought of self-denial—of the great pleasure she would receive from daily acts of love, scarce manifest in their unobtrusiveness, yet falling like dew and sunshine upon the heart.

And so it went on, the failing one never disturbing him with complaint or murmur, always welcoming him with a smile that, strange to say, did not impress him as growing feebler and feebler. All at once the light of life went out, dropping down suddenly like a spent candle. Now it burnt steadily, and now it was gone!

Mr. Fulton was stunned by the shock. He could at first only faintly realize the fact, and when a sympathizing friend said, "You have had time to prepare for this sorrow; the death-angel came not in suddenly," he scarcely comprehended his meaning.

From the hour of death until the hour of burial, when friends gathered in funeral solemnity, and all that dull machinery of burial that jars and rattles—be the adjustment never so carefully made—was set in motion, Mr. Fulton remained in a half-stupefied condition. Once, since the vital spark went out, he had looked upon the dead face of his wife, and shuddered at its ghastly whiteness. He could not force himself to a second view. But ere the coffin-lid was shut down over it for ever, drawn forward by a friend, he stood and let his eyes fall, in dread of a shock, on the features he might never again, except in thought, behold.

If sickness and pain and the throes of dissolution mar the countenance, much of beauty and sweetness is restored during that brief process of interior separation of soul and body which goes on after death in the sensational and external. With Mrs. Fulton this had been restored in a remarkable degree. Few signs of exhaustion or suffering remained. The mouth was gently shut and very placid. Her eyelids rested above the snowy cheeks, softly relieving their paleness with fringing shadows—not weighed down as by death, but with the seeming light burden of sleep. You almost expected to see them quiver, and then unveil the orbs which lay beneath. Not hardly back from the marble forehead had they drawn her hair, but in light, glossy masses gathered it about her temples, and laid it just away from each side of her face, yet touching it. One hand was drawn across her bosom, the other fell easily by her side. A few flowers, white and red, representing the pure truth and warm love of her character, lay upon her breast, as if dropped there without art and left where they fell.

Mr. Fulton let his eyes fall in dread of a shock. But there was no shock. The sight he feared to look upon proved a vision of beauty. For an instant it seemed as if the lost one were restored, and he bent down in haste to lay his lips to those which seemed as if just about to smile with love's warm invitation. Alas! in the icy touch delusion vanished. It was death—death! Death assuming the aspect of life, and mocking his sudden hope.

It was all over at last. The days of sad

preparation, in which the soul longs for seclusion and undisturbed self-communion, but finds them not, had passed with Mr. Fulton, and the time came when he could sit down alone and remember. She was gone, the tender, the loving, the patient, the true-hearted! Not much of the funeral services or the preacher's "improvement" of the occasion had entered his thoughts. Still, something remained. Of the departed he had spoken with much feeling, saying, among other things: "We who are in full health, in the flush of animal life, do not realize in any adequate degree the lonely experiences, the heart-weariness, the longings for day in the night-watches, and the longings for night in the tiresome days, of those whom God is preparing by wasting sickness to become angels in his kingdom. If you have any such in your homes, give them love, and care, and cheerful companionship. Make their beds soft in sickness. Give them smooth pillows. As for our departed sister, all that loving care, all that tender solicitude could give, were hers, and in the hearts that mourn her to-day there is pure grief only."

Pure grief only! Mr. Fulton was not deceived. He could not take this delusion into his soul. The picture had flashed on him with startling vividness. No, he had not realized in any degree "the lonely experiences, the heart-weariness, the longings for day in the night-watches, and the longings for night in the tiresome days," of her whom God had been preparing by wasting sickness to become an angel in his kingdom. But it was all revealed now to his dull apprehension. How stupid, how blind, how self-inverted, not to have understood this before!

Now, when it was all over, the long period of life's decadence, the unexpected death scene, and the low, dull, half-realized misery of intervening days until the time of burial came, and his heart lay bruised and helpless under the weight of its obtrusive ceremonials,—now, when it was all over, and he sat alone in the still chamber, shivering and in darkness, where for so long a time a low but sweet voice had made music for his heart and a pale face given out light warmer and purer than any sunshine, memory began to restore the past.

"Must you go out this evening, dear?" Mr. Fulton actually started and turned his eyes upon the empty bed, so clearly sounded the old familiar voice, not in a complaining tone—not burdened with weariness or suffering, or shaded with the anticipation of other solitary hours added to the many she had passed since morning—but with forced cheerfulness, yet pleading. If the pale face and loving eyes had looked over to him from the pillow now, would he have answered "Yes"?

Ah, memory, memory, unsleeping Nemesis! The pale face and loving eyes were not there, only the white pillow, smooth and full. But memory held to his sight the picture taken on a sensitive page, and he saw himself turning away while the pleading tones yet filled his ears—turning away and shutting the door! Oh, the bitter anguish of that moment! And evening after evening, answering to the earnest yet never chiding question, he had thus turned away, shutting the door!

White, and still, and patient! His eyes are closed. But no bodily form ever stood out more clearly defined than the spectrum now holding his vision. White, and still, and patient, as he had looked upon her so many hundreds of times, without once getting down into any just idea of her true consciousness. Now a new revelation had come to him. But it was too late! Her feet had gone down into the waters of Jordan, she had passed to the other side, and he stood weeping on the shore alone.

Not a complaining word, not a chiding look, haunted him. Always a lovelit face had brightened at his coming, and patient eyes just a little shaded held him up to the last instant of departure, never closing heavily and sadly until the door was shut. But conscience and memory haunted him now with crowding accusations.

Not a complaining word, not a chiding look. What was the record on the other side? Had he been always patient and uncomplaining?

"If I had not felt so weak, Henry!" Was there an accusing spirit in the room? No, it was in Mr. Fulton's soul. Memory had turned another leaf and hurt his vision with another picture. He was standing with hard eyes and stern mouth before his shrinking wife, who looked up with a hurt expression on her face and tears brimming to the eyelids.

"If I had not felt so weak, Henry!"

Mr. Fulton turned the page and shut his ears. But the book of his life was written over on every leaf, full of sentences and images from margin to margin, and the sentences had living voices.

"I am losing strength confined to these close rooms."

He had scarcely heeded the words when spoken. How distinctly they were remembered now! How mournfully prophetic were the tones in which they came back to him! "Losing strength!" And yet he had not taken warning — nay, accepted a friend's invitation for an afternoon's ride instead of going out with his wife! He fairly shivered now when he thought of it. And many afternoons the strong, wide-chested, full-blooded man had ridden out, drinking in the living country air, while she drooped at home, wasting graveward for the lack of that vital stimulant he was absorbing to himself. No wonder she lost strength. The mystery was unraveled now.

And thus it had gone on, he denying himself nothing, while her feebly uttered, scarcely obtruded wants were rarely if ever comprehended; she slowly drifting away the while, and he not perceiving the downward pressure of the current until it was too late to save the most precious thing that God had given to bless his life.

When it was over—the last scene in this mortal drama—and the sympathizing friends were gone away, leaving the mourner to his sorrow, his loneliness and to memory, thus it was with him. Ah, than heartache like this, so hopeless, so crushing, so beyond the reach of medicine, what pain is not easier to bear! The wrong, crystalized by death, is beyond all recompense. We may weep, grieve, we may repent, but there is no atonement. For, ever, out of the unrelenting past, it looks back upon us, stern, rebuking and accusing. It stands a skeleton in the house of our life, and we cannot clothe it with flesh nor soften the stony glare of its eyes. Its shadow lies always on our path, and it has power to darken our brightest days with a sudden cloud, though that cloud be no larger sometimes than a human hand or a pale, loving face that never looked upon us with rebuke or accusation.

THE END.